Ghosts
in the
Dark
Silence

ANITA KRISHAN

FiNGERPRINT!

Published by

FiNGERPRINT!

An imprint of Prakash Books India Pvt. Ltd.

113/A, Darya Ganj, New Delhi-110 002,
Tel: (011) 2324 7062 – 65, Fax: (011) 2324 6975
Email: info@prakashbooks.com/sales@prakashbooks.com

facebook www.facebook.com/fingerprintpublishing
twitter www.twitter.com/FingerprintP
www.fingerprintpublishing.com

ISBN: 978 93 5440 624 9

Processed & printed in India

To Arvind . . .

Love Forever

Life brought us together,
We carved us a path.
Across aeons we trudged,
through roughs and calms.
Fulfilling our promises
till death did us apart.
I saw pain in your eyes,
when your life began to ebb,
tough it was to bid goodbye,
but the ways of heaven are set.
My path is now lonely,
still my heart is at peace.
For I know,
beyond life love not abates.
It prevails and patiently waits.

You exist in time, but you belong to eternity.
You are a penetration of eternity
into the world of time.
You are deathless, living in a body of death.
Your consciousness knows no death, no birth.
It is only your body that is born and dies.

Osho

Lost

Confused spirits
lonely and astray,
trapped between
the astral realms,
the visible and the veiled.
They wander endlessly
amidst haze and reality,
cruelty and benignity.
Chasing lost ties
or buried dreams.
Seeking justice
and eternal peace.
Who'll unveil the passage
to their final release?

Foreword

Scientific belief in death being the ultimate end of one's existence stands in question when one considers people's intriguing encounters with ghosts. The idea of spirits dwelling inside bodies and then some going astray once they are out of it, is a topic most scientific minds find hard to accept. They credit the idea of spectral manifestations to have been borrowed from obsolete superstitions of the past.

In the foreword of my previous book *Ghosts of the Silent Hills*, I had expressed my doubts about the existence of the supernatural. I had also mentioned that since I had never had any direct encounter, and that I had based my stories on the episodes that occurred in the lives of friends or acquaintances––I was in no position to vouch for their existence. But I believed what others had recounted as their firsthand experiences.

An episode after the release of my previous book pumped in me the inquisitiveness to know more about our souls and the world of spirits.

It was the first week of August 2020. My husband, Arvind, was undergoing a surgery at Medanta hospital. By then, his body had gradually weakened due to serious medical conditions and his heart function was slowly ebbing. One evening, when he was wheeled back into the hospital room, he appeared confounded. He kept recapitulating a mystifying experience he had had. "I walked down on my own today and felt no pain," he declared with incredulity ostensible on his face. He had no idea how he had done it.

"Walked down? Where? How?" I asked. It was impossible for him to walk out of the operation theatre, when he was under anesthesia, undergoing a surgery.

"I walked down to the ground floor where I reached an empty white room. When I tried to return, four people appeared in that room and tried to stop me." He talked about this episode several times that evening. He was convinced that what he had experienced was real. It was an unmistakable case of his out-of-body experience, I realized.

He was still immobile when we returned home after two days. Almost immediately he began talking about the presence of many people in the room, people that only he could see. From my previous knowledge, I realized it was a very common occurrence in people about to pass over to the other side. On the morning of August 20, my life partner of nearly forty-four years finally relinquished this existence to join the divine. It was a great loss for me. But I realized that Arvind had intuitively been given signs about his approaching end. He had prepared me too, for this eventuality.

These incidents remained fresh in my mind. A few months later I picked up Raymond A Moody's book *Life After Life* based on case studies of thousands of his patients. In the book, the author, a psychiatrist and physician by profession, has recorded innumerable near-death experiences of people. The astounding fact that emerged from his research was that almost all of them spoke about similar out-of-body experiences. Many of those souls talked about having reached a brilliant divine light . . . the warmest, loving, and the most beautiful experience they had ever undergone . . . something unfeasible in the human world. Most didn't want to return from that comfort. But their time had yet not come to abnegate their physical existence, so they returned to their bodies.

Scientists explain this phenomenon as hallucinations of the oxygen-deprived brain. But my question to that is: why would all near-death experiences be almost identical . . . even in those who are atheists?

The Greek philosopher Plato (427 – 347 BCE), in his famous work *The Republic*, states that the soul is the source of life and mind, and it continues to exist and think even in the afterlife.

For us, who follow the Hindu codes of beliefs inscribed in our Vedic scriptures—which have promulgated the theories of life after death since time immemorial, the concepts of the liberation of soul after death, its imperishable existence, and reincarnation—such beliefs are deep-seated.

As I present *Ghosts in the Dark Silence*, once again based on actual supernatural experiences, I believe that there is a spiritual world, beyond human comprehension or scientific explanation. We are only a minuscule part of this vast mysterious universe, and the profound Divine Plan.

In the following pages, you will encounter the lives of five families that underwent some harrowing supernatural experiences. You may find many common factors in the stories, but then, most ghost encounters are similar, just like most near-death experiences are similar.

Once again, I confess that the incidents narrated to me acted only as an inspiration for me to write these stories— which set my imagination ablaze. An author needs just a spark to kindle a raging inferno.

Anita Krishan

Contents

The Eternal Ties

To say that I was irritated as I sat inspecting my room in semi-darkness, would be an understatement. My beautiful dream had been broken by a loud thud. I was now trying to locate the source of the sound.

Nothing seemed amiss. Perhaps my family was up and busy with their morning chores. I flopped back on my bed. *They should be more considerate, well knowing I study till late and I am a light sleeper.*

I had slept around two that morning after cramming a whole chapter of organic chemistry. I focussed better when the house was encompassed in silence.

I snatched the pillow from under my head in frustration and covered my head with it to block further noises. I wanted to return to my dream. But sleep eluded me. I tossed and turned for a few minutes and then once again sat up in my bed. It was still dark in my room. No light seeped in through the curtained window. I realized it wasn't even daybreak. That meant my parents and Raghu were still asleep. Then who had made that sound? I had heard it loud and clear, even though I had been in dreamland.

I switched on the bedside lamp and looked around. My room was as I had left it before going to bed. Had the sound come from outside? Had someone tried to break into our house? That seldom happened in Shimla. I had heard of thieves breaking into locked houses while the residents were away. That too was as rare as a meteorite falling on a house. Shimla was a safe town. Our suburban locality of Sanjauli was even safer.

Then I caught sight of my organic chemistry book lying on the floor. What was it doing there? I had kept it on the table just before going to sleep. I was sure. A mouse couldn't have moved such a heavy book, unless it had mutated overnight to become a giant. We didn't have cats running wild in our house either.

I stared at my book, unnerved. It seemed somebody had been to my room and had deliberately flung my book down. This was weird.

I glanced at the table clock. The time was 3:30 a.m. I had slept for a little more than an hour. Why had I been woken up at the finest moment of my dream? I moaned.

A beautiful girl had visited me in my dream. She had deep blue eyes like an ocean, a peachy complexion, golden hair falling in enticing curls, and a slim curvaceous body accentuated by a pale lacy gown falling till her ankles. Was she an angel visiting me from heaven?

I had also seen my room in the dream, the exact setting. She had come to sit by my side, caressed my face, and then had started to move away. She had stopped at the door of my room, turned, and beckoned me to follow her. I tried but my body was glued to the bed. I wanted to rush to her, hold her in my arms, like she was the love of my life. But I couldn't budge an inch. It was then that my dream had been broken by the loud sound.

Although I was baffled by it all, I wasn't scared. Not even close to it. I smiled and switched off the light. I'd solve the mystery in the morning.

I lay in my bed, thinking. There were a lot of pretty girls in my class and my college. I was infatuated with a few but didn't have the guts to approach even a single one. The norms of our society were strict—interaction between boys and girls in the college was discouraged, looked down upon. We sat on the opposite sides of the classrooms with a ten-feet gap in between. So, often my attention would stray from the blackboard to secretly catch a glimpse of a beautiful feminine profile. I would realize that I wasn't alone in indulging in this pursuit. Eyes continued to stray and furtive glances exchanged while the lecturer intermittently threw a chalk at the culprit caught in action to draw his attention back to his studies.

Only some bold couples, usually from the final year, dared to sit together in the college canteen. There were rumours of secret love affairs too and they became the source of jealousy for the rest of us. For we knew that if we were caught, we would be reprimanded by the college principal—a written complaint would be sent to our parents and a threat of rustication. Falling in love was considered the worst crime we youngsters could commit. The male students indulging in brawls or violent skirmishes, releasing their pent-up hormonal energies, were considered lesser crimes.

So, by and large, we had to be satisfied with shy glances and longing in the heart.

I secretly pined to befriend a girl in my class. But she wasn't as beautiful as the one who had just visited me in my dream. I wished she was real . . . my dream girl. What a beauty she was! Like someone from a fairy tale had suddenly come alive. I felt a strange attraction towards her, totally alien to me. Like I was in love with her. *If I find her in real life, this is the girl I'd like to spend my entire life with.* I chuckled at this thought. With such pleasant feelings traversing through me, I slowly drifted back to sleep.

For the next few days, the memory of the dream continued to linger, beautiful and exotic, seizing my mind and my body. Everything else had been driven out from my brain except one single thought, like the fragrance of the night jasmine prevailing in a garden overcoming all the other nightly fragrances. The beautiful face, like a snapshot, kept hovering in my mind, rendering me sad and wistful all the time. It began to hinder my concentration in class and my study at home. The result—I failed the next physics and chemistry class tests. My lecturers gave me stares of disbelief before handing me my answer sheets. "Madhav, what's wrong with you?" my physics teacher politely inquired. "I didn't expect this from you."

It was a jolt for me. I had never failed any test or examination. I had always been a topper. Throughout. I mean till now.

I then decided to embrace the real world. *After all, it is just a crazy dream! You don't cling to dreams. They break one day and make you fall flat on your face. Be practical, Madhav. Dreams are not reality. She is not real. Like a fool, you are chasing her in your naïve imagination.* So, I tried diverting my attention back to the girls at my college and my studies. Things became normal for a while.

A couple of days later I was once again woken up at night by a loud noise. I instantly switched on the light for I wanted to apprehend the culprit red-handed. My vision directly sought the floor. A shock navigated through me like an electric current. The same chemistry book lay on the floor. This time it was on my shelf, neatly stacked among the other books. Why only the chemistry book? Who had been in my room recently? And then instantly disappeared? And why would someone disregard my study material thus? Was someone playing a prank on me, to scare me?

I could hardly sleep for the rest of the night. I left my bed in the morning, tired and sore. The first thing I did was to confront Raghu, my younger brother, despite my doubts. I knew he loved his sleep more than anything else in the world—wouldn't sacrifice it even in exchange for a trip to the moon. Moreover, however mischievous he might be, he wouldn't do something like this to scare me. There was a good rapport between us.

He got startled by my allegation, which relieved me. He wasn't good at putting up such a convincing show of innocence. I then sought my parents. I found them sitting in our family room, sipping morning tea and chatting. They too were surprised at my questions. Then Papa Ji logically expressed, "Your book must have slipped from the shelf because of its weight." He rested the matter and picked up the newspaper.

I wasn't convinced. "Papa Ji, the gravity acts downwards, not sideways. Why didn't the rest of my books too slip down with this one? Why only my chemistry book?" Papa Ji shrugged and went deeper into the newspaper, hinting that the discussion was over.

If no one had been to my room, then what had made my book fly thus? It was all getting incredibly baffling and mysterious! This had happened for the second time. I was beginning to get scared. Whosoever had thrown my book down had done it with an intention. What could be the intention? Making its presence felt?

The next night I slept early, around eleven, for I felt exhausted. This was unusual. I hadn't run a marathon or anything even close that could have slurped away my energy. I had remained in the house studying, eating, and lazing round. I decided to wake up early to study for my approaching midterm exams and set my alarm for four in the morning.

I immediately fell into a deep sleep. Sometime past midnight, she came again. Was it a dream? I was unsure. Standing next to my bed, she smiled. Enchantingly. Bewitchingly. Was I awake? Was I really seeing her? It was the same beauty, the same curly golden tresses falling till her waist. She navigated her soft fingers on my face, lightly stroking it. I extended my hand towards her. I felt her holding it gently in hers. They were delicate hands, silky soft but icy cold. A feeling of ecstasy traversed through my body. And then the alarm went off, breaking my heavenly reverie. I woke up with a start and found my arm extended in the air.

My divine dream had once again been broken halfway through; the alarm had gone off at the worst moment. Even so, I was happy like a young boy in love—my first love. I was elated like I had had a wonderful date with a stunning girl.

I slowly sat up in my bed. A strange aroma was drenching the air of my room, a pleasant feminine odour, a soft perfume. The scent was familiar. How and where had I smelled it before? I just couldn't recall, but it awoke a strange sequence of emotions in me—from love to fear, from nostalgia to pity, from anxiety to longing.

Didn't the beautiful girl seem familiar, too? I was sure I had seen her before. I knew her, had met her somewhere. Where and how? My mind toiled to solve the puzzle.

I lay back in the bed. For the next few hours, I kept thinking, dreaming, trying to recollect what was evading my mind. I skipped my studies. I had no will, no concentration. I was in a strange mood. I was happily in love, yet sadness soaked me wet. I wanted to sing and dance, but I lay listless in my bed in a half-awake state.

Finally, I stretched my body, rubbed my eyes, and opened them wide. A bright light was seeping into my room through the curtains. It was one of those rare days of Shimla's rainy season—sunny and crisply bright. It was the day to enjoy the outdoors. I hopped out of the bed. No way should I miss this opportunity. The idea penetrated deep into my brain like a persistent worm.

It was also my birthday. On this beautiful sunny morning of August 25, 1970, I had completed eighteen years of my life. I had officially become an adult today.

For the past few days, the monsoon in Shimla had been at its peak. The whole of last week, thick dark clouds had assaulted the town ruthlessly—wringing out their entire load here that they had carried from the oceans thousands of miles away.

My college was closed. There was a strike going on which had become violent and the principal had declared the college closed till things could be sorted out. This and the rains had resulted in my house arrest—one whole week of confinement without much to do except study, and dream.

I was in my first year of college and was preparing to get into a professional institution. Like my father, I wanted to study medicine at one of the prestigious institutions in the country. My final exams were to be held in a few months, based on which I would get admission into a medical college. My preparations were far from adequate. Although the rains and the strike had come as succour, giving me time to devote to my studies, I wasn't able to focus. For the first time in my life, I would find my mind wandering, fantasizing. I would have my book open in front of me but would barely read a word. I would then shake my romantic thoughts out and remind myself that my future was entirely in my hands. Daydreaming would take me nowhere.

There would also be some or the other kind of disturbance at home—visitors, discussions, arguments, my noisy younger brother—all this was hampering my study preparations. So, the first resolution I made on my birthday was to concentrate better on my studies and get into a good medical college.

What I didn't know was that there are things in this world beyond our control. Things that the human mind can't comprehend.

More importantly, it obsessively infiltrated into my mind now that I must visit it—the quiet and serene place that I loved—situated on the next hill range.

After greetings and birthday hugs from my family, a quick bath, a special puja that my mother had organized and a sumptuous breakfast, I began my preparations to head to my hideout. I stuffed my bag with books and packed some sandwiches and nibbles. Picking up my umbrella to be safe in the whimsical weather of Shimla, I informed my mother that I wouldn't be home till the evening. She objected, "Madhav, stay at home, please. It's your birthday. I wanted to take you to the temple. You must get God's blessings today. Also, I am cooking your favourite dishes."

"No, Mummy Ji, I can't afford to while away a single day. Seriously, I need to study, prepare for my midterms and the finals. I surely need God's blessings, and I will pray to him on my way," I voiced cheerfully. "I'll be back early in the evening. Cook my favourite dishes for dinner." I gave her a peck on the cheek. "We'll celebrate together when Papa Ji and Raghav are home, too." Giving an affectionate hug to my crestfallen mother, I headed for the Christian burial grounds—the Sanjauli cemetery.

After twenty minutes of brisk walking, I reached the unpaved road that led to the cemetery. Trudging through the narrow pathway for another five minutes I reached a beautiful dense clump of towering pines and cedars. A small rickety gate at the entrance was open and creaking as it moved to and fro with the wind. I walked through the gate and into the cemetery, my footsteps disturbing the prevailing deathly silence.

Most of the graves in the cemetery were old. Moss and grass had sprouted on them utterly unopposed. The slithering creepers, which were cheerfully flourishing in the rains, had obscured most of the graves under their luxuriant green latticework. Flowering shrubs, which had once been planted around the tombstones, had now gone out of control, growing hysterically wild.

Inhaling the invigorating odours of the conifers and the wet earth, I walked around on the soggy ground looking for a suitable spot to sit, all the time avoiding stepping over the resting places of the dead. Finally, I chose a sunny spot on an incline and dumping my bag on the ground, sat down on a flat rock, the only dry spot I could find.

The tranquillity of the place was overwhelming. For the initial ten minutes, I sat in a trance—mesmerized by the splendour of nature. It had rained the previous night and zillions of raindrops hanging from the pine needles sparkled in the sunlight, rendering the trees studded with tiny diamonds. The hypnotic cobra lilies, that had crept out through the moist soil, swayed around me in the mild breeze, their hoods raised—uncannily mimicking the real cobras in their pattern and striking pose. A swarm of tiny purple, yellow, and white flowers had emerged from the emerald carpet of nature, mirroring the twinkling stars of the night sky. On the far horizon, a dark cloud hovered like a solitary bird of prey. A flock of yellow-vented bulbuls hopped and chirped as they dug for worms a little distance away. All of a sudden, they took off as if disturbed by an intrusion and flew down into the cavernous valley.

Having absorbed the beauty, the silence, and the warmth of the bright August sun, I took out my study material from my bag. I began solving tricky physics numericals that demanded my undivided attention. I must have studied for about half an hour when I was distracted. The light had become dim, having been annihilated by the thick clouds that were now racing to obliterate any left-out blue of the sky. I shivered as the cold drafts assaulted me. But more than the change in the weather, something else drew my attention. I heard a rustle and then footsteps behind me. They were crisp and clear, as distinct as the gathering army of the dark clouds threatening a spell of rain. Someone had walked past. I turned to check. There was no one around. Not a soul. Could have been a small scurrying animal, I concluded. *The scuttling animals don't sound like footsteps.* Shrugging, I returned to my study. But the mysterious sound had stolen away my attention. This unsettling impression of someone being there, in my proximity, made me anxious. Yet each time I roved my eyes around me, I only witnessed utter desolation and intense silence.

It was not the first time that I had visited the cemetery. This was my hideout whenever I desired peace. Apart from an escape from the noisy guests, it was the most suitable place to elude the pestering classmates when they hounded me for help with difficult math problems a day before the exam. I had spent many winter days sunning and studying in these peaceful surroundings. Unlike most boys my age, who loved spending hours in pubs in pointless gossip, I loved my seclusion and tranquillity. If that made me different from other boys of my age, it bothered me the least. But today, my different disposition was proving to be risky.

I now heard another sound—a mild, indistinct, soft sniffling. It came from behind the bushes. Just then, the clouds decided to release their vapour. Big drops of rain fell on my head.

Shimla's monsoons were so capricious—torrential downpour would often follow a burst of bounteous sunshine or vice versa. I shook my head in frustration and opened my umbrella. I needed to return home, for God alone knew for how long this rain would last. But then, it would mean termination of my study plan. At home, my mother was sure to pester me with this or that, trying to give me undue attention on my birthday. Attention was the last thing I sought from people. I was a reserved boy, a bit shy.

I decided to wait, keeping my fingers crossed for the rain to end and the sunshine to return. I knew the rain wouldn't stop anytime soon. I knew it was useless to wait. I knew I should leave this disturbing place immediately. Yet, I continued sitting glued to the rock, with my bag on my lap trying to save it from getting wet. I continued to receive a shower of tiny droplets filtering through the umbrella.

The sniffling sound was unremitting. I looked around. The cemetery was still starkly deserted. I had begun to feel unsettled, unable to solve the mystery of the furtive sounds in my vicinity. The splattering sound of the rain was rather soothing. It eclipsed the sounds that were making me edgy. Then all of a sudden I sat upright. The sound of footfall appeared right behind me. I turned to apprehend the culprit. But all I saw was the sheet of rain and the floating mist. How could there be footfalls of an invisible being? Was the cemetery haunted? I had heard some stories about spirits roaming the cemetery but never believed in them. A fleck of fear invaded my heart. I hurriedly stood up in agitation. I realized that it would be best to leave this spooky place immediately.

I traversed my eyes around to find a safe passage to the exit gate through the puddles that had begun to form. The desolate cemetery was bleak and unkind like stretches of a hostile desert. I strongly felt something ominous was around today. An inexplicable dismal feeling was creeping into me, seeping me with melancholy. I felt a deep sense of loss, the loss of something important.

I hurriedly slung my bag on my back and dashed towards the gate. I had barely taken a few steps when I heard it— muffled sighs of grief. Somebody was moaning softly. How silly of me to get anxious. There was a bereaved person here, mourning someone's death, someone dear to him. Or was it her? I realized it was a female voice, for the moaning had by now turned into soft wailing. Despite my hesitancy, my feet dragged automatically towards the sound. I didn't want to intrude into the person's privacy. I knew I shouldn't. Yet, I was unable to exercise control. It was as if a force was beckoning me, telling me to go and join in the mourning . . . grieve for the dead. It was a sensation—nothing like I had ever experienced in life.

I trailed the sound, gently, gradually, on tiptoes. I was still unable to see anyone, but the sound was now close, very close. It was slowly getting subdued. Sniffles again. I stood still, listening. Why couldn't I spot anyone? Then a moving white mass, shaped like the back of a woman, denser than the surrounding mist, hovered in the air right in front of me. I froze. What was that? A ghost? My mouth went dry and my heartbeat skyrocketed. Panic flared like a tsunami. I knew I shouldn't stay here any longer but my feet were like heavy iron, chained to the ground. I tried gulping air through my open mouth as I felt my lungs constricting. The white mass slowly twirled around. I gawked. My eyes widened with alarm and a frisson of fear ran down my spine. The beautiful girl with long hair, falling in curls, stood gazing at me. She was the girl from my dreams. Except there were no colours now. Everything was misty white—the body, the curly locks, the flowing dress—like a faint figure sketched on a white canvas. Was I in my bed, dreaming?

My feet became lighter and involuntarily moved towards her, drawn by a mysterious power. I knew I shouldn't. I knew I must exercise control. I knew for sure she was a ghost. Then why was I approaching her? Why did I have no control over my actions? It was as if I was being pulled by a high intensity magnetic force.

When I was about four feet away from her, the spectre suddenly dissolved. It seemed to have seeped into the earth like water into dry ground. I felt my dream had broken once again.

I stood shocked and bewildered, staring at the copious growth of moss, grass, bushes, and creepers, where just a moment ago stood an angelic woman I was in love with. Was she really there? Was I hallucinating? Was it just an illusion? My imagination? Another dream?

I had to confirm. My gut was saying that this was a sign for me to unravel, discover. For a few seconds I stood still as silence once again enveloped the cemetery. There was no sound except the rain strumming over the soft ground. I threw my bag and umbrella down on the ground. It had begun to pour heavily, as if the sky had opened up a torrent. I was soaking wet, the rain drenched me to my skin. Streams of water ran over my head, down my face, through my eyes—blinding me. None of this stopped me. I went down on my knees and began to remove the wild vegetation with my bare hands—frantically, desperately— uprooting bushes and grass and creepers and moss, all soaking wet and slimy. I worked on it like a possessed being, impetuously tearing away the slippery foliage, in search of the mysterious woman. She was down there somewhere. I knew what I was doing was wrong. Dangerous. But I had lost total control over my actions. My mind and body had become two divided entities now. Disjointed. Broken apart by an unknown force. Each controlling its action, ignoring each other, defying each other. Why was I pursuing her? I had no idea. I knew very well that what I had seen was not a person, not a woman of flesh and blood. She was a spirit of a dead person, an essence of what she once was. I had fleetingly sighted a ghost. My mind was discussing all this logic, but my hands continued to work frenziedly to unknot the mystery. The very persona of the figure was pleading me to see, to know, before she melted into the earth. But know what?

I toiled on hysterically, removing layers after layers of soil with my fingers and nails. The tips of my fingers were sore. Splinters pierced into my nails. Blood oozed from them. I didn't care. I carried on with my insane activity till I came upon a large gravestone—an old crumbling piece of a flat, frayed grey stone, underneath which lay a body. Buried. Decaying or decayed. Forgotten.

The rain continued to pound, helping me in my crazy endeavour. The water gushing over the gravestone washed away the loose dirt to reveal the etched words on it. Fear generated a painful knot in my stomach. Did I know her? With my heart palpitating and my hands shivering, I read the fading engraving on the stone—

ELIZABETH M. ANN
DIED
AUGUST 25, 1945
AGE - 18 Years
She lives with us in memory,
and will forevermore.

My heart stopped beating. My head swooned. Today was August 25, the year 1975. I had completed eighteen years of my life. Who was she who had died thirty years ago at the tender age of eighteen? Why was she appearing to me time and again? Why had she led me to this tombstone? What was my connection with Elizabeth? Was it her ghost I had just seen? And why on earth on my eighteenth birthday? What had happened thirty years ago on this day? How had Elizabeth died so young, even before life had really begun for her? What was she trying to tell me?

I was unable to answer any of the questions that were assaulting me one after the other. There was something in my subconscious, ringing bells, but it refused to emerge in my conscious awareness.

After all, I was a mere mortal! She lived in the world of spirits. The difference was large—the distance unfathomable.

As I slowly walked out of the cemetery, shivering and shuddering, with unexplained sorrow stabbing my heart, I somehow knew that she had led me here today.

From that day onwards my life changed drastically. An inconceivable depression seeped into my heart. I lost interest in everything life had to offer. I began to suffer terrible inexplicable headaches. I lay listless in my bed all day, eating only to survive. When my college opened after the forced break, I declined to join back. I even refused to walk out of my room. I didn't have the will. I didn't have the strength. I rapidly began to lose weight.

My parents were dejected and desperate. Their son, always a topper, ordained to go in the best medical college of the country, had all of a sudden braked midway, parking his life in an enclosed space of his room. More than that they were tense seeing me wasting away—turning into skin and bones. Papa Ji came to sit with me every day, to talk me out of my self-exile from life. A cardiologist himself, he was baffled by my condition. He began administering me some tonics to keep me going. He invited his colleagues to examine me, specialists in various fields. All were intrigued. No one could diagnose what was wrong with me. My tests were normal. There was no visible ailment.

Mummy Ji's perpetually red and swollen eyes saddened me, but I had no will to comfort her. Each day when she came with my favourite dishes, I refused to eat more than a few bites, which she fed me with her hands. Many a time I couldn't even retain the food in my belly. I knew how aggrieved she was. I didn't have the drive to help her or make any effort to help myself.

My books lay forlorn, gathering dust. They had lost meaning for me. Papa Ji went to meet the principal of my college to take an exemption for me from appearing in the midterm exams. I was extremely unwell, he justified.

I had no idea what had happened to me. It was just that I had lost the will to live. The incident at the cemetery had triggered in me a feeling of intense loss, of hopelessness. Life had become empty and meaningless.

I continued to be bedridden like a cripple. Was I dying?

Autumn arrived with its clear, cool days. From my bedroom window I viewed the nimbus sapphire sky and the soaring kites. Beautiful feathered visitors often sat on the branches of the oak, singing melodious songs. They failed to raise my spirits. The massive oak began to shed its leaves and tiny bright-green leaves erupted simultaneously. The brightness of the sky began to wane. The winter slowly crept in. It wasn't too long before snow and frost covered the landscape and the oak. I watched icicles dripping drop by drop, diminishing, getting ready to say goodbye to the world. Was I getting ready to do the same? I wanted to. I had lost the will to live.

My parents tried to do everything they could to make me feel better, but I refused to do anything more than the bare essentials. I even refused to bathe for days on end. It was as if I was slowly rotting, committing suicide in a slow motion. Days began to drag like the links of a chain made of solid iron. My soul, feeling bound by that rusting iron, fluttered for freedom. I yearned for the end.

Raghu often came to sit by me. He brought messages from my friends and tried cheering me up by narrating funny episodes and jokes. But I wasn't interested in anything. I would lie listlessly, completely ignoring him. I couldn't even pretend to show interest. Often, he would leave my room in tears of frustration.

I missed my final exams, leaving my parents in intense despair and pain. It's not that I didn't notice the drooping shoulders of my father and the greying hair of my mother.

They both had aged by ten years in just a few months. I cared, yet remained detached.

At the cemetery that day my heart and mind had become fractionated and turned into two separate entities. What my mind commanded, my heart denied. I couldn't make decisions, couldn't control my actions. In fact, there were no actions. I was like a paralyzed body whose life had come to a halt. Was I under a spell? Would I ever be able to break it?

It was at this darkest hour of my life, when it had reached an abysmal state, that Papa Ji met Dr. Rawat at a seminar in Delhi on modern medical practices.

Dr. Rawat was a renowned hypnotherapist. Since Papa Ji considered my ailment to be a psychiatric problem, he appealed to Dr. Rawat for help. Dr. Rawat agreed to see me. It would also be an enjoyable trip to a famous Himalayan town, he added. A week later he arrived in Shimla.

After the initial protests, I agreed to see the doctor. It was, as usual, tough for me to make my heart agree to my brain's command. But a nod was all that was needed.

By now, my muscles had atrophied due to disuse. A simple effort of changing clothes was a prodigious task. With the help of Papa Ji, on that morning of the summer of 1976, I bathed and changed into fresh clothes—ready to see the famous doctor.

When Dr. Rawat entered my room, I was in for a surprise. Contrary to my expectations, he was young, probably in his early forties. A tall, lean, and a handsome man, he had an overpowering personality. He smiled at me and I stared at him brazenly.

He began by asking me some generic questions. I knew he was trying to gauge my ailment. My patience was soon exhausted. I yearned to return to my world of indolence. "I'm getting tired," I declared.

Dr. Rawat stated politely but firmly, "Just bear with me for a while, chap. You are too young to waste away your life. You need some serious help." For the first time something clicked inside me. I realized I wanted help. I needed to get out of my infirmity. I wanted to live. I liked Dr. Rawat.

Dr. Rawat drew the curtains creating a semi-darkness in the room. He then dragged a chair to sit next to my bed. Only Papa Ji was allowed inside as long as he sat in a corner and did not cause any distraction.

"Madhav. What a beautiful name you have, Madhav— Lord Krishna," he said, offering me a benevolent smile. His words acted like water on fire. "You know my name is Keshav, another name for Krishna. Isn't that a coincidence?" I relaxed and smiled after a long time. "It is a wonderful beginning . . . one Krishna coming to another Krishna's aid. Perhaps ordained by that Krishna." He beamed amiably and pointed his finger up. Our eyes met. "I am hopeful I'll be able to help you. You too do not lose hope of being cured. Relax your body and mind." I nodded. He held my hand gently in his. "Madhav, close your eyes and try to find happiness inside you. Discover it. You don't need much to be happy, just the right attitude, simplicity of mind, and lack of desires. You need to fill your heart with pure love, for yourself and for everyone around you." I closed my eyes. "Now loosen each part of your body. Think of the most beautiful moments of your life."

And I began to think of her. I knew for sure she had visited me here, in my room. They were not dreams. She was real. Was she here now? I felt it strongly. I smiled.

"Be calm. Take control of your emotions." I heard a distant voice. "Relax. Let all the thoughts go out of the mind.

Try to find peace in your heart . . . nothing but peace." My body and mind relaxed, preparing to receive. Surprisingly, I could easily follow the commands, like an obedient child. Then I began to drift into a half-asleep, half-awake kind of a state . . . a stupor. Elizabeth was close, very close, beckoning me once again into another world . . . a new, strange world.

It began to play like a spool of a film, a whole saga uncoiling in my mind, the events of a life I once had. Another time. Another period. I saw it all. Dr. Rawat persuaded me, opening up a channel for me and I surged unbridled through it. I began to tell him a story that was emerging from the deep recesses of my mind. It was thirty years ago . . .

I see a young teenage boy—rustic, simple, poorly dressed, working in a garden of sprawling, grassy, terraced lawns and blooming flowers. That's me. Gopal. I see rows and rows of flowers—hydrangeas, irises, begonias, geraniums, fuchsias, phlox, stocks, foxgloves, lupines, dahlias, orchids, honeysuckle, morning glory.

I paused, for I was baffled. I had no idea how I knew all these names. But I was rattling off the names as if I was an expert horticulturist.

They are profusely filling the flowerbeds and the garden with their beauty and fragrance. I am happy. A middle-aged man is working with me, in the garden. I call him Pita Ji. He's my father. He's guiding me, so he must be the gardener and I, his helper. I see a middle-aged woman working inside the house. She's my mother—Mata Ji. She is a housemaid and also helps the cook in the kitchen.

I am a fair, good-looking adolescent boy, with a thick crop of curly dark hair and an appealing smile. I live with my parents in a small hut within the grounds of a large mansion. In the evening we three sit together in the dim light of a kerosene lamp in our humble abode, eating a modest meal of rice and lentils. We share stories and laugh together before retiring for the night. I see how much my parents love me . . . dote on me. I am their only child. Life is simple and peaceful.

I went quiet, overwhelmed by the pictures forming in my mind. They were beautiful. Were they true? I didn't want to come out of my torpid state. "Yes, Madhav, go on. What else do you see?" I heard Dr. Rawat coaxing me from somewhere far. He didn't need to. I was deep into it—into another time and place.

I am turning rebellious. I want to join the ongoing struggle in the country for our independence. We want the British to quit our country. They are bossy and at times brutal, I've heard. My father is worried for me. He keeps me with him, involved in the work.

A tall foreigner with an imposing personality now enters my perception. He's in the red uniform of the British Army and is riding a horse. He is the master. The villa belongs to him. Colonel Edward. Yes, that's how everyone addresses him. He lives alone, with an entourage of servants, my family being part of it.

We all are modest native folks, a bit in awe, a bit fearful of our master. Colonel Edward is a strict man, but also generous when he's satisfied with a servant's work. He spends a lot of time in the garden, with my father and me, giving us instructions. My father works hard to keep him pleased.

I have been to school . . . My knowledge extends beyond simple reading and writing. I have matriculated. I want to study in a college. Pita Ji is asking for this favour from the Colonel . . . increase in his salary so that he can send me to study in a college. The Colonel defers the answer. I am eagerly waiting for his response.

I converse with the Colonel in English. I am the only one who understands his accent. I have become a self-declared interpreter for the whole household. As a result, I deal directly with the Colonel. A lot.

None of us has any idea about the Colonel's marital status. We think he's a bachelor. Sometimes he brings home his lady friends who stay for a few days and then depart.

There's something special happening now. We are preparing to welcome someone . . . the ladies coming from England . . . Colonel's wife and daughter. I am curious.

The guests arrive one afternoon of the cold mountain spring. For some reason, the daughter comes alone. Her mother, the Colonel's wife, hasn't come. She fell ill just before their departure.

I see the complete household lined up to welcome the Colonel's daughter. My first glance at her and I am as if struck by a bolt of lightning. I haven't seen such a beautiful girl before. I stare at her impudently while the rest of the staff stands with their heads bowed.

"Oh! She's . . . She's . . ." I tried to speak, squirming.

"Who is she, Madhav?" Dr. Rawat probed in his comforting voice.

"Elizabeth . . . the same girl . . . she came here in my room . . . I also saw her in the cemetery."

"Hmm. Madhav, return to the time you were describing."

It was not difficult for me. I easily flowed back into that mysterious era that felt so real.

Elizabeth notices my reaction and she laughs at my brazenness. "Who are you?" she asks sweetly.

"I . . . I . . . I . . ." I get stuck like a jammed record player. I blush; my face is visibly red. She laughs heartily. My father, who's standing beside me, apologizes on my behalf. "He nervous, my boy. He speak

good English. Teach me some," he explains in his broken English and Elizabeth raises her eyebrows. She smiles at me and moves on.

I am unable to sleep that night. Elizabeth's beautiful face hovers in my mind like a gorgeous butterfly flitting in a garden. I know I can't fall in love with her—I, a mere Indian servant—I, a poor boy without a proper job. I know I am being impractical. The beautiful Miss will never reciprocate my love. I am way below her status. I struggle to keep my emotions under control.

That's how we all address Elizabeth—Miss.

When the Colonel goes out to work in the morning, Elizabeth is left alone under my mother's care. My mother can speak only a few words of English. In a few days, Elizabeth is bored and lonely. I am given ample opportunity to see her and interact with her. I hide my feelings but Elizabeth knows. She tries to be overfriendly, flirts with me—pinching me, putting her arms around me, bringing her face close to mine and I can feel her fresh breath on my face. It stirs me emotionally. I am cautious. I know my limits. I have heard of the stories of barbaric tortures that the Gora Sahibs are capable of. So many innocent natives or those fighting for our independence have been tortured, killed, or sent for Kala Paani—a distant land surrounded by a deep dark ocean. If you are sent there, that's the end. You can't escape. One of my uncles, my mother's brother, who had joined the freedom movement, was imprisoned and subsequently he disappeared. We have no clue about his whereabouts. We don't know whether he is alive, dead, or in Kala Paani. My mother remains sad because of it. We are afraid to reveal his relationship with us to anyone. There are traitors within us natives, who will do anything for a few silver coins, or even a pat on the back by a Gora Sahib.

My parents often caution me against being too friendly with the Gori Mem. It can be dangerous, they warn me. Keep your distance, my mother often tells me. Initially, I am vigilant. But I am a teenager—rash, impulsive, and juvenile.

I smiled happily. What I saw brought a glow of ecstasy to my face. "Yes, Madhav. Do you see anything else?" Dr. Rawat prodded softly.

It is evening. A dreamy glow of the setting sun makes the garden look heavenly. Elizabeth and I are alone in the garden. She kisses me on my cheek and expresses her love for me. I am on the verge of telling her that I too am infatuated with her—that she has seeped into my thoughts and into my dreams like the sweet juice of the wild berry that grows in abundance on the hilly slopes. I get flustered and hide my feelings. I tell her that it is impossible for me to accept her as my equal, as my lover. We are poor, no match for her affluent lifestyle. Besides, her father will kill me if he ever comes to know.

She makes a wry face. I catch resentment on it. She reveals to me that the Colonel is her stepfather and she dislikes him immensely. It was a mistake to have come to India but now she knows that she came because she was destined to meet me and fall in love. She tells me that if I do not accept her love, she would immediately return to London. But if I reciprocate, we both will raise a family and live together happily ever after. She tells me that her love for me is pure and deep. She has never felt like this for anyone.

I am on cloud nine. I let go of my guard, let our relationship grow. I don't want her to go back. I don't want to lose her. By and by we both fall deeply in love with each other. It's a crazy madness, we both know, but we drift along with the play of destiny.

The heavenly summers of the mountains bring sunshine, cool breeze, and romance. We furtively begin escaping to isolated places. We walk up and down the cattle paths in the forlorn divine forest nearby. We amble hand in hand through the tall fir and cedar trees and discuss our hopes and dreams—and our future. I have now opened up so much to Elizabeth that I can reveal my inner thoughts and my feelings to her without inhibition. Elizabeth often steals a kiss on my cheek and each time I blush with embarrassment.

We sometimes sit on a flat plot where fresh emerald grass and multitudes of colourful wildflowers grow on the slopes around. The heavenly fragrance of nature fills us with tranquillity. We spend hours talking to each other, eager to hold each other in our arms, expressing our love for each other, making promises to be loyal to each other forever. We are an innocent pair of young lovers—youthful, naïve, but loyal. I dream of marrying Elizabeth and then moving to London with her. I tell her this. She is on top of the world. We are happy in anticipation of the beautiful times ahead.

Those are such heavenly days.

My smile slowly faded. I lost my speech. The tale I was happily unfolding to the doctor who sat beside me, listening to me patiently, now lay muzzled inside me. I was fazed and restless, struggling to come out of my trance. Dr. Rawat goaded me on, "Go on, Madhav. What happened next? You have to go through it all. There's something more in your story that is causing you distress in this life." He was guiding me through an episode I was resisting to confront. Then, like a log of wood, I began drifting in a strong current. Nothing was under my control.

Elizabeth and I are lying together on a flat piece of the grassy patch, our favourite spot hidden in a thick grove of trees. Summers have ended. Monsoons have arrived from the far oceans in the southwest, and the sky is dark and dreary. Mist and clouds swoop around us, trying to hide us in their soft, protective layers. It rained earlier in the day. The grass is wet. Rain droplets collected on the leaves of the trees are continuously dripping down on us. We are getting soaked but we don't care. Lost in our dream world, we lie in each other's arms. Elizabeth snuggles close to me and nestles her face in the curve of my neck. She has never come that close to me. My heartbeat goes wild. I close my eyes in ecstasy. And then

I shriek in pain as I am jerked out of my tranquil world. Someone is holding my hair in a tight fist and rudely pulling me up. Elizabeth sits up and covers her mouth with both her hands to muffle her screams. She whimpers in fright.

I face Colonel Edward's blazing eyes. He is raving mad. "You bastard, you bloody Indian bastard. How dare you touch someone who's mine, how dare you!" Seeing a rifle in his hand, I begin to tremble. I know what is coming. He pushes me roughly and I fall to the ground. I try squirming away. He hits me on my head with the rifle butt. It is a hard blow. I swoon and fall flat on my back. Blood is pouring out from a big gash on my head. The Colonel doesn't stop. He lifts the rifle up to his shoulders and hits me again with such force on the other side of my head that I hear my skull crack. The world around me becomes dark. I lose consciousness.

I couldn't go on. I was shivering and crying. My head ached badly, as if I had been recently hit. Dr. Rawat sat still, gravely regarding me. "What happened then? Go on," he asked calmly. "It is important to see this part." He sent me back to my grim past.

I complied. Reluctantly. Nervously.

I see myself lying in a pool of blood. I moan and open my eyes. I have regained consciousness. I am alive. My eyes seek Elizabeth only to perceive the most horrid sight. It is something I couldn't have imagined even in my wildest nightmares. Elizabeth lies struggling on the grass. The Colonel, her stepfather, is on top of her, clobbering her into submission. She is crying, begging her father to let her go, to spare her honour, but it is as if the man is no more a human, but devil incarnate. When she is stunned enough by the beatings, the man rips her clothes and rapes her.

I had begun to tremble. "It's okay, Madhav. That's enough. You can wake up now." I heard a very distant sound. Dr. Rawat was trying to bring me back to the present. But I was not ready yet.

I can hear her calling my name. She is crying, begging for help. "Gopal, Gopal, please get up, please help me." She sobs pitiably. I see everything but I can't help her. I try to move but can't even lift a finger. I am barely alive. My life is fast ebbing out of my body. I will soon die, I know.

When he is finished, the horrible man stands up, smiling. I hear Elizabeth crying and shouting at him. "I will see to it that you go to jail, you bastard. I knew for a long time that you had your evil eyes on me . . . right from the day I made the mistake of coming to India alone. That's why I kept my door bolted at night and made sure I wasn't ever alone with you."

The Colonel straightens up his clothes and laughs. "So you knew? You should have surrendered to me instead of making me desperate."

"I don't know why my mother married such a depraved pervert like you. Once she knows about your evil deed, she will leave you forever."

I can hear the Colonel's evil laughter. "I don't give a hoot for that old hag. I married her because of you. I waited for you to become a woman. Why do you think she fell ill at the last moment of your trip here? It wasn't a coincidence."

I hear Elizabeth drawing in her breath. "I hate you."

"You better behave. I need you to be with me, in my bed every night. I can give you a decent life."

"A decent life? You pervert. You rape your stepdaughter and want her to be your concubine? Stay away from me, you dirty old man." Then she sees me lying in a pool of blood. "Oh my God! You have killed him. You have killed my Gopal. I love him." She falls on her knees near me. "I'll tell everyone. You'll rot in jail, you sick murderer."

"You have to remain alive to be able to tell anything to anyone. If I could have my way, you'd warm my bed each night, but now you have left me with no choice." Elizabeth instantly scrambles to escape. But her stepfather is quicker and more powerful. He holds her tightly in his grip with one arm, and his other arm goes around her neck.

"You'll be caught if you kill me. For murder." Her voice is hoarse. She is choking.

"Who will reveal my secret? It will be a clear case of rape and murder committed by an Indian bastard, who I killed in a fit of rage. This will be considered a rightful act of retribution by an upright British officer." His devilish laugh echoes through the air and reaches my ears. *"Who will punish a British Army Officer for getting justice, eh? Who'll be bothered for a mere Indian boy? Or even for you, an insolent adolescent?"*

The vile man has strangled Elizabeth, killed her. Once her body goes limp, he drops her. I hear the thud as she falls to the ground. I whimper. He again diverts his attention towards me. I try lifting my body in self-defence. It is futile. But that slight movement gives him a hint that I am not dead. He hits me again and again on my head, smashing it.

I can see my spirit leaving my body and floating away. There is no pain now, and no fear, no anger, no sadness.

It has begun to rain heavily. I can see water flowing from my body and running down the hilly slope in a bright red stream. All the shreds of evidence of the recent crimes are being washed away in the rain. The Colonel turns and leaves the place without as much as a glance at us. There is no remorse on the man's face. He's whistling as he mounts his horse, tied at some distance from us.

The body of the young girl I love with all my heart now lies limp, lifeless, getting soaked in rain and her blood.

I am looking around, seeking her spirit. She has disappeared into oblivion.

A painful sob escaped my lips as I squirmed to wake up. "That's it!" I was moaning in pain. I had a splitting headache. I heard Dr. Rawat's voice, still distant. "You may now return to the present."

I slowly sat up. Papa Ji came and sat next to me, holding me in his tight embrace.

"Was it his dream? Or, was it . . . true?" Papa Ji asked Dr. Rawat.

"It could all be true. I think Madhav just recalled the events of his past life."

"Does that happen . . . I mean, we don't know what happened in our past lives. We don't know for sure that we have a past life."

"It is all a matter of belief," Dr. Rawat asserted. "There's strong evidence of rebirth and reincarnation. My grandfather worked closely in the famous Shanti Devi reincarnation case. Don't you remember the girl born in December 1926, who claimed to be Lugdi Devi who had died in October 1925? It was all over in the newspapers in 1936, the time when her relatives got curious about her claims. They soon realized everything she had claimed about her past life had been true."

Papa Ji nodded. "I heard about it through discussions at home. I was a school-going boy then."

"So was I," Dr. Rawat stated. "My grandfather was in the commission appointed by Mahatma Gandhi that went with Shanti Devi to Mathura, where her husband and child from her claimed previous birth lived. My grandfather was convinced that the girl was speaking the truth. The stories that he told us got me interested in the reincarnation theory. That's why I became a hypnotherapist. I have come across many other cases where people remember their past lives. Madhav is now added to my list." Dr. Rawat smiled and patted me. "I am convinced about the authenticity of your story, son."

Papa Ji looked pensive. He couldn't say that it was a fabricated tale. He had seen for himself that I had been in a trance. And why would I lie?

Dr. Rawat addressed me, "Madhav, it was indeed a painful episode, I agree. But the past has vanished into obscurity. It is meaningless to wallow in it. You need to let it go and move on with your new life now."

"What about Elizabeth? She is still seeking my love," I whispered.

"What do you mean?" Papa Ji sounded surprised.

"She came here in my room many times. Remember I would find my chemistry book flung down on the floor? I mentioned it." Papa Ji stared at me without answering. "Then I saw her in the cemetery, too. I can show you her grave there. She disappeared on top of it. That's how I discovered her grave."

"You never told me that!" Papa Ji's tone became petulant. "Then what happened?" he asked hesitatingly.

"Then something came upon me. I lost interest in everything. I also continued to see her occasionally. I am not sure if they were dreams or reality."

Dr. Rawat intervened, "You have to make her spirit understand that, that chapter of her life closed long ago. She needs to go to her eternal peace." I suddenly felt a great sense of loss. I rested my head on my knees and wept like a child. Papa Ji put his comforting arm around me. Dr. Rawat continued, "You both are bound to each other. You both will meet again, in another time, in another life. Our love and relations do not last one lifetime. But you have to forgo her in this life. It is all God's plan."

After I had cried my grief out, I felt lighter. It was as if a mist had got lifted from my fogged brain. The realization as to what I had been doing to my life began to seep in. This life was as precious as the previous one, that had been lost to irrational violence. I couldn't waste the present one in my foolishness. "Dr. Rawat, I am so angry at that vile British Colonel who murdered us."

"Why should you be angry? Can your anger change the past? No! So why?" Dr. Rawat regarded me with raised eyebrows. "Anger, jealousy, and hatred are slow poisons. It's like drinking these poisons yourself and expecting them to destroy others." I nodded slowly. Dr. Rawat's pragmatic advice made sense.

"I understand, Sir. But the Colonel should have been caught and punished. Instead, he went scot-free and perhaps continued to enjoy his life," I said, unable to erase the image of the Colonel violating my Elizabeth.

"Nobody goes scot-free in the court of God. Karma is the law that governs us all. Our blissful existence, our rewards, or our doom—all are the play of Karma. That is the ultimate truth." Dr. Rawat got up to pull the curtains back. The sudden light in the room blinded me. He continued, "It's time for you to make your choices, friend. Seek your purpose in life and do your Karma. You are born to alleviate the pain and suffering of humanity. Go back to life and carve your path. The world is calling you."

After Dr. Rawat left, I sat pondering over my relationship with Elizabeth. Whether Papa Ji or others believed it or not was inconsequential to me. I knew what I had seen was real. I felt it in my every pore. The feeling of being connected with her even in this life was strong now. But here I was—reincarnated into this new life, whereas Elizabeth's spirit had gone adrift. She had been lost and lonely for so many years, till she found me. But why now? We humans do not have answers to so many mysteries surrounding us.

That day life acquired a new meaning for me. I learnt to cherish love and relationships. My heart was filled with gratitude and affection for Papa Ji, Mummy Ji, and Raghu—for their unconditional love, for all the efforts they had made to rescue me from the road I had embarked on, a road to my ruin!

I realized that my time was limited, and I must value it. I had already wasted a huge chunk of the precious moments of my life. I was going back to college and to my studies. I would become a neurosurgeon and help people with the most important organ of our body—the brain—the controller of our actions, reactions, and all other functions. It was the organ which in my former life was crushed into a pulp of tissue, bones, and blood, by a barbaric and debased human.

But first I had a strong urge to do something.

In a few days, when my body and mind were fairly healed, I visited the cemetery again. I gathered wildflowers on the way—white, lavender, pink, blue, all soft pastel colours, the colours I saw her wearing. I went to Elizabeth's grave. The green cover had grown once again to hide the grave under its gentle care. Without disturbing it I offered my flowers. They softly swayed in the cool breeze. I felt they had embodied Elizabeth's spirit and were waving me goodbye. "Farewell, Elizabeth," I whispered. "I don't know why you came back to remind me of a life we lived long ago. I do understand your attachment and your love . . . our love. But your spirit needs to go to its eternal rest now. So farewell, sweetheart. We shall meet again in heaven someday."

My eyes filled with tears. Wiping them, I got up and walked out of the cemetery gate. It was rocking and creaking in the gentle, cool summer breeze of the mountains.

The Sinister Invasion

The golden radiance of the setting sun bounced off the white facade of my house and penetrated directly into my heart, making it glow with happiness. I had no idea that this feeling of being on cloud nine was soon going to evaporate like a feeble cloud in the heat of the blistering June sun.

As Payal and I stood gazing at our house, the outcome of our tough grind of over a year, I smiled and tenderly wrapped my arm around her. "This is a dream come true, Payal. How many people our age manage to build their own houses?" I boasted. I was twenty-nine and Payal was twenty-six.

"And that too so beautiful!" Payal squealed happily and returned my hug.

I added wistfully, "You know, honey, if Papa hadn't lit a fire in me through his challenge, we wouldn't be standing in front of this beauty."

Payal chuckled and kissed my cheek. "You know what, Puneet, I love your appetite for challenges."

I laughed and returned her kiss. Instantly, my mind drifted away to the time I had just finished secondary school.

My family wanted me to be a doctor. I was a diligent student and earned a seat at the prestigious Lucknow Medical College. My parents were beside themselves with joy.

I left my home in Faridabad with a mixed feeling of anticipation and apprehension. But once in the med school hostel, things turned sour. I was a good-looking teenager. Also, docile and placid. I had no idea why I became the prime target of ragging for a small group of students at my hostel. Rumours were that some criminal elements were sneaking into the college in the evening. Nobody dared to report them.

With the onset of the evening, when it would be time for the sickening lot to invade my room, I would go hysterical with fear. My abuse was not only physical. I began to be subjected to sodomy. My dignity was in tatters. "If you even think of reporting the matter to the higher authorities, or anyone else, your parents won't be able to find your dead body." It was a serious threat. These criminals couldn't be doctors in the making.

When I couldn't endure more suffering and mental damage, I packed my bags and returned to the safety of my home. Those were the longest two months of my life. It took me much longer to expel the trauma from my mind. I coped with it alone. I hid the real reason for my return from my family.

Back home, in a charged atmosphere where everyone was against my decision, I began to lay blueprints for my future life. I loved travelling and writing, and was fiercely passionate about them. I joined a college in Delhi to pursue a graduate course in journalism.

Papa was outraged. "This is a profession for the vagabonds," he roared. The old man's dream of seeing his son as a renowned doctor lay shattered. He refused to talk to me. His silence was painful. When he finally spoke to me after a month, his words were like barbs, "Puneet, you are choosing to live like a pest in other people's houses. You could have built yourself a palatial house as a successful doctor."

The words cut me deep. "No, Papa, I will never be a pest. I'll earn well in whatever profession I choose. I'll build my own house one day. This is my promise to you."

"I'll be the happiest to see that day," Papa had retorted dryly.

I wanted to be a man of my words. So, I worked hard and had a brilliant record throughout college. With a first-class degree in hand, I was immediately offered a job by a popular magazine as its correspondent.

My sincerity and ability fetched me quick promotions and cash flow. I was careful with my money. Each morning when I met Papa, I was reminded of the promise I had made to him, although he never mentioned it again.

I was with the magazine for two years, when Payal joined as a junior journalist. She was a very pretty girl—vivacious, full of passion for work and zeal for life. I was immediately attracted to her. A few assignments together, and we fell in love. After a year of earnest romance, we vowed to spend the rest of our lives together and tied the knot with the blessings of our families.

I rented a small one-bedroom apartment not far from the place of our work. Immediately after the wedding, Payal and I shifted to the new apartment. A week later, after making the house liveable, we left for our honeymoon.

We had a great time in Langkawi islands in Malaysia, a trip that Vineet, my older brother, had sponsored—his wedding gift to us. When we returned after a ten-day bash, we were even deeper in love.

The next evening, as we sat sipping wine on our balcony after the day's hard work, I lovingly held Payal's petite hand in mine and declared, "Payal, I won't be able to give you a lavish life till we build our own house. It's a promise I made to Papa many years ago, and must uphold. We'll need to save as much as we can."

"That's a great idea, honey. To have our own house—our home sweet home." She added reflectively, "If we manage to build our house before our children come, that'll be perfect."

I quickly calculated. "Honey, I think in about six months we'll have enough cash to buy a piece of land."

"Why wait for six months, Puneet? Let's apply for a loan now. My salary can be used to return the loan. Your salary is enough to sustain the two of us."

I hugged her, delighted and impressed by her mature thinking. The next day we visited a bank and applied for a housing loan. The loan was approved and within a week we found this great plot in Faridabad and immediately bought it. It was just a fifteen-minute drive from my family home. The architect was Vineet's close friend and provided us with free professional help. The construction of our dream house began.

Payal and I spent many evenings and all our weekends at the construction site. After more than a year of hectic life—commuting through the jam-packed roads, stuck in traffic jams, verbal fights between us, arguments with the supervisors, mood swings, stages of financial crunch, stalling and continuation of work—we finally stood outside our brand-new house, relieved that a frenzied and tiring phase of our life was over. The result was stunning. Our house was a beauty.

"Which world are you lost in?" Payal's comment brought me back to the present. I was thinking and gazing at my house like I used to gaze at the stars as a child. Wonderstruck. I walked towards the rear of the house, secretly wiping the tears that were blinding me. Payal followed me, animatedly chatting. "You know, Puneet, I have seen a lovely dining set and a gorgeous sofa online. I'll pick up curtains from Fabindia. I have decided upon the colour scheme for our sitting room." Thus, she went on with her childlike delight, her happiness bursting through her heart.

On the first Sunday of November of the year 1995, when the fiery summers were long gone and autumn was slowly slipping into winter, we shifted to our new house. Our family and close friends joined us for the housewarming. We had a *havan* followed by a sumptuous lunch. By five-thirty our guests left. We cleaned the house and sat in our living room, blissful and relaxed.

The bay window of the room provided a magnificent view of the western horizon. We watched the changing colours of the evening . . . glowing coral, pink, peach, lilac and then the deepening grey haze. The night began slinking in slowly, and with it our good mood began to fade. Our happiness was replaced by an inexplicable sadness. I wondered at my penetrating sorrow. Something was wrong. We should have been happy—we were until nightfall—but now we sat listless and strangely miserable. We couldn't even muster enough effort to get up to switch on the lights. We watched the shadows in the room gradually moving, stretching, and then merging into a single dark drape.

Payal shivered. "Come on, Puneet, please switch on the light. I am scared."

"Scared of what?" I asked, annoyed. Why was I annoyed all of a sudden?

"The darkness. I don't like it. I don't know why."

"Don't order me around!"

"Puneet, I sense something frightening around, here with us . . ."

I looked around. The darkness began closing on me, menacingly. I shook my head to expel the feeling. "What's wrong with you? There's nothing frightening here. Just a figment of your imagination." I stood up crossly and turned on a few lights. What was making me angry? "Care for a glass of wine?" I asked and she nodded. I walked to the sideboard in the dining room and poured two glasses of Madeira, the wine I had been saving for this day.

We sipped the wine in silence, but depression continued to suffocate us, soaking our hearts with torrents of misery. What was wrong? Something needed to be done to uplift this strange melancholy. I played soft Hindustani classical music on my phone. It didn't help.

Half an hour later after two glasses of Madeira, Payal walked into the kitchen. As she moved towards the switch, she stepped on something mushy and slipped. She instinctively grabbed the counter to save a bad fall. She stood frozen. What was on the floor? We had left it spotless sometime back. She reached for the switch. As the light flooded the kitchen, she gasped. The box of *gulab jamuns* lay on the floor and she was standing atop a few of the mushed sweets. It was the leftover *prasaad* from the puja.

"How careless of Puneet," I heard her mutter annoyingly and then she shouted, "Puneet, you should have at least picked up the prasaad box if you had dropped it. How lazy can you be? It's all over the floor and I have stepped on it. Defiled it." My hands were turning into tight fists. "It's an ill omen to step on prasaad, you know," she yelled.

It was our first day in the new house and she was spoiling it. I walked into the kitchen in a huff but stopped dead noticing the mess. "You are saying I threw it down? Are you hinting that I have gone mad?" I shouted. Payal gazed at me in shock. I was never unruffled easily. What was wrong with me? I gulped a glass of water to pacify my blazing anger. "By the way, I haven't been to the kitchen all through the evening. You know it."

With deep frowns on our face, we cleaned the mess. As we ate our lunch leftovers, a strange hush hovered in our new house. Usually chirpy Payal sat listless, playing with her food. I wasn't happy either. "I think we both are exhausted, Payal. Months of hard work to build this house has taken its toll."

"Yep. Today has been exceptionally hectic. We should be fine tomorrow morning."

We cleared the table and went upstairs to our bedroom. Down in the dumps, we changed into our nightclothes and slipped under the blanket. Payal began to snore instantly. I remained disturbed—something at the back of my mind bothered me. I had no idea what it was that was making me so unhappy. Gradually, tiredness overtook me and I slept.

It was the most disturbing night. I was invaded by nightmares. I felt as if something dark and harrowing was invading our lives. I left the bed dog-tired.

The morning turned out to be gloomy. Thick, dreary clouds had obliterated the sun. Throughout the day a heavy downpour and intermittent thunderstorm lashed the city. Payal and I reached home late, soaking wet in the winter rain and shivering with cold. After changing into dry clothes, we sat with hot cups of tea and exchanged notes on the day's events.

As the evening slowly slipped into the night, once again we began to get uneasy. A cold unexplained sadness crammed every corner of our house. "Something's wrong, Puneet. I am upset. I feel like crying. I don't know why. I had a great day at work."

I shrugged at the shroud of gloom that was slowly tightening around me. "What's for dinner?" I asked, changing the topic.

"Come with me to the kitchen. Let's cook together." I nodded. "Puneet, please put on some music," Payal called out from the kitchen. "Some holy mantras or bhajans."

I played the devotional songs sung by my favourite singer, Jagjit Singh. The melodious notes in the deep baritone filled the house, gradually lifting our wistful moods. We cooked and ate dinner in silence.

The thunderstorm returned with a vengeance at night. The wind swished against the windows, rattling them. We decided to go to bed early.

In the middle of the night, something disturbed my sleep. Silver moonlight cascaded in through the slightly drawn curtain. The storm seemed to have receded, the clouds dispersed. An eerie silence hung in the air. I was about to turn to my side when I froze. Someone was standing next to the door.

I blinked my eyes a couple of times. I could distinctly see him—a tall, slim, turbaned male. Blurred. The eerie form slowly walked towards me and came to stand next to my bed. My heartbeat hit the roof.

A thief? A well-dressed thief? Are there more intruders with him? No sound escaped through my constricted throat. I wanted to warn Payal, but fear had me frozen.

After a minute or so, which seemed like an hour, the man stirred. He began walking away from me, around the bed—slowly, leisurely. My eyes followed him. He walked towards the dressing table. *Is he looking for Payal's jewellery? Take it all but spare our lives. Please!*

The man halted in front of the mirror momentarily and then walked towards the wall. I rubbed my eyes. Where was he? Did he seep into the wall? I was sweating like it was a scorching summer day. I sat up and switched on the table lamp. The room was peaceful.

The light disturbed Payal and she opened her eyes to peer at me. "Why are you up? What's happened?" she asked sleepily.

"There was someone in the room," I whispered.

"Who was in the room?" She became alert and raised her torso on her elbows and gazed around with a frown. "I don't see anyone."

"He . . . He walked past that wall." I pointed at the wall without looking at it as if that presence would rematerialize from it.

"Puneet, what rubbish? You must have been dreaming." She slowly sat up. "What do you mean, someone was in the room and then walked through the wall?" Seeing me nodding she stiffened. Drops of perspiration collected on my brows were ready to drip down my face. She took a tissue from the side table and wiped my forehead.

I was a sound sleeper and had never woken Payal from her sleep. She held my hand lightly and felt the shivers. "Are you sure you saw someone? Sometimes dreams seem real." She gently stroked my face.

"No, Payal, I wasn't dreaming." I held on to her like a child. "He came to stand next to my bed. A *sardar*, well-dressed, a ghost . . ."

"What rubbish, Puneet? Please don't frighten me. Are you doing it intentionally?"

Her comments vexed me. "What do you think? I'm out of my mind? Will scare you with some fabulous ghost tales in the middle of the night? There's something disturbing in our house!" With this, I switched off the lamp, pulled the blanket over my head and pretended to sleep. Payal slowly crept next to me. I wrapped my arm around her. We kept lying in each other's arms for a long time, awake and on the edge. It was only towards the morning, when the pale light began to brighten up the horizon, that we could doze off into a fitful sleep.

Throughout the next day, worry rendered me physically and mentally spent. I had to meet a deadline. My head throbbed terribly.

Payal and I returned home early and then stood outside the door, staring at the lock as if it would turn into a monster and engulf us. Our stomachs fluttered with fear. Finally, Payal bravely stated, "Come on, Puneet, open the door. It's our house."

The house was undisturbed. Perversely cold. And so unwelcoming. I felt like an intruder in my house. I sat down on a chair to take off my shoes, while my mind sought an explanation. It wasn't that someone had lived here before, or something disturbing had happened here. Then, what had gone wrong with our beautiful home?

I had bought a night bulb on our way back and while Payal made us tea, I fixed it in our bedroom. Perhaps keeping a light on at night would discourage the ghost. It could be the reason why ghosts appeared mostly in the dead of the night. I tried reasoning. I earnestly hoped that this would keep the ghost out of our bedroom. That night I bolted the bedroom door.

The turbaned man visited again at midnight. The bedroom suddenly went cold. Blood froze in my veins. A sudden whiff of flowery aroma hit my nostrils. I was half awake and instantly knew he was in the room. The fragrance lingering in the room was familiar . . . rose fragrance . . . the smell of the *Gulab attar* used in Indian weddings to sprinkle on the groom. My blurry eyes followed him. He walked straight past our bed and stood in front of the mirror. The light illuminated him. This was no hallucination. I could even see the turquoise colour of his *sherwani*. The *zardozi* work on it glowed in the dim light of the night bulb. It was all so eerie. I could see the reflection of the bed and other furniture of the room in the mirror but there was no image of the man who was standing right in front of it. Terror trickled down my spine. My heart pounded and dread gnawed my insides.

He was unmistakably a ghost.

After a minute the spectre evaporated in front of me. I instantly jumped up and switched on the table lamp.

"What's it, Puneet?" Payal slowly sat up, seeing me staring at the vacant space. "You're scaring me." Gently touching my arm, she inquired hesitatingly, "Are you awake?"

"Yes."

"Did you see him again?"

I nodded. Payal trembled under her cosy blanket. "Our house is not some old ruins or a haunted house! We built a new house!" she cried.

And then, the nightly visitations of the ghost became as regular as clockwork. Why was he upholding this daily unscheduled appointment in our bedroom? I had no idea. But I was also getting used to him. The moment I felt the apparition enter our bedroom, I would turn my back on him. I would only get a glimpse of him dissolving through the wall.

Simultaneously, the strong whiff of the gulab attar would wake Payal up. The fragrance was getting stronger.

The winds blowing over the snow on the mountains came visiting the plains, bringing penetrating cold with them. The new year arrived all wrapped up in a thick blanket of fog. Some days, when the visibility dropped to almost zero and it became impossible to drive my motorbike to office, Payal and I travelled by a cab. By the end of January, the foggy days departed and cold subsided a bit. But the visits by our ghost remained constant. Payal unswervingly refused to open her eyes for even a fleeting glance. I continued to ignore the supernatural intrusion as consistently as his dogged visits. Was there any other choice?

Then one night, when I had turned my back on him, the ghost stopped reaching the wall and slowly turned. I felt his piercing gaze, a handsome bearded face distorted in anger. The hostile vibes were so creepy as compared to his calm demeanour till now. The ghost continued to stare as I broke into a cold sweat. The apparition then turned and faded into the wall. "Puneet, is he here?" came Payal's subdued voice. I was breathless. Payal's eyes flew open, only to find me shivering. "The ghost is angry," I uttered in my shaky voice.

"What can a ghost do to us, Puneet? It hasn't done anything till now." Payal sat up and slipped her hand in mine. "It is just a bodiless form of energy that can manifest itself into a shape. It doesn't have solid strength like us," she spoke like a logician, trying to rest my anxiety.

"Ghosts are unpredictable, can harm. Haven't you seen *The Omen* or *The Exorcist*? Many stories and movies are based on true incidents. The malicious supernatural can destroy," I shivered at my statement.

"Rubbish! They are just movies, don't start believing in them." Payal shouted so loudly that I was afraid the whole neighbourhood could hear her. "Sometimes, I wonder at your common sense, Puneet. How can you be so inconsiderate? Reminding me of those horror movies in the middle of the night, just after the ghost has been in our room. What's wrong with you?" She was huffing and puffing. She then turned her back towards me and pretended to sleep. Both of us remained in our shells, awake and avoiding each other for the rest of the night.

The next day was Sunday. At the breakfast table, Payal was moody and grouchy. She only spoke in monosyllables. I felt desperate and disillusioned. Our new house had lost all its charm, had become a dreadful place to live in. Our relationship was suffering. We squabbled without reason. This conundrum would kill us. Perhaps some hidden ears were listening to us all the time. I held Payal's hand across the table. "I know, honey, it's turning into a traumatic experience for us both. Let's get out and spend the whole day in some nice, peaceful place."

"Sure, Puneet! Good idea." Payal instantly lost her grumpiness. In fifteen minutes, we were ready and out of the house.

We drove on our motorbike to Badkhal Lake, found a hidden green patch and sat under the shade of a willow tree. Payal seemed pale, squeezed of energy and happiness. However, we felt better when we were out of our house. "Never could I have imagined we would be living with a ghost. If someone had shared a similar experience with me, I would have mocked that person." Payal sighed.

I nodded pensively. "I don't know what's going to happen to our lives! We built our house with so much enthusiasm, with so many beautiful dreams for our future. And here is a ghost who insists upon living in it. We can't even plan to have children!"

My statement brought tears to her eyes. "Puneet, I so desperately wanted to start a family. I love children. You are right. How can we start a family in the house where lives a spirit of an unknown dead man?" She rested her head on my shoulder. "I am scared and sad, Puneet." I wrapped my arm around her protectively. We had every reason to be miserable. We had used all our savings on this house. There was a huge loan to be returned with interest. "Puneet, dear, have you shared this ghost affair with anyone?"

"No."

"There's no point. Who'll believe us? People will call it our imagination . . . cooked up stories to draw attention." I nodded dejectedly. "We shouldn't say a word about it to anyone, till we find a solution to get out of this mess."

The sun had reached the far west skyline. A peaceful day spent under the open sky and warm sunshine helped us both to regain our calm. It was time to return home.

I went to park my bike in the garage. Payal waited outside. Holding hands, we walked towards the entrance. As we reached the bay window of our sitting room, I stopped dead. Someone stood at the window. A tall dark shadow. A distinct human figure. Watching us. My hand tightened over Payal's. She looked at me in apprehension. "Payal, who's that?" I whispered. Payal turned to see but only had a glimpse of the chilling form. It then moved away and merged with the dark interiors.

"Was that the sardar's ghost?" Payal asked, holding on to my arm.

Her terror-stricken shudders plunged my heart into depths of anguish. "No. It seemed different." I stood breathing heavily.

Payal crept closer. "Puneet, is there really someone else in there?" I shrugged. "Let's not go in."

"Then go where, Payal? This is our home."

The night was rapidly enveloping us in its black cape. I opened the lock with my unsteady hands. Hesitatingly, we stepped into the dusky icy gloom of our house. I switched on a light. The house was at least ten degrees colder than outside. My eyes nervously surveyed the interiors. There seemed to be no one here apart from the two of us. I went to turn on a heater and Payal went towards the kitchen. Her scream had me arrested to the spot. She dashed out of the kitchen. "He . . . He . . . there . . ."

"What's there, Payal?" I then saw it. The same dark shadow. Formidable and hostile. It stood behind Payal. Towering over her. It was nothing like the ghost of the sardar. "Who . . . Who are you?" My shaky voice startled Payal. She turned to look. In that instant the shadow withdrew into the kitchen. I hesitated and then daringly walked into the kitchen. I turned on the light. "Look, Payal, there's nothing here. It was just a play of light." I didn't believe my own statement. I was frightened.

What was going on in our house, was outlandish. Were we going to live in a haunted house for the rest of our lives? God help us.

I didn't want to alarm Payal. I tried to act normal. "I'll cook dinner for us," I offered. We ate eggs and bread for dinner, and immediately retreated into our bedroom. It somehow felt warmer and safer here.

I tried to fall asleep, but my anxiety wouldn't let me. What was that dark entity—that frightening supernatural being? It emitted hostile vibes unlike the sardar's ghost.

Payal too kept tossing and turning the whole night.

In the middle of the night a cold waft hit my face like a whip. I was instantly wide awake. The air was saturated with the aroma of the rose attar—sharp and strong. I knew the sardar's ghost was in the room. I closed my eyes and waited for him to walk away. Then something unusual happened. I heard a ghostly whisper right in my ear. "Heeeeeelp." Instantly my eyes flew open. Terror stabbed my heart. The turbaned ghost's face hovered above mine. He was crying. The right side of his forehead was smeared with something dark. The dark viscous liquid dripped down his face. Blood? Plop. Something icy cold fell on my forehead. A shriek escaped my throat making Payal jump up in confusion. Our door rattled. The apparition shivered and faded in front of us . . . like dry ice turning into gas. My eyes caught the dark shadow next to the door. Erect. Immobile. Scary. My whole body turned cold. Payal's stammer drew my attention to her, "Pu-Puneet, th-th-there's something dark on your face." I caught raw panic in her voice. She hadn't noticed the dark apparition. My shivering hands struggled to switch on the table lamp. The shadow disappeared. "B-B-Blood." Payal's face had gone ashen.

"Where?"

"On your forehead."

I didn't believe her. Still, I picked up a tissue to wipe my forehead. The tissue was stained red. I ran to the bathroom. I applied soap and scrubbed my face as if I were cleaning a greasy pot.

In the morning, pale and frightened, we sat for our breakfast. I had one glance at my wife's shrunken face and declared, "Payal, we can't go on like this. Our fear will kill us."

"I too am sick of this daily trauma. Puneet, is there any escape from this mess? Will we remain stuck in this quagmire forever?" She sat supporting her head in her hands. "I feel like a mouse trapped in a cat's paw, about to die."

"Last night the ghost was bleeding and pleading for help. I caught despair in him. Maybe, he wants us to help him."

"How can we help him?"

"We'll have to do a bit of investigation."

"What investigations can we do?"

"Let's meet the person who originally owned the plot. Remember, we bought the plot through a broker and never met the owner directly. Maybe he can throw some light on the matter."

That evening I informed Payal, "I had called the broker from my office and got the name and address of the man who had sold us the plot. We need to meet this gentleman." I took the paper out of my pocket and read the address loudly. "Amarpal Singh. Lives in Mehrauli. I'll call him tomorrow morning and fix a meeting with him for Saturday." Saturday was three days away. "What do you say, Payal?" I asked as I pocketed the paper.

"Sounds good."

This ray of hope was like a flicker illuminating a gloomy, murky path. We sat down at our dining table with glasses of wine. We had barely taken a sip each when Payal suddenly sat up stiff. "Amarpal Singh? Is he a sardar?"

I smiled smugly. "I realized that the moment I read the name. There could be something fishy about the young man's, er, the ghost's death."

"Of course. I simply don't understand. How can a dead person produce blood?"

"There are so many things we don't know, Payal. My mind is tired of trying to find logic. But right now, I'm famished. What's for dinner?"

"Let me see what I can make. Come and help." Payal gulped the last sip of wine and walked into the kitchen.

From my seat, I noted her frozen hand on the kitchen light. She then rushed back to me and sank into a chair. She tried to speak but only gurgling sounds escaped. "Are you okay? What happened, Payal?" Payal was sobbing and pointing towards the kitchen. "S-S-Strange shadow, f-f-face, n-near the sink, and something dripping from it." I became paralysed. Was it the ghost of the sardar? I peered into the kitchen and then back at Payal. She appeared to be choking. Gathering courage, I got up. "No, Puneet, don't go there." Payal held my hand.

"Payal, we can't live here in fear all the time." Gaining courage from my statement, I walked into the kitchen. Payal followed me, hanging onto my arm, her body shuddering. I turned on the light. "See, there is nothing here. What scared you so badly?"

Payal was staring at a portion of the slab. I followed her gaze. "B-Blood. I saw it dripping down from that . . . that . . . something . . . like . . . a creepy face . . . without a body."

"Was it the sardar?" I looked at her probingly.

"No. S-Something else." She hid her face behind my back and shivered.

I quickly cleaned the slab with a wet paper towel. Instantly, a loud crash from the dining room made us rush out. The bottle of wine lay shattered on the floor. There was no logical reason for it to fall. It was sitting in the middle of the table. I cleaned and mopped the floor with ebbed spirits, my eyes darting around the house as if I expected an assault. Payal sat on a chair shrunk into a ball, her eyes wild with terror.

I decided to speed up our investigation. It was critically urgent to crack the mystery behind these chilling activities in our house. "Payal, let's meet Amarpal Singh tomorrow, though it will be tough to get another day off. I received a stinker from my boss today."

"I received one, too." Payal wiped her tears and sank into a chair. "Mr. Rao is dissatisfied with my performance. I'll lose my job, Puneet." She held her head in her hands and moaned. "Life has brought us to a dangerous crossroads. I'm unsure where to go. I hate it. I feel miserable. Seems like this is the dead-end."

"Come on, Payal, pick yourself up. Let's get to the root of this problem." Determined, I walked to where the telephone was kept. I took out the paper from my pocket and dialled the number. Payal came to stand next to me. I wrapped my free arm around her. The bell rang for a long time. No one responded from the other side of the line.

I felt uneasy. Cold air had begun to engulf us. Something was with us. Close. Payal's shivers were transmitted to me. Then out of the blue, the paper was snatched out of my hand. Before I could react, it floated away as if carried by a strong breeze. Who was carrying it away and where? I needed the address. I ran to catch it. At the kitchen door stood that gruesome shadow blocking my way. I didn't dare to move. Payal screamed.

I grasped that the dark entity was trying to prevent us from contacting the dead sardar's family. I rushed back and used the redial button to place the call. "Come on . . . come on . . . somebody please pick up." My desperation was rising. After a prolonged second ringing, I heard a soft voice on the other end. "Hello. How can I help you?" After a little vacillation, Amarpal Singh agreed to see us the next morning around eleven. He had barely given me his address when the house plunged into darkness. The phone line went dead. Power cut? I opened the door to check. In the entire neighbourhood, only one house was encased in darkness. Ours. I checked the meter. The main switch had been turned off. Who would do that? Was this spirit that strong?

We didn't have the courage to stay around the sinister presence after what had happened. There were some bananas in the fridge. I quickly grabbed them, and we rushed to the safety of our bedroom. Was it really safe up here?

The night passed in restlessness. Multiple sounds kept assaulting us. Footsteps on the stairs. A ghostly sound for help. Was it the sardar's ghost pleading? Was he in trouble? Was he afraid of the dark presence?

The morning was cold and cloudy, adding melancholy to our shrivelled spirits. When I went to the kitchen to make tea, shreds of the paper lay wet and stuck to the floor. I drew in my breath and stood stunned. The shreds had been arranged into a face . . . the grey tiles of the floor formed the eyes and the lips. The face had an uncanny resemblance with Payal. I began to shiver. But I could pretend to be brave at least, for Payal. I quickly washed the kitchen floor before Payal could walk in.

Hurrying through the morning chores we stepped out. A hazy layer of mist had wrapped the surroundings in its spectral cloak. Icy winds blew over the city. Zipping up my jacket and wrapping my muffler, I walked into the garage to take out my motorbike. It lay toppled. It had been thrown with such force that its front fork had broken, making it inoperative for now. Whoever was trying to create impediments in our mission, was strong and hostile.

With fright fluttering in my guts, I held Payal's hand in a tight grip and led her into the gloomy day to hail a taxi to ferry us to Mehrauli. We had barely travelled half the way when smoke began to emit from the cab's engine. "The engine is overheated and backfiring," the driver informed us. "I can't go further." I made no comments and stopped Payal from grumbling. I was in as much urgency to reach my destination as someone trying to create obstructions. An auto stopped to check if we wanted a ride. We hopped in. Someone may be trying to deter us, but there was someone helping, too.

At ten minutes to eleven, Payal and I were at Mr. Amarpal Singh's door. Just as we rang the doorbell, a flash of lightning accompanied by the sound of thunder shook the door. The rain came pouring down in sheets. A grizzled, gaunt, and slightly bent sardar, well into his seventies, ushered us in. He led us into a modest sitting room. "What can I do for you?" he asked once we were seated.

"Uncle Ji, we have come to your door to seek your help." Desperation in my voice was as clear as the cries of a dying animal.

"You seem worried, *puttar*. I'll do whatever I can."

A lady came to join us—a shrunk, wrinkled, and aged woman, bent with sorrow. A *dupatta* covered her grey head. Payal and I stood up to greet her. "*Satsriakal. Behtho puttar, behtho.*" Her voice was tremulous. She sat down beside her husband.

"He's the young man who called me last night," Mr. Amarpal Singh informed his wife.

She nodded gravely. "Is it something serious? My husband said you sounded panicky on the phone last night. And then suddenly cut off the call."

I didn't know how to begin. "We live in Faridabad, constructed our house there. We shifted in it only recently, about two months ago. Our house is in sector Z, on plot number 17." I gazed at the old couple expectantly, checking on their reaction. None came. "Don't you remember it?" I asked.

The lady shook her head. Mr. Singh narrowed his eyes. "Just excuse me." He hurried out of the room. The silence in the room grew heavy. The lady got up too. "It's cold. I'll make some hot tea for you."

Left alone, Payal and I surveyed the room. All of a sudden, I gasped and rushed to the bookshelf in a corner. Payal followed. A framed photograph on top of the shelf was what had drawn my attention. It was a photo of a handsome sardar in a black suit, white shirt, and a purple printed tie. "Payal, he is the same—the ghost," I whispered. Payal sucked in her breath. Hearing the shuffle of approaching footsteps, we both quickly turned away from the photograph as if we had been caught stealing.

Mr. Amarpal Singh had returned with some papers in his hand and now stood watching us. "That's the photograph of my son, Jagvir." He sighed and sat down on the sofa. "I don't know why you mention the plot, but yes, we had an association with it." We both eyed him eagerly. "That plot once belonged to my son."

"Why did your son sell it off? I mean it is an excellent plot, prime location."

Mr. Amarpal Singh hesitated and then sighed. "My son is dead. Murdered. That's why."

I stopped breathing. Payal almost fell off the sofa. "We are so . . . so sorry, Uncle Ji. Was the murderer arrested?"

"There were two of them, the woman my son wanted to marry and her lover." Mr. Singh's voice was packed with resentment. He suddenly looked up straight at us. Annoyance on his face was as clear as the rolling thunder outside. "So, why have you come? Why are you asking me so many questions? Are you investigators?" His sudden hostility took us by surprise. Payal and I exchanged glances. Mr. Singh further raised his voice, "What if you live on the plot that once belonged to my son? Why are you here?"

Just then his wife walked in with a tray and everyone fell silent. Tea and cookies were served but the awkward silence continued. The old lady looked from one person to another and then asked, "What's the matter? Is everything okay?"

Mr. Singh stated crossly, "These are the ones who bought Jagvir's plot."

The lady raised her brows. "So? Is there a problem?"

"I have no idea why they are here!" Mr. Singh shouted, looking daggers at us.

I looked down at the carpet, then at the photograph on the bookshelf. I saw it shake slightly. Was my troubled mind hallucinating? It gave me an indication that I must finish what we had come here to do. "Uncle Ji, your son, Jagvir . . . we've seen him many times inside our house. Even two days ago," I blurted.

"What? What nonsense!" Mr. Singh yelled, his nostrils flaring. He glared at us as if we were a pair of escaped convicts. "He's been dead for almost two years now." He redirected his eyes momentarily towards his son's picture and then back at us. His face had turned ashen.

This did not deter me. "He visits us at night, walks around in our house in a blue sherwani, with rich Zardozi work in silver and a matching blue turban. And last night, he was bleeding from his head . . ." The old lady's eyes expanded in horror. She covered her face with her dupatta and squealed.

"I don't believe you." Mr. Singh hit the sofa with his fisted hand. "You must have known him when he was alive. How do I know you are not imposters, and have come to cheat us?" he asked, staring at us accusingly.

"No, no, Uncle Ji, please believe us. We'd never deceive you. We are scared. That's why Puneet sounded panicky on the phone last night. We have seen him so often and, and know he's not alive, I mean he's . . . he's . . . Please, Uncle . . ." Tears streamed down Payal's cheeks.

"Uncle Ji, we are not here to add to your distress. We are here seeking your help. Please, help us—and help your son. He hasn't found peace. I appeal to you with folded hands." I was beginning to tear up. I joined my hands and pleadingly gazed at Mr. Singh and his wife.

"You think I'm a fool? Get out of my house." Shivering with anger, Mr. Singh sat on the edge of the sofa. I was crestfallen. Payal and I were in a hopeless situation now.

And then an unexpected thing happened. Jagvir's photo flew off the shelf and landed at the feet of the old man. We all stared at it aghast. Payal put her feet up and sat bundled on the sofa as if she had seen a real ghost. "He's here . . . He's here . . ." she kept mumbling in shock. The old lady whimpered. Mr. Singh seemed jolted by a thousand volts of current. I noticed a corner chair shift on its own by an inch. Was that where he sat now? Why wasn't he visible like he was at night? Could he control his appearance and disappearance?

Mr. Singh's shoulders slumped. The wrinkles on his face suddenly multiplied. A sob escaped his throat. His wife hid her face in her palms. The sound of her moans cut through the deathly silence that had now flooded the room. Then Mr. Singh raised his head to look straight at me. "That was the dress he was wearing that day—the day of his engagement, the day of his murder. A blue sherwani." He sighed and picked up Jagvir's photo and holding it close to his chest, he broke down. "Jaggi, why are you here? You should have been with *Rabb* now," he lamented.

Mr. Singh's wife choked with grief and kept repeating, "My Jaggi, my Jaggi." The pitiable sight broke my heart.

Payal added through her sobs, "It is obvious that Jagvir's soul hasn't found peace. It is seeking something. Maybe revenge! Were his murderers punished?"

"No. The court released them due to a lack of evidence. Although that wicked woman was the last person seen with him, nothing could be proved. It was a well-planned murder. The police too were in a hurry to close the case. Perhaps, they were bribed into destroying the evidence and keeping silent."

"We are sorry for what you have suffered, Uncle Ji."

"Jaggi had made a passing comment that morning, the day of his murder, that his fiancé was insisting the Faridabad plot should be registered in her name before their marriage." Mr. Singh wiped his eyes and sighed. "We were shocked. It was an unwarranted demand. It was so apparent that she was greedy. I told Jaggi sternly not to do it, at least not till he was married." He shook his head. "Our Jaggi was blind to her character. We advised our son to consider breaking off the engagement."

"And?"

"He got angry. He called us old-fashioned and narrow-minded. We decided to overlook what was obvious. It was a drastic mistake. I should have remained firm."

"After the engagement ceremony, Jagvir left with her. He never returned home." Mr. Singh's wife spoke through her sobs.

"Murder a young man over a piece of land?" Payal shivered visibly. "How evil!"

"That night we waited and waited." Mr. Singh choked on his words. His wife got him a glass of water. He sipped silently and tried to swallow his pain with it. When he spoke after a long gap, he was breathless, as if he had climbed many flights of stairs. "We tried his friends' phones. No one had any clue of his whereabouts. We both spent that night awake and worrying!" Tears trickled down his wrinkled cheeks. "The next day, the police found his body on . . . on his empty plot . . . now your house."

Payal audibly sucked in her breath. My jaw dropped. Mrs. Singh sobbed hysterically. "My poor son. That vile woman took him to his plot and killed him there. How I wish he had never bought that plot!" She wiped her tears with her dupatta. "You know, a month later she married the other man. The scheming bitch."

Payal got up to sit with her and held her hand. "We need to pray for the peace of his wandering soul."

The old man nodded. "When he died, we had a brief prayer session that my younger brother had arranged. We were inconsolable and didn't pay much attention. I'll arrange for a proper prayer session in your house now for the peace of my Jaggi's soul. I hope you won't mind."

"That's what we came to you for."

"We'll come to your house on Sunday with the priests. I'll go to the gurudwara today to make arrangements. Our Jagvir must rest in eternal peace now. We had no idea that he, he . . ." He got up with Jagvir's photo in his hand and kissed it before placing it back on the shelf.

"I strongly believe we need to open his murder case again," I declared. "My older brother, Vineet, is an advocate in the Supreme Court. I'll meet him to discuss the case. We'll not let the murderers go scot-free, I promise you that."

"Puttar Ji, we neither have the strength nor the money to fight long court cases."

"You are not alone now. Let me help you. I want to." The resolve in my voice surprised me. "I will request my brother to take up the case on no profit basis. You don't have to worry at all." Jagvir's parents had tears in their eyes. I smiled encouragingly. "Now I know why Jagvir hasn't found peace, what his soul is seeking."

"Justice!" Payal added ardently.

"God bless you, puttar. Yes. We'll together fight for justice now." Mr. Singh turned towards Jagvir's framed photograph. "Jagvir, if you are here, listen to this. We'll avenge you. You may rest in peace now." He then did the most unexpected thing. He got up, walked to where I was sitting and hugged me. As I hugged him back, he fell into my arms and wept like a child. "We felt so broken, so helpless, so lonely. Jagvir has sent you to us."

"Yes, Uncle Ji. You lost a son. Consider me your son now." I hugged the old man tightly.

"You are." Mr. Singh nodded spiritedly, wiping his tears.

"Will see you on Sunday then, Uncle Ji, Aunty Ji." I bowed to touch their feet. "And we'll keep bothering you with our visits." The old couple nodded and smiled.

As we were taking leave of the heartbroken parents, I glanced at Jagvir's framed photograph. My heart missed a beat. The photograph had turned to an almost 90° angle towards us from its original position. His smile was warmer.

It was lunchtime when we came out. The puddles and the overflowing potholes were everywhere. It had rained heavily. The clouds were now dispersing. Cold shivers were traversing through my body. It made me miserable that a young man had been murdered in cold blood on the plot on which now stood my house. My heart was bursting with sympathy for him. God alone knew what physical and mental pain that gentle fellow had undergone in the last moments of his life.

"Puneet, I'm not scared anymore of the ghost that lives in our house," Payal declared valiantly.

"You are like the Supergirl Kara Zor-El," I said, laughing.

"Not funny!" She frowned. The sun came out from behind a cloud to soak us in its warm dazzling light. We went to Nirula's to grab a quick bite before heading home.

The fading evening light wasn't too depressing today. We played our favourite music and cooked a simple dinner. As we sat at the dinner table, I took a large mouthful of the rice *pulao* and put down the fork on my plate noting Payal playing with her food. "A penny for your thoughts?"

"You know, Puneet, it broke my heart meeting the old parents. They have been so deeply wounded. We should do something for them."

"We are. Tomorrow I'll discuss with Vineet about reopening their son's murder case. I've promised them. Will fight tooth and nail to get them justice."

"You sound like a soldier going to a war." She chuckled. She looked so beautiful and cheerful. I blew her a kiss.

That night I grew restless. I was perhaps subconsciously waiting for Jagvir's ghost. He appeared. Earlier than usual. My eyes responded to the strong rose fragrance. The ghost stood next to my bed. He smiled. This time he didn't walk towards the wall. Instead, he rose towards the roof and then vanished through it.

He had come to say goodbye, I knew. I felt relieved and happy. Concurrently, I heard footsteps on our stairs. Someone was climbing up towards our bedroom. "Just a conjecture of my overworked mind," I concluded, turned to my side, and blissfully drifted off.

On Saturday morning, I woke up early. Payal was still asleep, completely burrowed under the blanket. She looked so beautiful and innocent that my heart went out to her. It had all been so stressful for her. I decided to give her a surprise. I would make the pancakes she loved and serve her breakfast in bed. I walked down. I was still on the stairs when something drew my attention. My heart leapt into my throat. I gagged. A blind terror shook my body. A woman was hanging from the ceiling fan of our sitting room. With my scream stuck in my throat, I turned to scamper back. Then I stopped dead. The figure was familiar. I realized with horror that it was Payal in her wedding sari. I collapsed on the stairway, crying with anguish.

Gradually, logic returned to my head. Minutes ago, I had left Payal sleeping in the bed. Then what was that thing hanging from the fan? I diverted my eyes back to the horrific scene. I could see better from this position. I realized there was no body. It was just Payal's sari draped as if around a body.

Who had done that? Who had taken her sari out of her closet? And draped it so dexterously? When? It hadn't been there when we had gone up to sleep around eleven.

I didn't want Payal to be traumatized. I rushed back to confirm if Payal was safe and intact. Then I ran to get the ladder from the garage. I removed the five-yard piece of my wife's clothing strung around the fan. I didn't want to put it back in her closet. It had been touched by something sinister. I heard Payal walking out of the bedroom. I quickly rolled the sari and hid it under the sofa for the time being and hurried to keep the ladder back.

I was not myself the whole day. What I had witnessed in the morning was running in my head in a loop. "All okay?" Payal asked me many times. Each time I gave her a weak smile and nodded.

As promised, Jagvir's parents were at our house at exact ten on Sunday morning. Two priests, known as *gurumukhs* in the gurudwaras, accompanied them. The gurumukhs supposedly have the ability to interact with troubled souls.

The devout men had brought some holy books with them. As I sat with the rest on our sitting room floor for the prayers, I noticed a corner of Payal's sari peeking out. I quickly shoved it back before Payal could notice.

The priests sang the *Gurbani*, followed by the *Sukhmani* Sahib and *Sahaj paath* for the liberation of the soul. After an hour-long prayer, they ordained the restless soul of Jagvir to break free from his earthly bonds and proceed on his journey to heaven. It was his time to go to Rabb, the Almighty, who is the ultimate deliverer, the Ultimate Father.

I knew that Jagvir's spirit had already gone home to Rabb.

"Halwa was my Jagvir's favourite," Jagvir's mother announced with tears in her eyes as she distributed the prasaad that she had brought.

Jagvir's ghost didn't visit us again.

Payal's sari remained hidden under the sofa. I hadn't forgotten. It was just that I wasn't been able to decide what to do with it. I couldn't throw away the cherished apparel that she had worn on her wedding day. Nor could I put it back among her clothes.

The prayers seemed to have mellowed down the paranormal activities in the house. Payal and I breathed easy for the first time since we had started living in the house.

Little did we know that it was the calm before a violent storm.

Even a fortnight hadn't passed when terror returned to ravage our lives. That ill-fated night, I woke up with a parched throat. I lifted the jug of water. It was empty. I had filled the jug to the brim before coming up for the night. Had Payal drained it all? How could she? It was impossible to drink a big jug of water in such a short span. She was sound asleep. I examined the floor for spilt water. It was as dry as a hot desert in the summer sun.

Picking up the jug, I walked down to go to the kitchen to refill it. I had covered only half of the stairway when I stopped dead. Payal's sari was fluttering in the sitting room, as if someone was playing with it.

A dark figure sat on the sofa . . . a human shape, darker than the surroundings, dark from head to toe. The top of the form slowly turned towards my frozen body. It was directly looking at me. The sound of eerie laughter that followed hit me like a blow. The jug dropped from my hand and rolled down the stairs. My scream got stuck inside my throat. Somehow, I mustered the courage to move and dashed back to my bedroom as fast as I could on my shivering legs. I shut the door with a bang. Payal was sitting up, having been woken by the noises.

"Puneet, be a little considerate. Why are you creating a riot in the middle of the night?" she chided me in her sleepy voice.

"Something . . . Someone is sitting on our sofa," words finally escaped my mouth.

"Who?" Payal's eyes expanded with fear.

"Th-The s-same d-dark . . . s-scary."

Payal muffled her scream with her hands. "The one that was in the kitchen?" she asked hesitatingly. I nodded.

We didn't sleep a wink afterwards. Our encounter with the world of the supernatural should have ended. What was this thing still lurking in our house?

At daybreak, I sneaked out of the bed and walked down, shaking with fear. I needed to check the house before Payal woke up. Eerie silence hung everywhere. I halted on the stairway, holding my belly that was being tormented by cramps. From the corner of my eye, I saw it again . . . Payal's sari hanging . . . like wrapped around a dead body. I didn't know what to do. I took a few deep breaths to steady myself, walked down, brought the ladder and removed the sari. Once again, I shoved it under the sofa. With my spirits in the gutter,

I went back and lay in the bed with Payal, cuddling her in my arms. I was extremely worried for her. I must protect her.

At breakfast, I fleetingly scanned the sitting room a few times. Everything looked normal, as if what I had witnessed last night had been a dream. Payal and I finished our breakfast and left for work early.

In the evening when we returned home, the usual cold hostile air greeted us. We changed and sat in our bedroom writing reports. That was an excuse to avoid being anywhere else. "Puneet, I don't want to go to the kitchen," Payal declared when it was time for dinner.

Neither did I want her to go down alone. "All right, dear. I'll quickly make us some grilled sandwiches," I offered.

In the kitchen I had a strong hunch that someone was watching me. Each time I looked over my shoulder, I felt a movement. Something invisible was hovering around. "I'm not afraid of you," I conveyed loudly. I wanted to at least sound brave even if I was trembling inside. I felt like I was trapped in a dark tunnel with no escape.

At night, I kept two jugs of water instead of one in our bedroom. I shut the door and locked it. Payal kept a booklet of Hanuman Chalisa under her pillow. She sat mumbling prayers for a long time. She seemed terrified of something. Was she aware of what was happening in the house?

I tried diverting her mind. "I forgot to tell you, Payal. Vineet has started the proceedings for opening the Jagvir Singh Murder case. Hopefully, Jagvir will finally get justice."

"Good," Payal replied.

In the middle of the night, Payal's moans woke me up. She was restless. I touched her. She was burning hot. I couldn't get a doctor this late. So, I decided to give her a paracetamol to bring down the fever. I needed to fetch the first-aid box from the sideboard in the dining room. Rushing down the stairs, I suddenly halted midway. The dark figure stood at the bottom of the stairway blocking my way. I cringed with fear and stepped back. The apparition slowly faded. I breathed easy. Just a step later, I received a forceful push from behind. I was holding the railing or else I would have gone tumbling down the stairs. I turned to confront the offender. The dark entity was right behind me now. For the first time I saw it from close. It had a dark, ashen grey, contorted face, vilely grotesque. What sent icy chills down my spine were the piercing eyes . . . bottomless holes exuding pure evil. I was taken aback. I wanted this thing to leave us alone. I gathered courage to remonstrate. "Get out of my house," I muttered. It began to move backwards, up the stairs, and then vanished. Payal's loud moans worried me. I didn't want to leave her alone. With loud prayers on my lips, I ran to fetch the first-aid box.

Within a minute I was back. I took out a pill and picked up the jug of water. It was dry like it had never been filled. So was the second one. How was the water disappearing from the jugs? Left with no choice, I filled a glass with unfiltered water from the bathroom tap.

The whole night Payal tossed and turned and moaned. The paracetamol relieved her for a few hours, but then fever and headache returned. We spent a sleepless night. Whenever Payal stopped moaning, I heard strange sounds coming from outside our room . . . the staircase creaking under a heavy weight, distinct footsteps outside our door and sniggers. What was stopping it from entering our bedroom? I lay listlessly in my bed, dizzy with fear and dejection.

When the morning came, the sunlight seeping in through the windows couldn't dispel my gloom. I left the bed depleted of my energy. I cautiously opened the door. The bright light gave me courage. I walked down to the kitchen to make tea for Payal.

I immediately knew I wasn't alone. Someone kept following me. Sharp footsteps. Without a body that owned them. How could I continue to live here, each moment in dread? My lovely house had now been turned into a bloodcurdling monster.

Payal was still burning with fever when I brought her down from the bedroom. She drank a cup of tea with great fuss. She was shivering uncontrollably. She seemed so unwell that I thought of admitting her to a hospital. Perhaps she would be safe there. I took her to see a doctor near our house for his advice.

By the time we reached the doctor's clinic, Payal was miraculously restored. Colour returned to her cheeks and her fever went down. I too felt like I had been released from a torturous prison.

The doctor couldn't diagnose what was wrong with her. He sent her blood sample to a lab for testing. "I will decide on the medicine only after I get the report. Keep her fever under control till then. She doesn't need hospitalization," he advised as we left the clinic.

It was a pleasant spring day. The azure sky was cloudless and the breeze was cool. The silk cotton trees were ablaze with fiery blooms. The new spring flowers were happily dancing, so were the grasses moving in unison in the pleasant gusts. It seemed the whole world was celebrating the advent of a new season, except us two morose souls. We went to the parking. Before I could kick start my motorbike, Payal held my hand. "I don't want to go back home yet. It's so beautiful here. Let's sit somewhere, in a park. I feel much better."

I drove her to a nearby park and we sat languidly under a massive *peepal* tree. Our rundown energies needed a breather.

Staying outside like this gave us short-lived relief. Payal rested her head on my shoulder and sat silently. I swallowed the pain that filled my heart, noticing the transformation of my lively chirpy wife into a mute, miserable person.

At lunchtime, we fetched some sandwiches and coffee from a nearby café and returned to the park. Payal gobbled down her sandwich and sipped her coffee with relish. Gradually she became relaxed and cheerful. I held her hands in mine and peeped into her tired eyes. "Look, Payal, if we keep getting frightened of every small episode, our energies will get depleted, and the evil will defeat us. Will you promise not to chicken out anymore?" Payal nodded faintly. "Come on, Payal, you have always been so strong."

"Puneet, I try to be. But I feel my strength is slowly fading, my insides are being eaten away."

"Payal, please listen to me. We have only two choices left with us now. Either we defeat the evil that has invaded our house or get consumed by it. What do you want?"

"Defeat it," Payal voiced weakly. "But how?"

"Maybe we should seek help." It suddenly occurred to me that I would have to take my parents and my brother into confidence now. Payal and I couldn't handle the situation on our own anymore.

A sudden change in weather diverted our attention. A strong breeze had brought thick clouds. It was time to return home. "Puneet, I don't want to go back to that house," Payal asserted in her feeble voice.

"Where else will we go?" I said, defeated, and forced Payal to get up. It hurt me to do this to her, but we couldn't pass the night outside. By the time we reached home, there was a full-blown hailstorm outside. There was one brewing inside our house.

After a simple dinner of *khichdi*, I proposed, "Let's watch a movie? Do you want to watch a Hindi comedy?" With raised eyebrows, I waited for Payal's response.

"Whatever," she shrugged and went to sit on the sofa with a gloomy face. I realized with concern that she was sitting on the exact spot where that dark form had sat the other night. Under the same spot lay hidden her wedding attire. I didn't want to frighten her, so I kept mum.

I inserted the cassette of the movie *Naram Garam* in the player connected to our TV and sat on a chair. Payal watched the movie hardly for five minutes. She then shut her eyes and loudly moaned. "What's it, Payal?"

Payal shook her head. "There's someone here. I can sense it. I am scared, so terribly scared, Puneet. I'm surrounded by something dark . . . please save me . . ."

I roved my eyes all around but couldn't spot anything. "Payal, stop this frightening dialogue. Let's discuss this in the morning."

She fell silent. I noted a glazed look in her eyes. Ignoring her, I diverted my attention back to the movie. I just needed us to pass the night without problems. I had decided to call my family the next morning. I would tell them everything. I urgently needed their help.

Payal got up to go. "Puneet, I am very unwell."

"Okay. You go." I casually waved at her. "I'll watch the movie. It's interesting."

"Come with me, please." She croaked in a hoarse whisper followed by a bad bout of cough. I was concerned. She had gone bluish pale and was shivering.

"Are you okay, Payal?"

"I have a terrible constriction in my throat and my chest," she managed to whisper and then walked out of the room.

I remained seated. "You change and get into the bed. I'll follow soon."

When I reached our bedroom some ten minutes later, a horrible stench hit me. It was a putrid smell of rotting flesh. Payal was lying in the bed shaking violently. I was staggered. "Payal," I called out to her nervously.

She slowly sat up. Her head was bent to one side, her body stiff, her hands twisted, her teeth exposed in a frightening grin. Wild fury oozed from her partially dilated eyes. On seeing me, she growled weirdly. I cringed with fear. My heart stopped beating and my mouth went dry. I gathered my wits and cried, "Payal, please wake up. What's wrong with you?"

"*Hutt.* Go. Beat it," Payal said, snarling like an animal. Frantic with fear, I realized that she was probably possessed.

My legs had lost all strength and felt like jelly. I was ready to slump to the floor with my weight. I couldn't handle this alone. I urgently needed help. Whom should I call? Couldn't trouble Papa this late. Vineet. I'd call Vineet.

Could I leave Payal alone even for a second and walk down? Something bad might happen to her. I stood flustered, unable to make up my mind. Payal picked up an empty glass from the side table and threw it at me with force. I ducked. The glass struck the wall behind me with a loud crack and shattered into splinters. Some pieces rebounded off the wall and hit me on my neck.

I stared at the mess in pure horror. The force with which the glass was hurtled, had it hit where it had been aimed, I could have been seriously injured. The spirit inside Payal wanted me incapacitated. I would have to constrain her quickly. I looked for something to use. Then I noticed the Hanuman Chalisa lying in a corner. It had been flung away. Had Payal done that?

She began to crawl towards me on all four limbs, like an animal, eyeing me like a creepy monster. I rushed to pick up the holy book. I had heard that demonic spirits had an aversion towards anything holy. I was convinced what was inside Payal right now was demonic. Holding the book in front of her, I started reading the Chalisa. Payal froze in her position. She snarled and then grabbed my free wrist so tightly in her hand that it hurt. She produced horrifying sounds—wild and raucous. Then baring her teeth, she lunged at my wrist and sank her teeth into my flesh. I was confounded by the sudden attack and tried shaking off her clasp. She stuck on like a leech. I jumped back dragging her along. She hung on relentlessly. A flash of terror traversed through my body. Blood began trickling down my wrist. The pain was becoming unbearable. I gave her a hard whack on her back and she released my wrist. There was blood on her face, around her lips. My blood. She chilled me to my bones. I needed to control her before she seriously hurt herself or me. I took a step towards her and extended my hands to hold hers. She was quicker and punched me hard on my chest. The force of her blow stunned me. The pain was so intense that I suspected my ribs had been broken. How had she attained such enormous strength?

It took all I had for me to stand up. "Payal, you are strong, stronger than the spirit trying to overpower you. Throw it out," I said. "You are not scared. You are very brave." I had rolled my final dice. I had no idea how else to control the situation. All of a sudden, she began to cough violently. Then she baulked and fell on the bed on her stomach. Instantly, I felt something breeze past me. An unseen entity—cold and sinister. The malicious spirit had left Payal's body. The smell of rotting flesh swelled in the room. I needed to take Payal out of here.

I had barely taken two steps towards Payal when I felt a strong push from behind and I went crashing down. My head struck the mirror of the dressing table, shattering it into pieces. I slumped on the floor. Blood poured out from my head in a stream, blinding me. How was I going to fight this? I mustered my strength and stood on my shaky legs. My eyes sought Payal. She wasn't on the bed. She wasn't even in the room. Where had she gone? I took a few wobbly steps towards the door. The door slammed shut on my face with a bang. I pushed it as hard as I could in my condition, putting my entire weight on it but the door wouldn't budge. I was trapped. How was I going to save Payal? What was happening to her down there? I was getting weak with all the blood I was losing. I sat down on the floor. I needed to gather my wits and strength. I needed to reach the telephone to seek help.

"Blood . . . I seek blood . . . heaps of blood . . ." An awful grating whisper filled the room. I looked up. What was Payal doing up there? How did she reach there?

Payal was up on the wall near the roof. Someone was holding her there, making her stick to the wall like a lizard. She glared down at me with wildly savage eyes. Her lips were still curled into a loathsome grin. My blood had dried around her mouth. Her hair fell all over her face. She looked like a demon.

"Payal, what's wrong with you? Please come down." I sobbed. "We need to leave the house, escape from the evil that has taken possession of you. Please—" I couldn't even complete my sentence. She leapt like a raging bull from the wall and landed directly on me. Both of us went crashing to the floor. Then, everything turned black.

When I became aware of my surroundings again, I was alone in the room. The room's door was open. My head throbbed, as if it had been hammered on and my whole body ached. The room was pitch dark, encased in an eerie silence.

I felt needles in my dry throat. I needed water. I took the support of the bed and with great effort raised myself to sit on it. I reached for the lamp's switch. No light came on. I needed to check on Payal. I limped out of the room, hoping that she had survived.

I reached for the light switch outside the room. It didn't work either. There was no power in our house. Step by step I crept down the dark stairs. In the kitchen, I lit a candle and drank milk straight from the bottle kept in the fridge. There was still no sign of Payal anywhere.

When I walked out of the kitchen, a cold draft hit me like a sharp knife. The streetlight was cascading in through the main door. It was swinging—opening and banging shut due to the furious wind.

"Payal! Where are you?" My voice was met with silence. Had Payal walked out of the house and into the dark blustery night? Why? Where had she gone? Who had taken her away from me?

I had lost a lot of blood and weakness was once again overpowering me. I took the right decision to call Vineet before collapsing on the floor and losing consciousness again.

I never saw Payal again.

I was admitted to a hospital with blood loss, a few broken ribs, a collapsed lung, a crack in my skull, and my body pierced by splinters of broken glass. The demon had tried its best to eliminate me. I had survived. Sometimes I wish I hadn't. I wish I didn't have to live in this world—a world that appeared colourless now.

After being declared fit by the doctor following six months of hospitalization, I spent six months harassed by the police under the suspicion of having murdered my wife and destroying her body. I don't know why Payal's parents were bent upon holding me accountable for her disappearance. I understood their anguish for having lost their only child. I wanted them to realize how heartbroken I was. Nobody cared!

Nobody except Vineet believed me. He thought it was obvious that I couldn't have murdered Payal. How would I have disposed off her body when I was seriously injured to even move? Vineet was positive that someone had attacked us. He did not mention it to anyone that it had been a supernatural incident, because he knew nobody would've believed us.

Vineet's efforts paid well in another case. He managed to get a life term for Jagvir's murderers.

It has been more than a year now. There's still no clue to Payal's whereabouts. Vineet tried his best, ran from pillar to post. He went to police stations, media companies, put up missing person posters, and even contacted people in influential positions. He visited a few persons dealing with evil spirits, but it was all futile. "Sometimes a demonic entity follows the lost soul and invades the space inhabited by it. The woman could be with it, with the demon," an expert exorcist told Vineet. My heart shattered into pieces that day. I wished Vineet hadn't given me that piece of information.

I live with my parents now. I am afraid to live alone. Darkness gives me panic attacks. I barely leave the house and work from home—writing weekly columns for the magazine. I have a huge loan on my head and have no idea how I would ever be able to pay it. Not in this lifetime.

Time and again my mind wanders to the unfathomable questions. Where was my Payal taken? What happened to her? How could she just disappear without a trace? Is she dead? Each time I think of her, I repent not taking her to a safe place on time. I repent having built the house that became the cause of my ruin, of the wretched life I now live. More than anything, it took away my love from me.

My house now lies abandoned. Nobody wants to buy it. People even avoid going near it. Many neighbours complain of strange sounds emanating from inside the house. Some claim to have seen a dark shadow lurking at the bay window of the empty house.

My house has notoriously acquired a new name—The Haunted House.

The Ouija Backlash

PART-1
SRINAGAR

Life was easy-going till I was sixteen years old. If I could turn back time to a period of my choice, that's where I would want to return and eliminate the mistakes I had made. For it was then on that those dark entities began to clasp my life in their terrifying claws and my escape became a gargantuan task for me, and for everyone around me.

My long altercation with the supernatural began on a pleasant, albeit ill-omened, autumn night when Vini Didi introduced us to the Ouija board. Her friend had given it to her. Without assessing the consequences, Didi brought it home and lured Vidhi Didi, my middle sister and me into summoning spirits of the dead through it. That innocent game threw my life on a prolonged rollercoaster ride of dreadful events.

The year was 1992. Dad, a brigadier in the Indian Army, was posted as the head of the anti-terrorist operations in Srinagar, Kashmir. That's where we lived—Dad, Mom, and I.

October of that year arrived as usual, all dressed up in the fiery colours of the autumn. The leaves of the gigantic chinars acquired stunning hues of auburn, red, golden, copper, and bronze, before shrivelling up—in their last effort to spread splendour before bidding farewell. This phenomenon coincided with my sisters coming home for Diwali. I was overjoyed. We sisters shared a special bond despite the age difference among us . . . Vini Didi was six years older than me and Vidhi Didi was four years older than me.

The whole cantonment dazzled in fairy lights and earthen lamps on Diwali. After puja at home, we all went to the cantonment dressed in our best outfits for the party. Vini Didi looked stunning in her turquoise and beige *lehenga*. I noted eyes of many young officers on her. Dad must have noticed it too for he instantly appointed himself as our sentinel on duty. He refused to leave our side even for a minute. Mom kindly kept busy with her friends.

Enjoying the fireworks after the lavish dinner, we returned home. Vini Didi was on top of the world. Captain Varun, the most handsome and sought-after bachelor had managed to hand her a love letter despite the fortification. This had happened when she had gone for a helping of the dessert. Though Dad's eyes had followed her, he had missed the exchange as an associate had momentarily distracted him.

I had watched the Captain follow Didi gingerly, time and again turning to check, waiting for the favourable time to launch his ambush. The moment Dad's attention was fleetingly diverted, he slyly slipped a piece of paper in Didi's hand. Vini Didi blushed, smiled, and quickly slipped the love note into her purse. Once at home, I told Vidhi Didi about it. In retrospect, I wish I hadn't. For that's how the supernatural invaded my life.

It was close to our bedtime when Vidhi Didi and I went to Vini Didi's room to tease her. "I know your secret, Didi. Captain Varun handed over a love letter to you. Didn't he?" Vidhi Didi goaded her.

Vini Didi nodded with a bright smile and twinkle in her eye, "Don't tell Mom, Dad. He's head over heels in love with me."

"Wow! Vini and Varun. Sounds great. Doesn't it?" Vidhi Didi held Vini Didi's hands and waltzed around. She seemed more excited than the one who had received the declaration of love. Vini Didi laughed delightedly. There was a special glow on her face.

We left Vini Didi to her dreamland and returned to the bedroom that Vidhi Didi and I shared. We had barely settled in our beds when Vini Didi marched into our room with a packet in her hand. With a big grin she posted herself on the floor-carpet. "Come Vidhi and Vriti. I've something interesting here. I had forgotten all about it. My fused bulb just got lighted." That was inviting enough for us to hop out of our beds and join her.

"What is this?" I asked, curious when I observed Vini Didi take out a board from its box. It was a rectangular plank, had alphabets A to Z written in the centre and numbers from 0 to 9 below them. On the left top corner was written "Yes" and on the right side "No". At the bottom was written "Goodbye". There weren't any dice or counters of any kind. She put a heart-shaped flat plastic piece below the written stuff and happily announced, "It's a Ouija board, pronounced as 'weeja'."

Both Vidhi Didi and I stared at her blankly. "How's this game played?" Vidhi Didi asked.

Vini Didi chirped, "It's not a game. It's a spirit board . . . calls spirits. Don't take it as a joke."

Her bright smile was in complete contrast to the expression on my face. "Calls spirits . . . you mean dead people?" I had goosebumps. I roved my eyes around the room. It struck me that there must be hordes of spirits around. So many people had died or were dying every day in Kashmir valley. It began with the killing of hundreds of Kashmiri Pandits. But the butchery didn't stop there. It was going on in the name of Jihad—of people with dissimilar views, of so-called informers or traitors. Innocents were not spared either. Bombs were being detonated to kill them while they were out shopping for the daily necessities. Some were getting killed in encounters. The killing spree was going on like Roman gladiators' bouts unto death. The spirits of the dead, who had died unnatural deaths, must be hovering all over the valley and around us. My dark thoughts made me jittery. My heart filled with dread as I scrutinized the room. The room, however, appeared warm and peaceful.

Vini Didi nodded seriously. "Yes. We'll all focus our minds and call a spirit. The moment the spirit is here, the planchette will begin to move to the alphabets and numbers, answering our questions." She picked up the plastic piece and waved it at us. "This is a planchette."

"It'll move on its own? How's that possible!" Vidhi Didi narrowed her eyes and regarded Vini Didi suspiciously.

"The spirit will move it, silly."

"Will we see the spirit?" I shivered.

"Vriti, stop asking stupid questions. You know that the spirits are invisible."

Vidhi Didi screwed up her face and asked cynically, "Why would a spirit come at our beckoning? This sounds fictitious."

"They do, the spirits do come. I have seen it."

"When? Where?"

"In my friend's room. It's her Ouija board. We called spirits in the hostel. It gave us correct answers."

"What answers?"

"Please, girls. This isn't something new. People have been calling spirits since olden times. Many famous personalities have communicated with the spirits."

"Which personalities?"

"Hmm . . . for example . . . there was this novelist—Emily Grant Hutchings. She claimed that her novel was dictated by the spirit of Mark Twain through the Ouija board. Then, Pearl Lenore claimed that all her literary work had been delivered through a spirit named Patience Worth. She was in touch with this spirit for twelve years. Even William Butler Yeats' poetry was inspired by the Ouija board that his wife used. Mary Todd Lincoln, the wife of President Abraham Lincoln, contacted her dead son through seances conducted in the White House."

"Oh really, Didi?" I was impressed. "Can we get all our questions answered by the spirit?" My fear now turned to excitement, like we were on a treasure hunt.

"Yes. I just told you so."

"What questions will we ask?" Vidhi Didi too was entrapped now.

"Like, will we be rich? Will we do well in life? Who will be the man we'll marry?"

"Oh! All that?" Vidhi Didi grinned. "Now I know. You want to check if you'll marry Captain Varun or not. Why involve us? You could have done that on your own. Secretly."

"You need more people, more human energy for a spirit to come. It's safer too."

"Safer means? Is it dangerous to call spirits? Will they harm us?" My eyes once again inspected the room.

"Of course, silly. It isn't child's play."

Vidhi Didi too looked around with her narrowed eyes. "That sounds scary. Weren't you scared?"

"A bit unnerved the first time. But it's easy. You just have to politely request the spirit to go back to its realm, saying 'thank you and goodbye' at the end of the session."

Vidhi Didi and I sat staring at the board like two cats staring at a bowl of tempting milk. My brain went into hyperactivity mode, trying to think of the questions I would like to ask. I wanted to study economics and become a famous economist like Amartya Sen. "Vini Didi, I want to know if I'll be able to study at the London School of Economics."

Vini Didi nodded. "We will ask some generic questions. Shall we begin?" We nodded.

She had brought along a candle and a box of matchsticks. She lit the candle and placed it next to the Ouija board. "Vriti, please switch off the light." I refused to budge. I was afraid. Vidhi Didi gave me a hard stare and got up to do the needful. The room suddenly plunged into darkness and I shuddered.

"Okay sweeties, now be serious. No one will laugh. It annoys the spirits." I heard her taking a deep breath. "So, we'll call the spirit nearest to us, in our vicinity." My heart began to race. My eyes were getting adjusted to the dim eerie light. "Only I will ask questions, even on your behalf. You both will maintain complete silence. Is that clear?" I nodded nervously.

"Also, I will first check if it's a good spirit. If the planchette goes to 'No', I'll immediately ask the spirit to leave. You too will quietly pray for it to return to its realm."

"What if the evil spirit is a liar? It may say it's a good spirit, whereas it is evil." I voiced my opinion nervously.

Vini Didi glared at me. "Vriti, shut up. No more discussions." She squared her shoulders. Her voice sounded distant and spooky. "Put your index and middle fingers on the planchette and close your eyes. Appeal for a spirit to come."

Vini Didi and Vidhi Didi put their fingers on the planchette. I followed, hesitatingly. I closed my eyes and began to repeat in my mind, 'Come. Oh spirit, please come.' I peeped at my sisters through half-closed eyes. They both sat composed. I tightly closed my eyes again. Then, an uneasy feeling began to drench me. A hand brushed against my cheek. I cringed and instantly opened my eyes. Both my sisters were concentrating on the board. Who had done that? I turned to look behind. In that subdued darkness, the empty space and flickering ghostly shadows on the wall stared back at me. I shrugged and brought my focus back on our game. The moment I closed my eyes, a hand clutched my right shoulder. I squealed. There was no one around except the three of us. Yet I could see my nightshirt crumpled as if it had been grabbed. Instantly the planchette shivered and came alive. It began to move in circles. Our fingers were no more touching it, yet it was forming the figure 8 again and again. A blind terror gripped me. Vini Didi was staring at the planchette as if it were an alien insect that had bizarrely landed on our board.

And then a disaster befell. The door of our room flew open with a bang. I screamed. In breezed Mom followed by Ravi.

Ravi was a private in the Army and helped Mom in his free time. He carried a tray with cups of hot saffron milk for us.

It took Mom a few seconds to get used to the dim light of our room. Then she froze on the spot noticing us sitting around the Ouija board. "Girls, what are you all doing? Stop that. I say, stop that."

Vini Didi hesitated. Mom switched on the light. The sudden light in the room blinded me. Mom took the tray from Ravi and gestured at him to leave. Then she stood hovering over us like a hawk. Flustered at the surveillance, Vidhi Didi picked up the Ouija board with a quick movement and shoved it in the box even before Vini Didi could stop her.

"What have you done? We didn't even say goodbye," Vini Didi whispered agitatedly.

Mom's face was a multitude of reactions . . . disbelief, shock, anger, concern. "What are you girls doing?"

"We were calling spirits to answer our questions," I declared timidly. Vini Didi and Vidhi Didi glared at me through their bent heads.

"Calling spirits?" Mom's eyes popped out of their sockets. "My God! Why would you do that? What questions do you need to ask?"

Vini Didi and Vidhi Didi maintained unnerving silence. "About our future," I announced timorously, also worried that I had committed a blunder by revealing our secret. Both my sisters might be angry with me now.

"Future? No one has ever seen the future," Mom's voice boomed in the room. "Hard work, sincerity, determination pave the way to a bright future. Not calling spirits."

"Mom, don't lecture, please," Vidhi Didi complained. "We were just having fun. A simple innocent game." She shrugged.

"A simple innocent game? Playing with the spirits? That's dangerous." After a momentary silence, Mom shook her head.

"I don't believe in all these things, and neither should you. Now go to sleep. It was a tiring day."

Had Mom known then how close to the truth she was about it being dangerous, she would have done something about it. But everyone let the matter fizzle out like soda vapours from a bottle . . . to become a hornet's nest for me.

Vini Didi walked out of our room with a deep scowl on her face. Mom followed her after leaving our cups of milk on the table. Vidhi Didi got up with a glum face, picked up the Ouija board, packed it and shoved it into my almirah. She then gulped down her milk and marched to her bed without another word. Throughout all this, I hadn't shifted from my seat on the floor.

Why had the room suddenly gone cold?

"Vriti, switch off the light and go to sleep," Vidhi Didi ordered like a commanding officer, and, like a sullen soldier on a penalizing duty, I stood up reticently and followed her command. Why was I being made to feel as if it was entirely my fault? I hadn't asked Mom to barge into our room. It wasn't I who had started the game!

I couldn't sleep that night. I kept hearing strange sounds from my almirah. I called out to Vidhi Didi a few times, but she was blissfully asleep.

In the morning I left my bed exhausted. No one mentioned last night's fiasco. After breakfast, Vidhi Didi and Vini Didi went shopping with Mom to pick up the essentials they needed to take with them. They were leaving for their respective hostels the next day.

I went to my almirah to get my stuff and gasped the moment I opened it. It seemed as if it had been a battleground of wild cats. This mess must be Vidhi Didi's doing, I presumed—a display of her annoyance. But she was not the vengeful type.

As I looked for the clothes I needed, I noticed the Ouija board lying on top of the messy pile. The planchette sat on it—like an invitation to play the game. I shook my head to eradicate the alarm bells that had begun to ring in the deep recesses of my mind. "Don't be a chicken," I told myself. I shoved the board inside the box, closed it firmly, and put it in a back corner. Hurriedly taking out my clothes, I banged shut my almirah as if something deadly was about to materialize from it. I must remind Vini Didi to take the board with her.

The next day my sisters left. Their departure caused an unnerving stillness in the house. The Ouija board, having slipped out of everyone's mind, stayed in the corner of my almirah.

From that day onwards, I began to sense a distinct presence in my room. Once the night triggered silence, I would hear sounds. They would erupt from inside my almirah . . . as if someone trapped inside was trying to get free. I knew it had something to do with the Ouija board. But where would I keep it if not here? I couldn't discard it without Vini Didi's permission. Mom had forgotten all about it.

As days passed, that thing inside my almirah began to get stronger. Every morning, shivers would traverse through my body seeing the almirah door wide open and the Ouija board with the planchette on it lying on the floor. Who was doing it? Who wanted me to play? I was frazzled. This was unnatural. I wondered if I should discuss this with Mom. But I was afraid of her adverse reaction, afraid that she would admonish me for being imprudently superstitious.

In early November the high mountain ranges received their first snowfall. The winds blowing over them brought nips of chill down into the valley, offering the first flavours of the winter. A bizarre chill had begun to encompass my life too.

Winter was my favourite season, especially when it snowed. This time an untainted melancholy assailed my spirit. At night, after I switched off the light, eerie whispers assaulted me like a haunting wind blowing around me. Someone seemed to be calling out my name . . . that's what it sounded to me . . . my name echoing through the air . . . Vriiiiitiiii . . . I would wrap myself head to toe in my quilt and tremble.

I tried telling Mom about the Ouija board creating problems for me, but she was dismissive. "What's the big deal? Throw it away." She shrugged. "I don't like it sitting in our house. And Vriti, please pay more attention to your studies." With this, she went back to her busy schedule . . . running the house, attending functions, and seeing her friends.

A few days later when I woke up in the morning, I found the Ouija board lying on top of my quilt. I stifled my scream. Nobody had come to my room.

It now struck me that Mom was right. I needed to get rid of this creepy thing. I could explain to Vini Didi later. So, instead of keeping the Ouija board back in the almirah, I sneaked to the backyard and threw it in the trash-can. Why hadn't I thought of this simple solution earlier?

I was relaxed the whole of that Saturday, assuming my problem was over. The following morning when I went near my almirah, the smell of rot hit me like a tight jab. The Ouija board lay on top of my clothes, smeared with rotting waste. My mouth fell open and I froze on the spot.

With my whole body in shivers, I took it to the bathroom, cleaned it, and hid it in the bathroom cabinet, behind my other stuff. I realized that it wasn't the board but something else attracted by it that was creating this havoc in my life. Hadn't I felt a hand on my shoulder when we were inviting the spirits? I needed Mom's help to get rid of it.

Mom had friends visiting her and that kept her busy the entire day. Since she seemed tired in the evening, I decided to speak to her the next day.

Somehow that next day kept slipping into the next and the next. My school kept me busy as well. Each evening when I tried talking to Mom, we would be interrupted by someone— the cook, the cleaning lady, guests, or the telephone. Someone was causing these obstructions, I believed, to safeguard the Ouija board.

December came, and with it the first heavy snowfall. The colours of the entire city got buried under a thick layer of pristine white. The valley shivered in minus temperature. Schools closed down for the winter vacation. An uncanny hush enveloped the valley and my house in its shroud. I stayed indoor most of the time, clinging to Mom when she was home, avoiding being alone. I was afraid of something. I didn't know what.

One cold cloudy day, feeling down and having nothing much to do, I raided Dad's bookshelf. I found Bram Stoker's *Dracula* in his collection. I loved reading fiction and immediately became interested in it. By the evening I had read till where the English solicitor Jonathan Harker, visiting Count Dracula in his castle in the Carpathian Mountains, encounters three vampire sisters. Though the Count rescues him, Jonathan soon realizes that Count Dracula is a vampire too and his life is in danger.

After dinner, I continued to read in my bed. It was a bad idea, I knew, but it kept my mind distracted. Around eleven I inserted a bookmark, closed the book, and kept it on the table. A strange unease had begun to embrace me.

It must have been sometime in the middle of the night that I woke up with a start. A sudden grating sound of a chair being moved was distinct. I slowly turned my head towards the source of the sound. My chair had been shifted and a faint transparent figure sat on it. *Dracula* lay open on the table. And then, the page of the book turned on its own with a rustling sound. I whimpered. The figure's head slowly turned towards me. I screamed. Both Mom and Dad instantly responded and rushed into my room.

Mom wiped the sweat off my forehead. "What's the matter, Vriti?" My whole body was shuddering in reaction to what I had seen. I mumbled some unintelligible words and pointed towards the chair. It was now empty. Mom and Dad exchanged glances. "She's seriously ill."

"H-He was sitting on my chair and reading my book." The words finally escaped my mouth. I was stuttering and shivering.

"Who? Who was sitting in your chair?" Dad looked around.

"A ghost."

Mom looked annoyed.

"It's only your imagination," Dad stated casually and closed the book. I stared at him in disbelief. "And who told you to read the Dracula story?"

"No wonder you were frightened. You had a scary dream." Mom lovingly stroked my face. "You are too young to read the horror stuff." She tucked me into bed, kissed my forehead, and sweetly bid me goodnight. Mom and Dad stayed with me for a few minutes more. The room deceptively seemed calm and safe. They then left me alone to cope with my terrors.

I tossed and turned for the rest of the night and got out of my warm bed only when the sun's warm rays penetrated deep into my room.

When I walked into the dining room like a zombie, Dad had already left for work. Mom gasped, "What's wrong with your eyes? They are so red and swollen. Are you well, dear? Have you been crying?"

"I'm fine," I replied coldly and got busy buttering my toast. I avoided meeting Mom's eyes. I was angry at her. She wasn't even trying to understand what I was going through. Adults never take children seriously. The first thing I did after finishing my breakfast was hold *Dracula* from a corner like a defiled object and place it back on Dad's bookshelf. I never dared to read horror stuff again.

I spent the entire day doing my homework to remain distracted from the terrifying thoughts occupying my mind. After dinner I sat in the parlour adjacent to my parents' bedroom to watch TV. Mom was in her bedroom, reading and relaxing. I decided to watch a league football match. Diego Maradona, my favourite player, was playing against AC Milan. Dad too joined me to watch the second half of the exciting match. Around nine he declared that he was tired and went to his bedroom.

With a bowl of popcorn and my favourite fleece blanket, I was cosy and engrossed in the match when somebody tapped on the front window. My attention was on the TV as AC Milan had been given a penalty corner that could be converted into a goal. I walked to the window, shoved the curtain aside, and peeped out. The moment I did that, I shrieked. I had seen her. The light from the fixture on the opposite wall had fallen straight on her face. Mom and Dad came running from their bedroom to find me sweating and shivering.

"Vriti, what's wrong? What happened?" Mom was scowling.

"I thought you had been electrocuted," Dad said, standing cross-armed, frowning at me.

"Th-There's someone outside."

"Who?" Dad became alert.

"A . . . A ghost . . . woman . . . a witch . . ."

"Okay. What else?" Dad remained impassive.

"Grey-haired . . . like creepy crawling snakes . . . protruding red eyes, white face. A . . . A ghost."

"Vriti, good imagination! Late nights aren't good for you. Go to—" Dad hadn't even completed his sentence when the front window rattled. Then the windows of my room. A split second later the noise came from the kitchen windows opening into our backyard. Almost instantly, someone knocked on the windows of my parents' room. I trembled. Mom turned pale. Dad stood dazed. Just then Ravi hurried from the kitchen with anxiety written all over his face. "Sir, the kitchen windows shook and then someone knocked on the door. When I opened the door to check, I received a hard punch on my face, but I couldn't see anyone. I mean, whoever punched me was invisible."

Dad gazed at Ravi's swollen left cheek and frowned. It was turning blue. He wasn't lying. And then the windows of my room rattled with such ferocity that it seemed the panes would explode. "Who's there?" Dad roared. "Ravi, call the QRT. I'll go out and check." He ran to pick up his gun from his bedroom and then dashed towards the main door.

"Dad, please, don't go out alone." I held his hand.

"I have faced tougher situations, darling. Don't worry. I'll be fine." He extricated his hand and rushed out.

"I am coming with you, Sir." Ravi hurried after Dad. He had sent the message for help.

Mom shouted, "Be careful, dear." Dad had already disappeared into the dark night. My heart quivered with worry. Mom shut and bolted the door. We both sat on the sofa, waiting.

Our house was one of the four houses built on a flat area atop a hill, all occupied by high-end army officers and their families. This small plateau had an underground ammunition yard and was always in danger of an attack if the terrorists got a hint about it. But would terrorists first make noise, putting the occupants on high alert before carrying on? Or was this an ambush on the senior army officers? How could the terrorists walk past many layers of heavy security of numerous army camps below?

Dad was surprised to see his associates Col. Sen, Col. Bhupinder Singh, and Lt. Col. Rastogi, along with a few armed sentinels already out, cautiously scanning the area. "Someone has been knocking at our windows, Sir," they apprised Dad. So many windows had been knocked on instantly. There had to be many invaders to do that.

The Commandos arrived and skimmed the whole area. Dad returned home after half an hour, all satisfied that there were no intruders. He sat with us on the sofa and breathed out loudly. "Nothing," he shrugged.

Ravi brought Dad a glass of water. He hadn't even taken a sip when someone rapped on the window in front of us. All four of us froze. A weird screech followed. I clung to Dad, refusing to let him go. Dad put his arms around Mom and me. We waited with bated breath for something to happen, but all that followed was silence.

"I won't sleep alone," I declared, snivelling. Terror had turned my limbs cold and numb.

Dad nodded. "Ravi, bring the folding bed and get it ready in our room. Vriti will sleep in our room till we solve this mystery."

Ravi nodded with an expression oozing with worry. "Sir, may I also sleep here tonight? It's dark outside and I would rather not walk down alone."

Dad allowed him to stay. He thought there is strength in numbers, so having Ravi would only be helpful.

Two days later Dad got me a new companion, a six-month-old chocolate brown Labrador whom I named Coco. I loved Coco right from the moment I set my eyes on him. Perhaps he would help combat my fears now. I wouldn't be sleeping alone. Also, Coco would bark and frighten the ghosts away.

I cradled and cuddled Coco the whole day. He gave me the confidence to return to my room that night. Digging himself a nice globular depression on my quilt and curling into a ball, he happily snuggled at my feet. His presence was so comforting that I fell asleep almost instantly after switching off the main light.

In the middle of the night, sound of falling objects in my bathroom woke me up. Coco was sitting tight on my bed, growling at the bathroom door. *Creeeeeeak.* The door began to open slowly, inch by inch. I sat upright with a jolt. My eyes almost jumped out of their sockets as they watched the unbelievable scene . . . as if directly out of a horror film. The Ouija board emerged from the door, floating in the air, hovering like a vampire bat. It then headed straight towards me. I was so terrified that momentarily I remained glued to my bed, frozen in shock. Coco whined, sprung away, and scooted out of the room. My scream finally escaped my throat. I stirred into action and jumped out of my bed before the creepy thing could reach me. I rushed out of my room and dashed into my parents' bedroom. Both their bedside lamps were on, and Dad was sitting on his bed hurriedly trying to get into his slippers. Shaking and whimpering, I slipped under their quilt, as if it were the greatest defence shield in the whole world. Coco stood with his tail between his legs, looking at Dad, trying to express something. It was then that we all heard it—the sound of a loud crash in my room. Something in my room had been thrown down with force. Next came the sound of a door being slammed in anger. It was the bathroom door.

"Who's in your room?" Dad turned to look straight at me. Concern and anxiety were written all over his face.

"Gh-Gh-Ghost," I stammered. "I t-told you!"

Mom's eyes widened. Dad shook his head disbelievingly. He then marched out of the room like what he had been trained to be—a fearless soldier. He was back in a minute. He shrugged his shoulders and got back into the warm quilt. I noted a shadow of doubt on his face. "Dad, we need to invite exorcists and get rid of that thing in my room."

Mom kissed my cheek. "Go, sleep now. We'll see what to do about it in the morning."

"I am not going back to my room." I slipped further into the blanket. Dad patted my head. It was his way of giving me permission to sleep with them. Coco curled into a ball on the floor-carpet.

Through the rest of the night, we kept hearing sounds from my room. All three of us tried ignoring them, but they wouldn't allow us to sleep. In the morning when I woke up, Dad had already left for work. Mom was busy in the kitchen giving instructions to the cook. I needed my stuff. I didn't have the courage to go alone. I picked up Coco in my lap and tiptoed towards my room. At the door of my room, Coco howled, squirmed out of my grasp, and dashed away. He was afraid, I realized.

My room's door was tightly shut. When I had rushed out of it at night, I had left it open. Perhaps Dad had closed it. Mustering courage, I opened the door and shoved my head through the two-feet gap I had managed. What I saw turned me into jelly. My almirah door was wide open and it was completely empty. All my things—books, notebooks, clothes, diaries, my titbits collections—everything was scattered on the floor. I had never seen my room in such a mess.

I shut the door with a bang and screamed so loudly that it brought everyone in the house running to my door. Mom took one look at my shivering body and boldly shoved the door open. She then stood rooted to the ground, staring at the mess. "Vriti, who did this?" She gazed at me with her eyebrows raised.

"Mom, I . . . don't know." I wiped my tears with the back of my trembling hand. "Dad visited the room at two. It happened after that." Mom gasped. "I told you, there's a ghost in my room."

Before Mom could react, the bell rang. Ravi let in our nearest neighbour, Mrs. Sen. "I heard a scream and thought you were under attack. I called for emergency help before rushing here. What happened?" She joined us and tried peeping into my room.

Mom stood shaking her head and pointed at the mess inside my room. "Someone did that last night when we slept." Then she turned to glare at me. "You have been playing with that thing again?"

"What thing?" I roved my eyes around the room peeping from behind Mom's back, where I had taken shelter ever since she had responded to my scream.

She pointed towards my bed. I stopped breathing. The Ouija board and the planchette were lying on top of my quilt. "It-It was in my bathroom cabinet," I stammered.

Mrs. Sen's curiosity was at its peak now. "What's it?" She shoved me aside and tried to enter the room.

Mom held her hand and stopped her, "No. Don't go in, Debika."

"But why?" Mrs. Sen asked as she gaped at the mess.

"There's something strange . . . something mysterious in there." Mom turned towards me. "Vriti, you really didn't take it out last evening and tried calling spirits?" She eyed me and then the Ouija board as if it were a venomous snake about to strike us.

Mrs. Sen reacted instantly by covering her cheeks with her palms. "Calling spirits? That's dangerous. Very dangerous. When I was in high school, a few friends played this game. The spirit took away the four-year-old sister of the girl in whose house we played. I saw it."

I shivered. Mom's eyes expanded in fear. "Took away the child means?"

"The child died. An absolutely healthy child! The spirit conveyed that it was taking the child."

"Do you hear, Vriti? Do you realize the danger?" Mom shouted.

I burst into loud sobs. Mrs. Sen shouldn't have mentioned the death. I now felt that the Ouija board was after my life too. "Mom, I don't even know how it works." I spoke through my snuffles. "After Vidhi Didi hurriedly shoved it in my almirah that day, after you caught us, it keeps coming out of my almirah on its own. I even threw it in the rubbish bin, but it came back. I don't know who's doing it. I don't know what to do with it. Lastly, I had kept it in the bathroom cabinet. It floated out of the bathroom and into my room last night. I didn't tell you, but that's why I had run out of my room."

Mrs. Sen shivered and clicked her tongue. "Oh my God! Many strange things are happening around. Knockings on the windows and now this!"

Mom put her arm around me. "Ravi, take some help and clean the room. But first, throw that thing far away. Get rid of it immediately." She pointed at the Ouija board. "Burn it," she added as an afterthought and then guided me and Mrs. Sen away from the scene of the chaos.

Mrs. Sen refused Ma's offer of a cup of coffee. She stood for a while in our parlour scanning our interiors. Judging from her expression, I knew that she was seeking the ghost, convinced that our house had been invaded by a supernatural force. "Take care, my child. May Kali Ma protect you." She stroked my head lovingly before leaving.

After Mrs. Sen left, Mom suggested that I shift out of my room to Vini Didi's till the time she and Dad could come to a decision about what to do about this alarming situation. I gladly agreed. Most of that day went in settling down in my new room.

Dad took the next day off. He and Mom visited the Shankracharya Temple to seek the head priest's help. Two days later we had a prayer session at home, conducted by a handful of priests. Mom insisted that the puja be done in my room. She believed that the whole problem had originated from there. Dad wasn't so sure, because the Ouija board secret had not been disclosed to him. Was there any point in making him more anxious? It had already been burnt. A good riddance!

The puja proved to be ineffective. I shifted back to my room after the puja, and within a day the sounds returned, though furtive and subdued. I often felt a light touch . . . a graze on my back and sometimes on my arm. A few times I also felt a soft brush on my face. My intuition warned me that something was lurking around me like a prowler, waiting to strike. Coco seemed fully aware of the unseen presence. He refused to sleep anywhere but in my parents' bedroom. I felt ditched.

I tried telling Mom, but she brushed aside my claim. "Vriti, the Ouija board has been burnt to a crisp. Our prayers have driven away the mysterious presence. There's nothing now. Expel it out of your mind."

Summers arrived. The valley got dressed in fresh emerald slopes, vibrant wildflowers, and clear blue skies. The cornucopia of beauty around would uplift anybody's spirits. But melancholy soaked me wet. Life was being unfair to me. It was as if I was caught in a trap from where there was no escape. I tried obliterating my dejection by playing happy love songs on Vini Didi's transistor radio that I had snitched out from her room. I wondered if it was my imagination running wild, but I often heard a male voice humming along with the songs. It was perhaps the echo or the vibrations of the radio, I told myself.

In mid-May, Dad left for Delhi to attend an important meeting with the defence ministry. He would be away for a few days.

It was a warm moonless night. After serving us dinner and winding up his work, Ravi was about to leave when Coco rushed to the door and whined to be let out. He had already had his evening walk. However, Mom requested Ravi to take Coco out. Perhaps he needed to pee.

The moment they both stepped out, Coco got agitated. He struggled to free himself and managed to slip out of his collar. Immediately, he dashed away down the hill and into the pitch-dark wilderness. Ravi rushed back for a torch and then scouted the whole area. Coco didn't respond to his calls. Mom would not allow me to step out. We both sat on a sofa, waiting. After an hour's search, Ravi returned shaking his head. "I wonder what came upon him." Noticing my tearful eyes, he offered me a pale smile and added, "He'll come back on his own. Soon. Dogs do. I'll stay in the house with you. If Coco doesn't return, I will once again search for him in the morning."

Mom and I kept awake the whole night . . . nervous, worried, and waiting. My ears were alert for Coco's bark. All I heard were the familiar sounds and screeches that came from my room and outside. By the time the sun rose, I was physically and mentally drained. There was still no news of my Coco. He had run away. But why?

In the morning when Ravi opened the kitchen door to throw the garbage, he stood aghast . . . frozen in serious shock. The limp body of Coco lay next to the garbage bin with his neck twisted. He recoiled, shut the door, and rushed to us.

Who was so inhuman to have killed an animal so mercilessly?

I was stunned. I was angry. I was frightened. Mom instantly asked Ravi to bury Coco in the backyard. She didn't even allow me to touch my dog to bid him goodbye. It broke my heart.

We remained disturbed the whole day. I was inconsolable and cried for hours. I vowed never to keep a pet. They weren't safe with me. Perhaps my life too was in danger. Was Coco's killing a warning? Would I be the next victim? Maybe Mom was having similar thoughts, which is why she barred me from stepping out of the house till Dad returned.

When the sun slipped behind the mountains and the night began creeping in, dread began to gnaw my nerves. Every slight sound made me and Mom jumpy, even though Ravi was staying with us. Mom called and requested Col. Sen to send someone. "Our dog has been killed. We are all a little spooked," she explained.

"Yes. I know. Debika has updated me about some Ouija board incident. Don't worry, I will send someone strong and reliable," Col. Sen responded.

An hour later the bell rang. Ravi ushered in our guest for the night, Captain Varun. He walked in with a small duffle bag in his hand and a dazzling smile on his face. I stared at him open-mouthed. "Col. Sen has put me on guard duty till your husband returns, Ma'am," he apprised Mom, grinning from ear to ear. He seemed keen to please her and I knew why.

I felt secure with him staying with us in the house.

We had a leisurely dinner. Captain Varun continued his efforts to impress Mom with his witty yarns. I left them at it and went to my room to prepare for my maths test. Gathering my study material, I sat at the table. Almost immediately the light began to flicker. It had never happened before. "Mom," I called out, "something's wrong with the light in my room."

Mom came. "There must be a loose connection. I've asked Ravi to check it." She had barely finished her sentence when my bathroom door groaned on its hinges and began to open slowly. Mom stood motionless, staring at the door. I shrank in fear and then gathering my wits, rushed to her.

Just then Captain Varun, on his mission to please Mom, reached my room. "I can check what's wrong with the light, ma'am," he offered with a smile. His smile instantly vanished and his eyes dilated in horror as my geometry box flew off my table and went straight for him, hitting him on his forehead with a loud thud. I screamed. He flinched. "Who . . . Who threw it?" His eyes inspected my room nervously. No one was near my study table. Mom held my hand and rushed towards the door. Captain Varun turned to follow us. He staggered. Someone had pushed him hard from behind. Ravi, having heard my scream, reached just in time to prevent his fall. Captain Varun collected himself and ran out. He banged shut the door behind us. The door rattled angrily. Ravi dashed to bring a table and placed it next to the shut door. The door shook more violently. Someone behind it was feverishly angry. Ravi raced and returned with an idol of Lord Hanuman. He placed it on the table, lighted a diya and a bunch of incense sticks, all the while reciting Hanuman Chalisa. The rattling subsided. Mom, Captain Varun, and I watched from a distance, in a haze of fear. Blood had completely drained from Captain Varun's face. I had never seen a soldier so frightened.

"Ma'am, I have never witnessed something so eerie, never believed in ghosts. But now . . ." Captain Varun exhaled loudly. Sweat was dripping down his face in streaks. "The . . . The enemy guns aren't half as scary. This is so bizarre." He shuddered.

Mom, Captain Varun, Ravi, and I sat the whole night in my parents' bedroom, chanting mantras and hearing strange sounds erupting from my room.

The next morning Mom decided to make my room out of bounds for all. Ravi assembled a few army men to assist him. The team chanted loud prayers whilst carrying on with their work. All my belongings were removed quickly, and my room was sealed. Finally, the table with the Lord Hanuman idol was placed back in front of the door.

Mom didn't let me out of her sight even for a minute. She mumbled prayers the whole day. Captain Varun seemed still in shock when he returned in the evening. He couldn't greet us with his usual smile. "Why was that thing hostile towards me?" he asked me when Mom had gone out of the room. I shrugged. "Vriti, how do you people live in this haunted house? I was not myself the whole day. Couldn't share it with anyone. Colonel Sen has instructed me to keep my mouth shut."

Ravi, who was serving us coffee, added, "Didi, you should talk to your Daddy Ji when he returns tomorrow, about changing the house. This is an *ashant aatma* residing here . . . a restless dangerous spirit. Apart from yesterday's incident, I have felt it many times, especially after the sunset, when it gets dark . . . it has whacked me several times. I thought I was imagining it, but now I know for sure it was real."

"You too were victimized by this fierce ghost?" Captain Varun winced. "Any more casualties?"

"No," I replied. I didn't want to tell him that I had also seen it, felt it touching me. Fortunately, it hadn't hurt me. Not till then.

The voices in my room had gone silent. We were all tired after a sleepless night. Mom and I slept in her bedroom. Captain Varun and Ravi posted themselves on the floor in the parlour just outside our bedroom. They both had surrounded themselves with a lot of holy pictures. That night passed without any incident.

The next evening Dad returned. Vidhi Didi, having finished her semester, came home along with him. "I don't see Coco. Where's he?" Dad inquired when he didn't receive his usual frisky welcome from him. My eyes were wet with tears. I looked at Mom. She remained silent. She probably wanted Dad rested before she revealed the ghastly facts to him. Dad didn't notice our reaction and went to his bedroom to change.

After dinner, as we sat in the parlour, I presented my proposal to Dad about changing our house. "We aren't safe here, Dad. Let's move out as soon as possible, please, before the ghost harms one of us." Mom nodded.

Vidhi Didi expressed her view before anyone else could speak, "Changing the house because you think a ghost lives here? All your fabricated stories!" She made a face at me.

Mom looked at her sternly. "Vidhi, please be quiet. You don't know anything."

Dad declared, "I am expecting a new posting soon. So, what's the point? And things are okay now, aren't they? After the puja?"

Vidhi Didi looked at us in amazement. "What puja? What are you guys talking about?"

"There's something in this house," Mom reiterated. "Something that killed Coco two nights ago."

"What? Killed Coco?" Dad almost fell off his chair. After the shocked silence that filled the room, he got up and walked into his bedroom without another word. Mom followed him.

Vidhi Didi and I sat for a while in silence. I realized Didi wanted to know more but was afraid to initiate the topic. Finally, we went to sleep. My sister's presence in the bedroom was comforting. As soon as we switched off the light, we heard sounds from outside our bedroom door—like someone dragging feet. Vidhi Didi sat up in her bed. "No, Vidhi Didi, no. Leave it alone."

"I'm not scared."

"You haven't seen the geometry box flying and hitting Captain Varun on his forehead. He's still shaken. You didn't notice the big lump on his forehead. See it tomorrow."

"Oh! Captain Varun stayed with you? We must tell Vriti Didi."

"I will. Let's sleep now." I turned and tried to fall asleep. I don't know why I had this uneasy feeling in the pit of my stomach.

In the middle of the night, I woke up with a start. A gruff sound rumbled through the air all around me. Someone was calling out my name. The dim light of the table lamp spread an eerie aura in the room. The door of our room was wide open. Someone was close now . . . I heard a whisper in my ear . . . in a strange language. As a shiver ran through my body, I distinctly felt a hand on me . . . on my neck . . . a gentle touch. I couldn't see a soul. My body shuddered. I heard Vidhi Didi snoring softly. I wasn't dreaming. The hand began moving, caressing me softly. It navigated from my throat to my breasts and then slowly down my stomach. I froze. The hand reached down between my legs. Someone was molesting me. I shrieked and squirmed fiercely. I heard a growling sound of irritation. Then my bed shook. I kept lying dormant, trying to figure out what was happening. The bed shook again—more violently now. "Earthquake," I shouted.

Vidhi Didi woke up all flustered. "Vriti, why are you creating ruckus in the middle of the night?" She rubbed her eyes and glared at me.

I sat up in my bed. "You didn't feel anything, Didi?"

As Vidhi Didi shook her head with annoyance, somebody dragged her quilt away aggressively. Her eyes opened wide in terror. A moment later my bed began to shake violently. Everything else in the room was still and silent as the grave. Vidhi Didi muffled her scream.

As Vidhi Didi stared in shock, my bed began to rise. It rose up gradually, inch by inch . . . till it was about a foot above the floor. It hovered in the air like a bird of prey over an imminent victim. My mouth opened wide in a soundless scream. I began to choke. Vidhi Didi dashed out of the room. How could she abandon me thus, when I was about to die? Within seconds, Didi was back with Mom and Dad. As if disturbed by the intrusion, my bed dropped down with a thud, trailed by a snigger. Someone unseen was laughing at my plight. A calm male voice spoke into my ear in a distinct voice—"It's okay." The bathroom door then opened a few inches. My family stared aghast as a shadow slipped past it. Dad had seen it for the first time. An immense shock arrested him briefly.

He gathered his wits and rushed to me, picked up my frozen form in his arms, and dashed out of the room. Vidhi Didi and Mom scampered behind us, whimpering in fright. Once in his room, Dad hugged me tightly and kissed my cheeks so many times. He was making an effort to control his tears. Mom sat frozen like an icicle. Vidhi Didi sat next to her, shivering and crying. For once, I wasn't reacting much. It was a big relief that we were safe.

We spent the entire night together in my parents' bedroom. Sleepless. We continued hearing footsteps outside the shut door. Mom had kept holy pictures next to the door. Someone kept scouting our house the whole night. Mom kept praying loudly. As the first ray of light declared the new morn, the sounds faded. We were drained by then. I had never seen Dad so anxious. Mom was pale and exhausted. Vidhi Didi's eyes were red from crying. I was running a high fever. We were panicky. At least we were together.

What Dad had witnessed last night galvanized him into action. He dialled umpteen numbers. Soon we had a regiment at our house, guarding us against an unseen enemy and helping us pack. We moved to the Army guesthouse, our temporary residence till we got a new accommodation. We bid goodbye to the house that had become no less frightening than hell itself, running away from the chilling entity that had come to inhabit it and had targeted me.

PART – 2
AMBALA

Within a month Dad received orders for a new posting. We shifted to Ambala Cantonment, to the core Army area. Peace returned to our lives. The memory of the disturbing days in Srinagar began to wane. They now seemed like scary nightmares that were finally over.

I went on to study in a girls' college at Ambala that also offered plus-two classes. The college was situated on the outskirts of the Cantonment area. My focus was completely on my studies in those days, and I passed standard eleven with a good grade.

Six months later, Dad retired. My parents decided to move to our ancestral house in Chandigarh. I was in my decisive year of schooling—in standard twelve. Shifting to another school in the middle of the session would hamper my studies, that's what Dad believed. So, my parents decided to leave me behind in Ambala to continue my studies.

I had never lived by myself. I didn't want to. But Dad was insistent. "It is a matter of just a few months. Things are okay now. We have left the problem behind . . . in Srinagar."

I joined the college hostel reluctantly.

I was allotted a room in the smallest building on the campus which had just two floors and twelve rooms per floor. It was meant exclusively for the plus-two hostellers. Mine was the last room on the first floor of the west-wing of the hostel. Adjoining it was our hostel warden's house and next to it the west boundary wall of the institution. Right across was a garden displaying colourful blooms. Massive peepals, neems, banyans, and gulmohars lined its periphery. From my balcony and through the dense foliage of these trees, I got a fragmented glimpse of a row of servant-quarters next to the south boundary wall. A ten-foot-high boundary wall fortified the campus on all sides. Beyond the boundary wall was an endless infertile rocky stretch of barren land. Thorny bushes sporadically grew here on the arid soil for as far as I could see.

In my initial days, I missed my parents immensely. Eventually I settled down to my new independence. I shared the room with Amrita, a gentle and friendly girl from Patiala. Amrita was a science student. We instantly bonded. Though we didn't share our classes, we began spending all our free time together—going to the library, evening strolls in the garden, eating our meals in the hostel mess—we were soon inseparable.

Despite our growing friendship, I didn't share my spooky past with Amrita. Was there any point in recapping something I wanted to forget and eradicate from my life?

Both Amrita and I were cleanliness freaks. Before leaving for classes, we made our beds and left the room spick and span. Then one evening as I entered my room after a tiring day, with my shoulders drooping under the heavy bag on my back, Amrita made an odd comment. "Where had you gone?"

What kind of question was that? "Amrita, I just finished my classes."

"I thought you had gone somewhere after resting on your bed."

"I have entered the room now, after leaving it in the morning."

"Are you sure?"

"Of course. Why do you ask?" I dumped my bag on the table and sat down on the chair to unlace my shoes.

"Then who has been sleeping on your bed?"

I instantly froze in my hunched position. Then I raised my head slowly and stared at my bed. The cover was crumpled. There was a distinct impression of someone having lain on my bed. Someone of a large frame.

Our room had been locked the whole day. No one could have entered it except Amrita.

"You are playing a prank on me, aren't you?" I smiled at Amrita, earnestly wishing for her to answer yes. I also knew that the size of the depression on my bed didn't match hers.

"Why would I?" Amrita was genuinely annoyed. "I came back just ten minutes ago and sat on my chair, settling my books. I have an important biology test tomorrow."

"So?" I asked a bit brusquely. I wanted to digress from what was buzzing in my mind.

"So, I didn't have time to lie down. And even if I had, I like to do that on my bed. You know it." Amrita stood defiantly, with her hands on her waist. It was the first-ever spat between us despite having stayed together for months now.

"It's okay. Not such a big deal." I shrugged and quickly smoothed my bed. Shivers traversed through my body. I didn't want to alarm Amrita. No way should she know of my past encounters with the supernatural. I had come to like her so much. I didn't want her freaked out to the extent that she should decide to shift to another room.

This incident rendered me extremely nervous. I began finding the same depression on my bed often. My things were being moved. Sometimes I felt a touch, the same one I used to feel back in Srinagar. It was evident that someone else was living with us in our room now . . . silent and invisible. It had followed me here.

A month later, in mid-January, our classes were suspended. All the girls of my hostel, including Amrita, went home to prepare for our board exams to be held in March. There were tearful farewells. I was going to miss Amrita. We promised to remain in touch. I happily accepted her invitation to visit her in Patiala after our exams were over. She too promised to come see me in Chandigarh.

Mom and Dad were away in Australia visiting Dad's

younger brother who was settled there. So, I was left with no choice but to continue staying in the hostel for a week more.

The sudden change in the hostel environment was unnerving. Intense silence had replaced the laughter and feverish activities. When I returned from my dinner that evening, I realized I was the solitary soul residing in the now-empty hostel.

It was a freezing cold night, my first day alone in the deserted building. The deathly hush was disconcerting. Distant noises from the other hostel building too ceased after ten. The silence was like gathering thunderclouds—hostile and threatening. I had never in my life felt so isolated.

To keep my mind from wandering off to alarming thoughts, I decided to solve tough maths problems. It was when a distant church clock struck two that I once again became cognizant of my isolation. I recited a quick prayer to grab some pluck and switched off the light. Some light seeped into my room from a lamppost at some distance. I slowly drifted into a disturbed sleep.

Sleep came, but the nightmares followed soon and went on for what seemed like hours. I was back in our Srinagar house, sleeping in my old bed when it began to levitate. It exploded through the roof and surged into the desolate sky. I floated through intense darkness. Strange forms began to gather around me. They pounced on me and vied with each other for my blood. I was desperate to escape.

As I struggled to come out of the terrifying dream, I felt a strong pressure on my chest. Someone was atop me. I flapped my arms and legs. That horrible familiar growl woke me up.

I was panting and drenched in my sweat. It was then that I unmistakably heard it. Was it still a dream? I used my arm sleeve to wipe the sweat off my face. In the penetrating hush, the sobs were blaring, piercing through the semi-darkness of my room. They were coming from Amrita's empty bed. I mustered courage and sat up. A girl was lying on Amrita's bed and crying. How did she get inside? I looked towards the door. It was securely bolted. Fear began to encompass me in its tight grip, like a tight iron cast. "Who . . . Who are you?" I uttered.

The girl slowly sat up.

"Amrita? When did you come back? Why . . ."

Amrita slowly got up and walked towards the door. Why was she walking like a zombie? She halted and turned towards me. She was crying bitterly now. "What's happened, Amrita?" She extended her arms towards me . . . like beckoning me to join her. Then, I was once again alone in my room. I rubbed my eyes. Was I awake? Or was I still dreaming?

I spent the rest of the night shivering and chanting. Who had come to my room impersonating Amrita? And then dissolved like mist? Do ghosts change forms to mislead?

By the time the sun rose to offer its reassuring light, I felt half dead. I got dressed hurriedly and left my room. As I stepped out of the mess after my breakfast, one of my lecturers accosted me. "Vriti, there you are. I have been looking for you. Ma'am Bhullar wants to have a word with you. Go to her office immediately."

I got worried and hurried towards the principal's office.

"Come in, Vriti. I was thinking of you," Mrs. Bhullar said as I stood at the door of her office.

I walked in and slowly lowered myself onto a chair. Noticing her gloomy expression, my heart skipped a beat. I knew something untoward had happened. My immediate concern was for my parents and sisters.

"I believe you were very close to Amrita Kapoor," Mrs. Bhullar commented.

"Yes, Ma'am. She is my best friend."

"I have bad news for you." She hesitated and then added softly, "She died last night in Patiala."

I couldn't speak. For a few seconds, I simply stared at Mrs. Bhullar. Then I looked down. I didn't understand. Amrita couldn't be dead. She was in my room last night. Wasn't she?

I took a deep breath to compose myself. "How?" I asked hesitatingly.

"Nobody knows how she died. She had walked out to her garden after dinner. Her parents went to sleep thinking she would be back. But this morning they found her dead in their garden. Her mother thinks something horrid must have happened to her. Her eyes were bulging, as if she had been extremely frightened before she died. It's very odd that there are no injury marks on her." She looked at me with narrowed eyes. "Do you have any clue? I mean, do you think she may have been mixing with the wrong sort of people? Boyfriends? Did she ever tell you about any problem?"

I couldn't respond anymore. My body had gone into involuntary tremors. It was indeed Amrita crying in the room last night. Her ghost. I began to feel suffocated and rushed out of the principal's room.

Outside, I sat on a bench and gasped for breath. It was so uncanny. She was well and healthy when she left the campus yesterday morning. There was no reason for her to die.

Had my best friend been killed because of me? Because evil entities surrounded me? And they targeted others too . . . those close to me? Like Coco had been killed? I freaked out. I was alone and helpless, and now was being haunted again. Soon, it'll be my turn.

I couldn't concentrate on anything that day and kept roaming around the campus in a daze. When night fell, I reluctantly returned to my room, lonely and scared. Amrita's beautiful face kept hovering in front of my eyes as I lay on my bed. Would she be back again tonight? I opened my book but didn't read a word. Soon I dozed off. I don't know how long afterwards it was, but a loud wail woke me up. I sat up confused and agitated. Someone was crying on the balcony outside my room.

Amrita again?

My heart was racing. I sat curled into a ball in a corner of my bed. The sound slowly faded. My restlessness surged.

I couldn't stay here alone, I realized. I might not be safe. I needed human company. I needed help. Where could I expect to find help in the middle of the night? Maybe, I should go to the warden's house and request her to shelter me for a few days . . . till I could go home. Why didn't this brilliant idea strike me before? Mrs. Walia was a kind and caring lady and would not refuse my request. She might not like being disturbed at this hour. I hoped she would understand.

It was reckless of me, but it was the only action to take. I wore my warm jacket, got into my shoes, and opening the door walked out into the deserted night.

A garden light partially vanquished the darkness outside. That gave me courage to walk down the stairs. I reached the open ground, looked around, and walked nervously towards the warden's house. Absolute silence covered the campus.

A few yards away from her house I drew in my breath and froze. I wasn't alone. There stood a woman facing the house. Her dishevelled hair fell till her waist. She wore a long, thin dress and was barefoot. I was shivering in my jacket in the freezing cold. "Who . . . Who are you looking for?" I blurted. The face slowly turned towards me, a deathly, pale, shrivelled face. Her head was dangling from her neck. I stepped back in fright recalling with a sudden shock that this was the face I had seen through the parlour window of my Srinagar house. The woman curled up her lips in a hideous smile, exposing a dark hollowness. "Yuuuuu?" Her eerie croak vibrating through the air hit my senses like a water jet. "Kiiiiiiill . . ." She menacingly stepped towards me. I stood frozen in fright, trembling like a strummed wire. Then all of a sudden she became motionless. She was looking at something behind me. I followed her gaze and turned to check. I had a strong sensation there was someone else there, apart from the two of us, someone standing right behind me. The creepy woman made a weird screechy sound, turned, and ran towards the Warden's house. Within a split second, she vanished.

I mustered my wits and reversed my direction, away from the dreadful ghoul. It was perilous outside. It was a big mistake to have left the safety of my room. I sprinted up the stairs on my shaky legs, slipping and stumbling several times, dashed into my room, shut the door, and dived inside my blanket to hide in it. My whole body was shuddering in serious convulsions. Who was this ghostly female? Was she the one who had killed Amrita? Why? I cried till my pillow was wet with my tears. Gradually I became comatose, lost to the world. Sleep, like a shot of anaesthesia, overpowered me. I have no recollection of the rest of the night. Had I passed out due to exhaustion and fear?

When I woke up, bright sunlight lanced through the tiny window in my room and fell on my bed in streaks. It was late in the morning. I had planned to meet my economics teacher at nine for revisions. Jumping out of my bed, I rushed toward the restrooms to get ready.

I stopped dead in my tracks halfway. A mournful sound emerging from the warden's house hit me like a welt. I peeped down from the balcony. A crowd had collected outside the house. I spotted our college principal and vice-principal among the crowd. Something serious seemed to have happened. I rushed down. "Can't believe Rita Walia is dead," I heard someone remark as I approached the group. A cold current swept through me. She was young, barely in her mid-forties and fit. The previous evening, I had spotted her heading home with her daughter.

Her husband stood at the door with his shoulders hunched. "The doctor says she died of a heart attack. She didn't even have high blood pressure. She was healthy." The people standing around to pay their condolences clicked their tongues. "She must have gone to the bathroom and God knows what happened. When I went there around six in the morning, I found her lying near the door that opens to the outside. The door was wide open." People looked at the door and shook their heads. "Why would she open the door in the middle of the night? She had never done that," he said with tears streaming down his cheeks.

"Perhaps she wanted some fresh air," someone suggested.

"Yes, maybe she felt hot, suffocated. You know, that happens before a heart attack."

"No. Something's wrong. I can't put my finger on it. But this is not natural," the husband stressed.

I was the only one who had seen that dreadful woman outside my warden's house last night. I knew he was right. I didn't wait to hear more and scurried back to my room—inconsolable and distraught.

Once I had changed into fresh clothes, I rushed to the main office. After much coaxing, the clerk allowed me to place a call to Australia on payment basis. Fortunately, my parents were at home. I requested them to return to India immediately. I wasn't too well, I pleaded. I needed help. I couldn't reveal more in front of the office staff.

"Vriti, it's not easy to change tickets now. If you're unwell, get medical help from your college dispensary. You are not a child anymore. Learn to look after yourself," Dad said.

"It's just a matter of few more days, dear. Concentrate on your studies," Mom advised. That was it. My parents refused to understand. I was facing mortal danger here. Alone. The way that creepy thing had moved towards me, she meant to kill me. She had killed Amrita and my hostel warden. The only puzzle I couldn't solve was why she had spared me.

I was too scared to be alone. The whole day I hung around in the most crowded areas of the college. I loitered around for as long as I could, till the nightfall. I had no appetite but went to the mess for dinner anyway because at least I would be in a crowded place. The food lay untouched on my plate. When I was the last person left in the dining hall, I was left with no choice but to return to my room.

As I slinked towards my hostel, my breathing accelerated and my heart hammered against my chest. The area was glaringly deserted and frightening. A strange hush enveloped the surroundings . . . not a bird chirped, not a dog barked. Everyone seemed to have gone in hiding. I sprinted through the foreboding darkness and cursed myself for being an idiot.

My hostel building was unusually dark. It looked bleak, forsaken, and haunted. It *was* haunted. Now. With that sinister creature lurking around. I hurriedly climbed up the dark stairs on my shivering legs and reached the corridor. I stopped dead here. Someone was standing in the far corner . . . in front of my room . . . a dark silhouette of a female figure. It wasn't Amrita. She didn't look like that scary witch either.

I gathered courage and walked a few steps. The woman turned to face me. "Did you come to check on me, ma'am?" I relaxed and asked softly. "Carefulllllll . . ." a spine-chilling voice echoed through the air. The figure walked off the balcony into the empty space and dissolved.

How could I forget Rita Walia was dead?

Terror coursed through my veins. I rushed to my room and locked it. I stood panting, resting against the door. People were dying and their ghosts were hanging around me. I had no escape. I recalled what Ravi had done once. Shifting my chair next to the door, I lit a diya and incense sticks. I needed to keep the diya burning throughout the night.

Gayatri Mantra, Hanuman Chalisa, Om Jai Jagdish Haré, I chanted everything that came to mind till my brain switched off. I was rudely wakened by a sound. My eyes flew open. The diya had burnt out and the room had plunged into darkness. I didn't remember having turned off the light.

My door rattled. Someone was trying to enter it. I rushed to relight my diya with my shaky hands. There was shuffling outside. Were the ghosts vying with each other to seize me? A wail resounded, just like it had done in the nights before. That eerie woman was here again. Lurking. She was ominously closing in on me.

The dreadful sound began to withdraw. It continued intermittently, from a distance. Then there were screams. They sounded almost . . . human. Hysterical. Then everything went deadly quiet. I kept awake for a long time till my mind, heavy with the burden of fear, anxiety, and apprehension, shut down in the morning hours.

I left the bed late, exhausted. As soon as I opened the door, I saw commotion ensuing everywhere on the campus. *What now?* I rushed to the toilet to relieve the terrible cramps in my stomach.

There were policemen everywhere, inspecting the campus inch by inch. What were they looking for? I dared not show interest in them. I went back to my room and shut the door. After changing into my jeans and a thick pullover, I sat on my chair and wondered what to do next. My gut was telling me to stay inside.

Fifteen minutes later there was a knock on my door. I stiffened. The knocking became persistent. I couldn't ignore it. I opened a book, took a few deep breaths, and went to answer the knock. The vice-principal of the college along with two police personnel stood there.

"What time did you come back to your room last night?" Mrs. Singh asked me without exchanging morning courtesies. She looked pale and distraught.

"Ma'am, immediately after dinner, around eight."

"What did you do after that?" one of the policemen asked.

"I studied for some time and then slept."

"Did you hear any noise, like someone shouting for help?"

Should I share with them? Will they be able to help? Will they believe me? I shook my head. "No."

"Nothing?"

"Nothing."

"Hmm . . ."

"Why do you ask? What has happened?"

They ignored me, shook their heads, and turned to go. I overheard one of the policemen comment, "Ma'am, why is this young girl staying alone in this building? She could be in danger, too."

Something serious had happened. I waited for ten minutes and then left the room to go to the hostel mess for breakfast. Although I had no appetite, I had to act normal.

Navigating through a posse of policemen, I walked towards the mess. No one stopped me.

The mess was buzzing with heated discussions. Clearly, nobody was going to the classes. The first-year graduation hostellers sat huddled together around a single table.

"Apparently, there are no injury marks on the girls. How could they just drop dead?" a first-year student said, shrugging her shoulders, and I shuddered. *Oh, God! Please spare me more torments.*

"I was the one to discover them," a final-year student spoke like a crime reporter. "My God! It was the most harrowing sight of my life. It will traumatize me forever."

"What were you doing there?" someone asked.

"I had gone for my morning jog and there they were lying, cold, frozen." I heard a few gasps. "I screamed and almost collapsed. I can't get that gruesome image out of my mind. They were holding on to each other." She pressed her cheeks with her palms and shook her head. I began to shiver. "The expressions on their dead faces were of pure fright. Mouths wide open and the eyes bulging out. Before dying, they had seen something that had terrified them."

Their breaths have been sucked out by something not human. This thought struck me like a thunderbolt.

"Scared to the extent that they died."

"Together? Doesn't that sound odd?"

I sat in a corner and listened. Unobtrusively.

"Where were they found?"

"In front of the Vyas hostel."

My heart skipped a beat. That was my hostel.

"That hostel is vacant these days. Isn't it?"

"What were they doing there late at night?"

Thank God nobody knew that I was still occupying my room.

"Reckless of them to have walked to that lonely area, soon after Mrs. Walia's death."

"Their poor parents will be heartbroken."

"Inconsolable."

"Jasbir, they were your friends. You must know why they went there," someone asked, and everyone's attention went to a girl who sat among the first-years. She replied through her sobs, "They had gone to see if there was something mysterious there. Our floor sweeper had mentioned that some eerie, bloodcurdling sounds had recently been heard at night in that area."

"Oh. Then?"

"They had asked me to accompany them, but I refused. They laughed and called me a chicken. That was the last time I saw them. I went to sleep, didn't realize till the morning that they hadn't returned."

"They encountered something."

"Something chilling."

"So many deaths in the same area in less than a week? Doesn't that sound bizarre?"

"Terrifying."

"Do you think there's something paranormal going on there? An evil ghost that strikes at night?" How accurate the speaker was in her deduction!

"Or there's a maniac, a psychopath on the loose?"

A senior student stood up. "Whatever it is, I'm going back home. Can't live in this spooky place. I want to stay alive."

"Me, too. Won't stay here any longer."

"I'll prefer to live in a PG than in this foreboding place."

"Me, too."

"Me, too."

The agitated girls left their seats and began to march out. They stopped at the entrance seeing Mrs. Bhullar posted there. "Girls, please, calm down."

"Calm down? When people are dying unnaturally everywhere on the campus?" a senior student raised her voice.

The principal remained poised. "Look here, girls, what has happened has been very unfortunate. But we need to think with composed minds. Let's not come to unwarranted conclusions. The police are doing their job. I request that we maintain the decorum and reputation of our beloved institution."

"The reputation has gone to the dogs," someone muttered. The principal ignored the comment and continued, "The parents of the deceased girls are about to reach. Let's be considerate and not add undue anxiety to their grief." She threw a forced smile at her students—a tacit request to stay calm. She left and the students dispersed. I remained in the mess for as long as I could. Thinking. Only I knew that a malign spirit . . . a ghostly woman that followed me everywhere, was out on a killing spree. I had no idea what she wanted, or why she killed. It could be my turn next.

It struck me like a kick on the face. What if someone had seen me standing in front of the warden's house in the middle of the night, probably just about the time she had died? I could become a suspect. A psychopath on the loose! I was the only girl in the hostel around whom these incidents were taking place. The police had come to inquire. If they got suspicious, no one would believe in my supernatural theory. I was like a cat on a hot tin roof.

I didn't want to stay a minute more in my macabre hostel. I ran back to my room, packed my bags, lied to my teacher that my parents had returned, and caught the afternoon bus to Chandigarh. Since my house was locked, I requested the neighbours to accommodate me till my parents returned. The kind people happily obliged and accommodated me in their guestroom.

My parents were alarmed at the ordeals I had endured at the hostel. I had become skin and bones in just ten days. "It's good that you decided to leave the hostel," Dad said, his brows creased. Mom hugged me umpteen times. She arranged another puja at home. That helped me to calm down. The biggest relief was that I was never going back to that sinister campus again.

I did well in the exams and four months later, in the summer of 1996, I joined a college in Delhi to study economics honours.

PART - 3
NEW DELHI

I refused to join the college hostel in Delhi. I insisted on taking a room, not even a PG accommodation. It was a very brave move on my part, but I was resolute. I couldn't jeopardize lives. I was carrying a heavy burden of guilt for what had happened on my Ambala campus. I couldn't forgive myself for all those deaths. For Amrita's death.

"I have survived till now. Perhaps I'm meant to survive," I argued. Mom and Dad were helpless in front of my resolve. They found me a one-room *barsaati* apartment in Hauz Khaz Village. The place thronged with shops, restaurants, and people, and was near my college. Mom and Dad accompanied me to Delhi, to see me settled in my new house before I began my classes.

I fell in love with the area. On one side there was exuberant bustle on the high-end market, and on the other, calming quiescence. I was delighted with my apartment. My sitting room extended into a terrace that offered an aerial view of South Delhi's green belt—District Park and Deer Park. My bedroom's balcony faced the ruins of the fort and the royal water tank built in the thirteenth century during the Delhi Sultanate reign.

My parents got me a landline connection so that they could regularly keep in touch with me. Dad also insisted upon buying me a car. "Dad, I can take an auto to my college. I don't need a car. I'll buy one with my money when I begin to earn."

"You need it now, a small hatchback. You won't have to worry about safety," he asserted.

"You know, Dad, you want to reduce your worry more than mine."

Dad laughed heartily. "You're right, sweetie."

And surely, the Daewoo Matiz proved convenient for commuting to and from college or meet friends during the weekends.

Time flew by during my college days. Classes, assignments, fieldwork, library visits—I was happy that there was no time to pause and look around. The evil spirits seemed to have slipped out of my life. I believed it was good riddance.

Towards the end of my first year of college, Vini Didi got married to Varun—a major now. She settled down in Chandi Mandir Cantonment, where Major Varun was posted, not far from Mom and Dad. Vidhi Didi was a doctor now, doing MD in pediatrics.

I was in the second year of college when I met Vihaan at a friend's party. He was a tall, handsome, good-looking man with a demeanour of unruffled poise around him. I was instantly attracted to him. I earnestly wished someone would introduce us. Fifteen minutes later he reached out to me. "Hi, I'm Vihaan. Can I know the name of this gorgeous lady?"

I don't know why I blushed. "Vriti," I replied softly.

"What a lovely name! Well, Vriti, I waited for someone to introduce us till my patience got exhausted." I smiled. "You know, my eyes have been following a beauty in the party— drawn like a hummingbird towards a flower." He looked deep into my eyes.

Is he a habitual flirt? "I love hummingbirds. They are cute." I chuckled.

He threw back his head and laughed. He looked strikingly handsome when he laughed. "I don't know why but I think you are a special girl, Vriti."

Is he being honest? "Really, Vihaan? That's sweet of you."

"I'll fetch us some drinks and then let's find a quiet corner for ourselves. I want to know more about you."

While I waited, my friend Amaya rushed to me. "Wow. I have never seen Vihaan so interested in a girl. You lucky one!"

"How do you know?"

"He's my cousin, silly. A real gentleman. So many girls want to be introduced to him, but he has never shown such keen interest in any of them. And I like you too. You'll both make a perfect couple." She smiled and slipped away seeing Vihaan returning with two glasses of chardonnay.

We sat sipping wine and talking.

Vihaan was four years older than me. We spent the rest of the evening engrossed in each other. He invited me to dinner the next Saturday, and then the Saturday after that. Soon, all my free time was booked solely for him.

Vihaan had graduated from Delhi College of Art and was now a professional painter and sculptor. His artistic inclination fascinated me. After the initial attraction, we both fell deeply in love with each other. I loved Vihaan's sense of humour and he would leave me in splits with his anecdotes. However, I never disclosed my scary past to him. When life was going on so beautifully, why disturb its tranquillity?

It was a drastic mistake, for barely three months after meeting Vihaan, I was jolted out of my succour.

It was a muggy August evening. Vihaan and I had eaten a delectable dinner in a restaurant at The Village. We finished around eleven and then Vihaan walked me to the entrance of my apartment. We stood talking for a while. A gentle breeze made the heat less oppressive. Around half-past eleven, Vihaan left. His car was parked on the other end of The Village.

I turned and had barely climbed a few steps up the narrow dingy staircase when someone called out, "Vritiiiii." It was a familiar rasp. I turned to behold the chilling presence. The electric bulb of a distant pole lighted her messy white hair. Her head, as usual, was cocked at a strange angle. She emitted that horrible chortle and my panic swelled like a turbulent river. I screamed and scrambled up the two floors of the dimly lit stairway, staggering and slipping several times. In a minute I stood outside the door of my apartment—breathless, dripping with sweat, and fumbling for the keys in my bag. I kept looking back lest the horrible creature had followed me upstairs. I struggled to open the lock. The keys kept slipping out of my trembling hands. Sweat was trickling down my forehead and into my eyes, burning them, making me blind. I managed to open the door. As I rushed inside, I felt someone brush past me . . . an ice-cold draft. I banged the door shut. Someone had certainly entered my apartment with me.

I switched on the light and sat on a chair shell-shocked. She had found me again. My apartment seemed undisturbed and peaceful. So peaceful that it bothered me.

Soon I was bathed in my sweat. I had forgotten to switch on the fan in the despotic heat. My throat was parched.

Gathering my wits, I turned on the cooler and went to the kitchen for a glass of cold water. There seemed nothing amiss in my apartment, yet the impression that I wasn't alone pungently invaded my senses.

I picked up the phone's receiver to call Vihaan. What was I to tell him? Could I tell him that I was perpetually followed and haunted by ghosts, and that no rituals or pujas had been able to shake these chilling entities off me? What if he decided to end our relationship? That would break my heart. He was the first man in my life I was so deeply in love with. I realized if Vihaan refused to come to my help, I would be alone, fighting a losing battle of my life unaided. I put down the phone receiver, dejected.

I kept awake for a long time. Strange sounds had again invaded my peace. I kept hearing subdued creaking and shuffling. I lay listlessly in my bed, rationalizing varied logical explanations for my dilemma. What had gone wrong that fateful night when I had played the Ouija board game with my sisters? The planchette had moved like crazy. Why was it only me who had become the target? My sisters had never experienced anything.

The next morning, I ate breakfast in a hurry and left my apartment. I decided to miss the first few classes and go to the state library. I needed to know more about the Ouija board, from where all my troubles had initiated.

I found several books on the topic, of the people's attempt to commune with the dead, with the spirit world. It had been a practice since ancient times. Some religious books forbade this practice. They expressed that it was a tool of Satan and revealed information that should only be in God's hands. According to the Old Testament, God forbade people to seek mediums. Later, the catholic bishops banned the Ouija boards, warning people that they were communicating with the demons using it and opening the gates of hell. The scientists had different viewpoints. That was natural. The world of spirits was mysterious. It had no logical explanation. Only a few people like me, who had had supernatural encounters, knew the reality of its existence.

I realized that in my case, too, the Ouija board had opened doors for the demonic spirits that had then hooked on to me. I had no rationalization for why it had happened.

That evening I half-heartedly returned home around seven-thirty in the evening. The daylight was fading. The night was slithering in, ushering along the nightly creatures. The stairway leading to my apartment was dark, deserted, and foreboding. I climbed up hesitantly. As I reached my apartment, I found the stray brown cat that sometimes roamed on my terrace or visited me for a treat, lying right in front of the door. "Kitty, kitty, get up," I called out. It didn't respond. My hands were full, so I shoved it lightly with my foot. Still there was no response. My heart skipped a beat. I hurriedly opened the door and switched on the light. The cat was dead. Someone had twisted her neck and thrown her there. The ghastly sight of Coco lying dead in a similar position flashed in my brain. Sobbing with fear, I slammed the door shut. It was a deliberate act I knew. The killing spree had begun, the warning rang in my head. With my shivering hands I dialled the landlord's number, requesting him to send someone to remove the dead cat.

The evil was once again closing on me. I urgently needed to find help to get rid of it before it went out of control. I couldn't think of anyone but Vihaan. Would I be jeopardizing his safety?

He was strong and the person I was closest to now, I reasoned. Who else could I seek help from? I needed to spare my aged parents more anxiety. I decided to take Vihaan into confidence and tell him everything. We needed to sit in private to have this crucial discussion. I didn't waste another minute and called him, inviting him to dinner the following Saturday.

My plan got deferred. On Friday, Vihaan urgently needed to go to Jaipur to see his ailing mother. He was to catch a late-night train and I offered to drop him at the railway station.

We reached the station much before the train's departure time and strolled on the platform to while away our time. "Vihaan, I need to discuss something very important with you," I conveyed casually.

"What's it?"

"Not here, Vihaan. We need to sit in peace, for it is a serious matter. That's why I wanted you to come tomorrow to my place. But now you're going . . ."

"Now I am curious. Is it about someone else in your past?"

"Vihaan, there's nothing like that. Go with a peaceful mind for I am and will be yours forever."

Vihaan squeezed my hand cheerfully. "I should be back in three-four days. What about the next weekend? Is your dinner invitation still on?"

"Of course. Next Saturday." I instinctively turned and gave him a peck on his cheek.

Just then the train entered the station. It was going to stop here for just two minutes, so Vihaan rushed to board it. As the train chugged out of the station at 12:30 a.m. and I stood waving at Vihaan, he blew me a kiss and shouted, "Next Saturday, your apartment. *Pukka*."

I reached my place at around one. I was tired and sleepy. Hurriedly changing into my nightclothes, I slipped into my bed after a quick prayer, a vital lifesaving habit now. I was slowly drifting into a blissful sleep when I heard a male voice command, "Hey, go down. Your car window is open. Close it."

I got out of my bed, put on my slippers, picked up my car keys from the table, and walked down the steps onto the lonely road—all in a trance. As I reached my parking slot, the elderly night-guard accosted me. "Don't come on the road alone at this time, *beti*. It's not safe." His words acted like iced water on my face, rendering me fully awake. What . . . What was I doing there, on the deserted road in my nightclothes, in the middle of the night? I slowly walked to my car. The window on the passenger side was open. I recalled Vihaan had opened it to pay the parking attendant at the station. He must have forgotten to close it.

I started the car's engine and closed the window. As I locked my car and retraced my steps homewards, my uneasiness had amplified. Whose voice had I heard in my bedroom? Had I been dreaming? The outside temperature was around 35 degrees, and I was shivering like a reed in a gust by the time I reached home.

My apartment door was wide open. I shut it and rushed to the refrigerator. I guzzled down a glass of water and sat on my bed—alert and hassled. The room was peaceful and undisturbed. "Good girl." The voice came suddenly from the chair opposite my bed. Someone sat there, I now saw—a faint shadow. This time the masculine voice was crisp and terse. The sound of sneering laughter that followed gave me a heart attack. I stifled my scream and jumped off the bed. With my shivering hands, I picked up my phone and called my friend Puja who lived in Malviya Nagar, as a paying guest. The next thing I remember, I was rushing out of my apartment and down the stairs with just my purse that I had earlier dropped on my bedside table. I drove like crazy, whooshing through the empty roads. Thankfully, the traffic police were missing at this hour.

I had no option but to share my experience with Puja, evading the history of the horrible events. I told her about my apartment being haunted. Puja was supportive. I spent the weekend with her but couldn't impose on her for long. On Sunday evening she came with me to the house, to see me safe. "Vriti, you have a charming little joint. It doesn't look haunted at all."

Did she think I was lying? "It's only at night."

"In that case, change your apartment."

If it were the solution, I would have done it long back. I couldn't tell her that. "I will."

After a cup of coffee and spending half an hour with me, during which her eyes continuously inspected each corner of my apartment, Puja left. She seemed in a hurry to leave before the night sneaked in.

What if Vihaan weaselled out like her? The thought sent my mood down the dumps.

I called Mom and Dad. Mom was running a high fever. She was also suffering from arthritic pains. I couldn't request them to come. Mercifully, the week passed without more disturbance.

Next Saturday morning, I woke up ruffled, as Vihaan was coming over for dinner. Worry about where our discussion would lead, dampened my excitement. The torrential monsoon rain too had thrown cold water on my spirits. I kept wondering if Vihaan would be able to make it through the jam-packed waterlogged roads of Delhi.

I was glad I had shopped for the groceries the previous evening on my way back from college. During the week I had got recipes for some exotic dishes from Mom. "Why do you want the recipes now?" Mom was suspicious. I knew she was wondering if I was in a relationship.

"Mom, a special friend is coming over for dinner." It was time to throw her a hint.

"Does your friend have a name?" Mom probed further.

"Vihaan," I replied. I never lied to Mom.

"Just be careful, Vriti. Don't trust people blindly."

"Don't worry, Mom. You know me. I am very cautious and selective about my friends."

Just then I heard Dad's voice in the background and Mom quickly changed the topic. I knew Mom would reveal things to Dad only after she was satisfied.

I spent the entire morning cooking and cleaning. After an hour's rest in the afternoon, I dressed up for the most special dinner of my life. I had picked up an ankle-length dress from a nearby boutique—a white and leaf-green dress with a delicate touch of gold. I applied a little make-up and wore a delicate ethnic necklace to go with my dress. I wanted to look special for Vihaan.

Vihaan came on time despite the rain. He breezed in with an enticing smile, a big bunch of red roses, and a bottle of champagne. A heavenly smell exuded from the roses . . . the smell of love. Vihaan handed the bouquet to me, and I couldn't help but bury my face into it.

"I was saving this bottle for a super special occasion," Vihaan said, beaming as he placed the champagne bottle on the table, my makeshift study and dining table. I had spread a new silver-embroidered, white tablecloth on it. In the centre stood the silver candlestand that Mom had given me. I had planned a romantic candlelight dinner.

Super special occasion? Was Vihaan going to propose to me tonight?

I placed the flowers on the table, fetched two glasses, and rushed to bring the platter of starters—cheese, olives, and pineapple nibbles. I lit the candles before switching off the lights.

The candlelight induced an aura of passion. Vihaan reached for my hand from across the table and my heartbeat matched the flickering lights of the candles. On an impulse, I took the decision not to discuss my supernatural encounters with him. Not tonight. Tonight should be reserved for our love.

Vihaan gazed into my eyes. "Vriti, how lovely you look in the candlelight!"

"Only in the candlelight?" I teased him.

Vihaan laughed and stroked my hand lovingly. "You are the most beautiful girl I have known in my life." A loving smile played on his lips. I stood still in anticipation, my heart pounding wildly. I was sure Vihaan could hear it. "My life acquired meaning only when you came into it." He kept his hand lightly on my cheek. "You have added a spark to my vagrant soul. I am deeply in love—" Vihaan couldn't even complete his sentence. The tablecloth was whisked away with such violence that everything on it went crashing down on the floor. I felt the impact of a few flying objects on my body too. The room plunged into fearsome darkness. I sealed my lips to prevent my scream and ran to turn on the light.

The floor of the room was smeared with broken shards of the glasses, the food, the red roses. Streaks of smoke rose from the extinguished candles. The bubbling champagne ran in streams on the floor, soaking my prized tablecloth. Vihaan stared at the mess, horror-struck. "Who did that?"

My legs turned into jelly. I gaped at the mess like it was a pit of vipers. "Maybe, maybe the table tilted," I managed to speak.

Vihaan shook his head assertively in disbelief. "We were standing still. Someone pulled the tablecloth aggressively." He was breathing heavily. My lie was exposed instantly. "Get out," an unseen voice growled. Vihaan's eyes expanded in fear. He surveyed the room with unease. I froze like an icicle. The light began to flicker. Vihaan staggered as someone pushed him. "Out," the ghostly voice resonated. Vihaan stirred into action. He rushed to pick up his jacket, held my hand, and pulled me towards the door. "Let's get out of here. Hurry."

Within seconds we were rushing down the stairs and bundling into Vihaan's car. As I turned to look back, I saw a distinct hazy figure standing in the middle of the deserted road, watching us.

Once we were safely away, my sanity returned. "Vihaan, I didn't even lock the house. We left the door wide open."

"No problem. There's someone in the house, guarding it." He gave a nervous laugh.

After a brief silence that I spent taking deep breaths to regain my composure, I asked, "Where are we going?"

"To eat dinner."

"Vihaan, I have cooked some nice dishes for you."

"Donate them to him. Whoever he is."

Was Vihaan angry? I didn't have the pluck to ask him. Though he sounded calm, I felt as if my dreams now lay crushed like a snail squished into pulp under a heavy boot. I was frightened. I was angry with myself for not sharing my troubles with Vihaan earlier.

Vihaan drove to Siri Fort in the mild drizzle. Once out of the car, I noticed that my dress was soiled. Various pieces of cheese were stuck to Vihaan's trousers too. We rushed to the washrooms to clean the mess and then Vihaan led me to the Chinese restaurant.

Once we were seated, Vihaan gazed straight into my eyes. "Vriti, what's going on?" He looked pale and shaken. My shivers hadn't subsided either.

I deeply loved Vihaan. I also knew that strong relationships were built on trust. We couldn't start a new life on veiled truths. So, that night, I unlocked my past for him, even though I was afraid of losing him forever.

My long saga of the supernatural invasion into my life left Vihaan shocked. He was also genuinely concerned. "I love you, Vriti. I can't think of my life without you. I am ready to share all life's problems with you." Tears trickled down my cheeks. He passed me a tissue and continued, "You know, I never believed in the supernatural . . . till today. I confess I'm shaken. Scared too." He shook his head. "But I admire your guts, living with the ghosts for so long and surviving the ordeals." He reached out for my hand across the table and patted it assuredly. "You have suffered alone for too long. Not anymore." His soothing words made me burst into loud sobs. Fortunately, the inclement weather had rendered the restaurant nearly empty.

Outside, it had begun to pour heavily. I could hear the rain spattering against the windowpanes. Flashes of lightning intermittently permeated through the windows followed by loud cracks of thunder that rattled the fragile glass panes. Was this a bad omen?

We lingered over our dinner till the storm passed. As we walked out from the air-conditioned restaurant into a dark night, the viscous warm breeze brushed against our faces. I took deep breaths to overcome my breathlessness. My heart began to quiver. I didn't have the courage to go back to my apartment. God alone knew what waited for me there. We reached the parking and dilly-dallied for a bit. "I'll check into a hotel for the night," I proposed.

Vihaan vehemently shook his head. "Then, after that? Don't be silly. You are coming with me." Discerning my hesitation, he laughed. "Vriti, don't worry. You are safe with me. I am a bit old school. No intimacy till we get married." He wrapped his arm around me and kissed me on my cheek.

Had he just proposed to me? My heart fluttered like the wings of a Sunbird. I wanted to rush into Vihaan's arms and stay there for the rest of my life. I controlled my emotions. Life's major decisions shouldn't be taken in haste, I told myself. "I don't want to jeopardize your life, Vihaan. Perhaps you don't realize what you're getting into. I encounter the paranormal wherever I go. It follows me. I'm sorry that I kept it hidden from you."

He tenderly gazed into my eyes, took a deep breath, and stretched his chest to tower above me like a valiant knight obliged to rescue a damsel in distress. "I don't mind the paranormal. For you, I'm ready to face any challenge."

I restrained from giving him a tight hug. "Vihaan, living with me won't be easy. Let's not walk on a tightrope and build our dreams on fragile threads. Don't take decisions you may repent someday and then change your mind. I will be completely devastated if we break up later. Not that it won't hurt now. But let's take that decision now." Deep in my heart, I didn't want Vihaan to agree with me.

"Come on, Vriti. Do you think I am that fickle? We are in it together now, and we'll defeat these ghouls, once and for all. I promise." Vihaan's conviction brought hope to my morose spirit. I smiled through my brimming eyes.

"Mom and Dad have tried so many times, doing pujas and whatnot. Nothing has worked."

"We shall see." He patted my back like an old wise man.

We spent the entire Sunday in Vihaan's house—lazing, idling, cooking, talking. I couldn't avoid going back to my apartment. I had been wearing Vihaan's T-shirt and ill-fitted shorts since the morning. I needed my things.

My dilemma was killing me. I didn't want to expose Vihaan to the supernatural that had obviously been hostile towards him. "My parents aren't going to approve of our live-in relationship. Maybe I'll change my apartment," I suggested after thinking things through.

"I don't care what your parents or other people think. You are not living alone anymore. Let's go and fetch your things. We also need to clean your apartment before you hand it back to the owner." He added with a smile, "Do you think the ghost cleaned the mess he made?" I frowned at his comment and Vihaan laughed. "I am serious. He should at least offer to help to compensate for his nasty behaviour."

"Don't expect good things from the nasty one."

"Hmm. Now let's hurry. We must leave that spooky place before it gets dark."

I gave one month's notice to the landlord and shifted with Vihaan. Surprisingly, when I broke the news to my parents over the phone, they weren't even surprised. They were worried and alarmed that the paranormal had once again invaded my life. Dad said he had forever been uneasy, wondering if I were safe living alone. It was a good idea to shift with someone reliable, he added. Mom was pleased that I had finally met someone I liked, someone capable of protecting me. "When do we get to meet Vihaan?" They both wanted to know.

I happily settled with Vihaan. He began dropping me off and picking me up from college like my bodyguard. We were closer to each other than ever before.

A month passed like a beautiful dream and then, as often in life, we woke up to the despotic reality.

We began to hear loud ghostly growls that kept following Vihaan everywhere. Was he the ghosts' target this time? I didn't want to lose him. He could be killed, like so many others had been. I was in a state of total panic.

Not long after, one Sunday morning Vihaan got out of the bed looking very unwell. His face was flushed. Had he caught a bug? "Are you okay, Vihaan?" I asked with concern. He went straight into the toilet without responding.

I made tea for us, and then I sat at the dining table waiting for him and cutting an apple to eat.

Vihaan came and sat directly opposite me. I poured him a cup. He ignored it. A strange, twisted smile played on his lips. Was he happy or angry?

"I want to marry you. Now." He sounded like an intimidating police inspector.

"What are you saying, Vihaan? Of course, I want to marry you. Eventually."

"Today."

"What? How can it be today? I have to finish my graduation at least. It was your suggestion that we'll get married once my studies were over. We have already discussed it. We both want a proper wedding for us. Our parents have to be involved."

"No. Today," he growled angrily. His flaming red eyes glared at me and I suppressed my shiver.

"Are you joking?"

"No."

"That's not possible. Vihaan, what's wrong with you? Why are you acting so weird?" An intense silence ensued. Vihaan sat glaring at me like a hyena ready to kill. "Vihaan? Are you listening?" I raised my voice.

"Stop calling me Vihaan. I'm not Vihaan." His strange voice hit me like a forceful spurt of water. I drew in my breath. It was indeed not Vihaan's voice.

"Then who are you?" I asked hesitatingly.

"Ayaan."

I laughed.

"Don't laugh." Vihaan furiously hit the table with his fist. The cup filled with tea toppled. "I am serious."

"I have never known any Ayaan in my life."

"Don't you remember me? I carried a red rose for you . . . waited outside your school every day. I loved you!"

I stared blankly at Vihaan. His crooked smile was unnerving me. It was horrible, lusty kind of a smile. I had never seen him smile like that. Was he serious? Or was he taking me for a ride? Why was he saying he was Ayaan? Did he just make that up?

Vihaan's blazing eyes glowered at me. "I have been following you everywhere, shielding you from harm, saving you from the other wicked ones, so many of them who sought your body. I had to constantly fight with that old witch who had taken a liking to your beautiful body and wanted to seize it. I have got rid of all of them now. I've been living with you . . . saving you for me. You are mine."

My body began to get numb.

"You kept getting lost to me . . . running away, and I had to find you again and again. Now you can't escape. Do you realize? You can't escape." He again hit the table with his fist. "You cannot love anyone else."

"Please, Vihaan, you're scaring me. It's not funny."

"Shut up. I'm not trying to be funny," Vihaan shouted, glaring at me. "I was . . . am without a body. Something happened in the market . . . bullets. Anyone I tried talking to ignored me, including you. Then you opened a door for me . . .

called me and the witch followed. I have been with you ever since. It's I who protected you. That witch would have killed you long ago, like she killed others. This fellow Vihaan has done nothing. I'm going to destroy him."

Bells began ringing in my brain. I saw a man in my mind—a good-looking, fair, well-dressed Kashmiri guy, in his early twenties, who would daily stand where I would board the army truck after school that ferried us home. This was a little before the Ouija board incident. My friends would point him out to me. I did notice his passionate gaze. At times he held a red rose in his hand to give to me, but dared nothing more than display it. I would giggle like a typical teenager feeling thrilled at the attention, and board my vehicle. With the army guards around us, he never dared to approach me. Perhaps he wanted me to understand. But I wasn't interested in him. After about a few months, he stopped coming and vanished from my life and my mind. I now realized that something serious had happened to him. Had he died in one of those frequent terrorist attacks or army encounters? Was his spirit inside Vihaan now? Would it harm him?

"Yes, I'm the one." Oh my God! He was also reading my mind. "I tried to tell you for a long time. I wanted you to use the Ouija board. But you burnt it. I was angry." Vihaan stared at me, his eyes blood red and scary.

I had not told Vihaan about burning the Ouija board. "You killed Coco?" I managed to ask.

"You too have no escape. I will not be satisfied till my dream is fulfilled, till you become mine."

I needed the spiteful spirit to leave Vihaan's body, to leave us alone. I was desperate for help. I stood up and stepped towards the telephone. Vihaan turned and kicked the small table on which the phone was kept. The table along with the gadget went crashing down. Instantly, Vihaan let out a cry and leapt from his chair. I was taken aback by his speed. He reached me in a second and grabbed both my wrists. He held them tightly in his grip. "It's our *nikah* now. Are you ready to marry me?"

I looked around desperately for an escape. "What do you mean? I am a Hindu. We don't have nikah."

"You will marry me now."

"Leave me alone." I struggled to get free.

"*Manzoor?* Do you hear me? Speak. Manzoor?" Vihaan shook me like a rag doll. He was hurting me. My head swooned. I became limp and slipped out of his hands. As I lay shivering on the floor, Vihaan picked up the knife from the table and approached me slowly, eyeing me like a predator eyeing a kill.

"What are you doing, Vihaan? Stop it. Throw this mad spirit out. Please. It's not you. It's making you do horrible things." I grovelled through my sobs and tried crawling away.

"I want to take you with me now, to my world." He followed me menacingly.

"Where?" I needed to buy time. I looked towards the door. It was not bolted. After picking up the newspaper I had carelessly left it open. That carelessness might be my gain now. It was the single escape route I had. Vihaan continued to approach me with murder in his bloodshot eyes. He was going to kill me. Vihaan, my beloved Vihaan, would spend the rest of his life rotting in jail for a murder he didn't commit at his will. Nobody would believe that a spirit had forced him to murder me. My parents would be heartbroken. Inconsolable. My spirit would forever remain restless, controlled by this horrible selfish ghoul. "Dad. I need your help, Dad," I cried pitiably.

"There's no help for you here." A horrible chortle followed the vile comment.

I began to slink towards the door, trying to make my movement imperceptible. "Stop." The horrible raspy voice commanded. I must ignore it if I wanted to survive. I slowly stood up and then dashed towards the door. Vihaan was quicker. He leapt, caught my arm, and violently twirled me around. His brutality stunned me. He savagely raised his hand holding the knife to strike me. I stared at his wild eyes and trembled like a flag fluttering in a violent gale. "Vihaan, no. Don't! Please!" I begged and sank my teeth into his arm that held me. His grip loosened. I freed myself and dived under the table. Vihaan went down on his knees and crawled after me. I tried scurrying out from the other side. He managed to grasp my hair and tried dragging me out. I screamed. It was my end, I knew. I closed my eyes.

At that precise moment, the door opened with a bang. My eyes flew open. The spirit inside Vihaan got distracted. My jaw fell open as I watched the six-foot muscular figure of Dad breeze in, followed by the robust frame of Major Varun. I stared aghast. Had Dad heard me? How could he respond so quickly? Were they real or was I hallucinating?

The two men rushed to hold Vihaan in their powerful grips. Varun wrenched the knife out of Vihaan's hand. He fought back—snarling and clamouring like a monster. It was difficult for the two robust men to control him. Then with a quick move, Major Varun pinned Vihaan down on the floor. Vihaan struggled to get free. Dad held Vihaan's wrists and tried tying them with his scarf.

All of a sudden, Vihaan was speaking in a language he didn't know. "*Mein seeth karkhe Khaandar? Aa? Tvahi chaa phikiri taraan? Mae choe ameeseath Khaandar karun. Maay muhabbat,*" he voiced vociferously, and struggled to get free. He spoke so fluently in Kashmiri that we all were taken aback. I understood he was saying something about marrying me.

"Just shut up," Dad roared, knowing that this wasn't Vihaan speaking. Vihaan was a Punjabi like us and didn't know a word of the Kashmiri language.

Vihaan resembled a savage brute as he broke free. He pounced on Dad. Dad was thrown flat on the ground. I screamed and rushed to help him. Varun was quicker. He locked his arms into Vihaan's from behind and controlled his attack. Vihaan stared at Dad and drivelled insanely, "You were there, weren't you, sitting in your jeep and ordering the shooting?"

"You bloody terrorist!" Dad jumped up and punched Vihaan on his chest.

"Get something to tie him with. A rope. Hurry!" Varun's desperation made me rush towards the pantry. I found a synthetic clothesline. Varun, with Dad's help, tied Vihaan to a leg of the heavy dining table. I was aghast at the sudden strength Vihaan had acquired. If Dad and Varun weren't two trained army men, it wouldn't have been possible to control Vihaan.

Meanwhile, Dad took out a booklet from his pocket, drew a chair close to Vihaan to sit on, and began chanting mantras from it.

"Dad, this spirit was a Muslim when it was alive. These mantras may not work on him," I said.

"Vriti, there is only one God. You may call Him Brahma, Shiva, Paramatma, God, Allah, but He's the same Highest Holy Spirit. Religions are man-made. There's no religion in the world of spirits." I nodded and he continued, "All evil spirits are afraid of the Holy Name, in whatever form it is taken." Dad then took out a small packet from his pocket. It contained some ash. He rubbed it on Vihaan's forehead. "It is holy ash given to me by a pandit," he said.

Instantly, Varun forcibly poured a liquid from a small bottle into Vihaan's mouth. "This is Holy Water. We came prepared to purify your house, though this was not what we expected," he said, shaking his head as the liquid went inside Vihaan's mouth.

Vihaan continued to release angry growls and carried on with his efforts to break loose from his constraints. Dad's chanting became louder. To my surprise, a few minutes later, Vihaan began to pacify. Then he coughed violently and went limp. We heard an angry growl heading towards the bedroom. I saw the blurry shadow, the same figure I had seen sitting on my chair in our Srinagar house. Dad rushed to shut the door of the bedroom. Varun sprinkled the left-over Holy Water outside the door.

"What . . . What am I doing on the floor? Why have you tied me?" Vihaan's voice captured our attention. He was looking around, utterly perplexed. "Who are you?" he asked, looking at Varun.

"It's okay, chap. Get up now." Varun untied Vihaan and helped him sit on a chair.

"Dad, you were on time." My voice quivered as I sat on a chair next to Vihaan. "Were you both visiting me just like that?"

Dad exclaimed, "No, Vriti. I saw this strange vision yesterday when I had dozed off after lunch. A girl visited me in my dream, a beautiful young girl with light brown eyes and brown hair tied in a high ponytail. She seemed so real." *Oh my God! He's describing Amrita.* Dad had never met her. I had told my parents about the other incidents except for the death of my friend and roommate, Amrita. I hid it because I knew it would have worried them. Dad continued, "She was crying and warned me that you were in danger and must be rescued.

The dream made me nervous. I tried calling you but your phone was continuously engaged. Out of order?"

"No. It never rang."

"Strange." Dad shrugged. "Your Mom insisted that you could indeed be in danger and needed help. She too had been having bad dreams lately. I took a good decision in asking Varun to come along."

"You must have left very early."

"We did. Thank God! At that hour, there was less traffic on the roads and Varun is an excellent high-speed driver. If we were late even by a minute, we would have lost you forever." Dad had tears in his eyes.

"And I thought that the arrival of heroes in the nick of time happened only in the films." Varun smiled and breathed out loudly. "What a save!" He turned to me. "Both Vini and I have been constantly worried for you, Vriti. After Dad called last night, Vini got anxious and insisted we leave as soon as possible."

A loud bang from the bedroom broke our discussion. All eyes were on the bedroom door. "How do we get rid of this problem?" Dad wiped his face and moaned aloud. "I cannot allow my baby to live in this horrific danger, in unending fear. How do I bring normalcy in her life?" He rested his head on his palms in utter helplessness. "This ghost is becoming more and more savage and treacherous."

Tears trickled down my cheeks, despite my brave front. "Yes, Dad, I need help desperately," I said, brushing away my tears with the back of my hand.

Varun nodded at me, came to sit next to Dad, and patted his hand. "Don't worry, Dad. Vini and I have been doing intensive research and have found someone with potent powers against the evil spirits. Sometime ago, my friend posted at Shimla had sought his help. He is highly impressed with him. I requested him to seek help for us too, and the holy man has agreed."

"Who is this holy man?"

"He's a hermit. Lives in a small ashram in a forest near Theog, thirty kilometres from Shimla—called Swami Niketanand. Apparently, his powers to deal with the supernatural are known far and wide."

"Can you get in touch with him? Now?"

"Yes, I'll call my friend. He can pass on the message to Swami Ji."

"Can he visit us here?"

"I think so. There's a lot of army movement on the Hindustan Tibet Road. I will take special permission and arrange for him to visit us."

"Call him right now." Dad stood up with a purpose. He picked up the instrument from the floor. "I will talk to the GOC-in-C Western Command, and arrange for a conveyance for Swami Ji. We must destroy this demon, once and for all. Till then, we'll stay here with Vriti and Vihaan and arrange for *akhand* pooja from today to keep the evil at bay."

Fortunately, the telephone was still working. Dad handed the receiver to Varun and stood next to him as he dialled the number.

I sent a silent "Thank You" to Amrita for being a true friend even beyond life. *I'll also request the holy man to help her beautiful soul attain peace.*

Vihaan sat bundled on the chair, shivering and sweating. I had never seen him so weak . . . so frightened, shaken, and confused. I held his shivering hand in my shaky one and wrapped my other arm around him, comforting him, conveying to him that he wasn't to be blamed for what had happened, assuring him that I loved him with all my heart.

A Misled Spirit

We were a happy family, living a modest life. Things were good. But it was not meant to be. Overnight, we were carved into tortured voodoo dolls.

I think the warning had come to me through that disturbing dream. Was it an omen of the dark days to come? The nightmare had felt so real, as if I had seen something that had a strong connection to my life.

I dreamt of a woman being torched alive. Her painful screams and pleadings for help pierced my heart. No one stepped in to help her. The spectators watched her being consumed by the soaring, crackling flames and laughed, as if it was a kind of show to be enjoyed. I tried to reach out to her, but my legs were chained. I sobbed with pity for the burning woman.

I woke up squirming in my bed, and sobbing. What kind of dream was that? Ghastly. Grisly.

Creepy. My clothes were wet with perspiration. I sat in my bed frozen in shock. I couldn't sleep afterwards.

The dream I had had kept playing in my mind. I tried to distract myself but it didn't help. I began to feel afraid of something. I was tense and jittery all the time. My happiness was being slowly wrung out like water from a sodden cloth.

And then, my life turned into hell.

This had happened for the third time that week. An unknown fear, like a worm wriggling through my veins, woke me up. The green phosphorescent needles of the table clock were at 3:32. The time proved to be a portent of the horror to come. My stomach was knotted with fear. A cold cloud of gloom began to envelop me. I began to drift into a trance. I struggled to remain awake. I heard Samir moan in his sleep. Riya, my two-year-old, began to cry all of a sudden. And then she was there at the doorstep—the scary form with a sallow chilling face, the woman who appeared in my nightmares. I shivered in fright and tried to sit up. I couldn't even move. I was fettered to the bed with invisible chains. I lay helpless, like an etherized patient on a surgery table.

Samir's agitation grew. I heard him thrashing his limbs and sobbing like a baby. I wanted to wake him up. Help him.

The woman continued to stand at the door, her eerie stare sending shock waves through me. Who was she?

Then the nightmare broke. I sat up in my bed. Fully alert. My heart was pounding against my chest. I glanced at the clock. The time was 3:37.

I have never had recurrent dreams. This was a first. I took little comfort in the fact that the eerie woman had remained standing at my doorstep. She never stepped beyond it.

Samir's moans now subsided. I left my bed, filled a glass with water from the jug, and had a few sips. Then I gently shook Samir. He stared at me blankly, half awake. He looked pale, paler than the woman in my dream. "Samir, are you alright? Drink some water. You'll feel better."

"Where is she?" he asked in a whisper.

"Who?"

"The woman in red."

"Which woman?"

"I . . . I don't know. She had come again."

I was stunned. Samir had seen her, too. She was real.

A woman in red? Was that the colour of her sari? It had been loosely draped. In the dim light, the colours were not perceptible. Everything was dark except her pale face. Had Samir seen the same apparition in his dreams?

My limbs were getting numb. "What did she want? Did she say something?" Samir shrugged his shoulders and tightly pressed his lips. He traversed his eyes around in a daze and then accepted the glass of water from me. "What time is it?"

"Quarter to four."

"I have to be up at six. I am going to the office early today for an important meeting. Don't disturb me till then. Go back to sleep." I nodded as he slipped under his coverlet and turned his back to me.

I stayed awake and worried till I left the bed at half-past five. I felt exhausted, as if I had run a race. I had to send my son Rohan and my elder daughter Ila to school, and then cook and pack lunch for Samir. Riya would be up and demanding attention soon. Listlessly, I carried on with my morning chores.

At breakfast, Samir was silent and withdrawn. I wanted to discuss my nightmare, but I hesitated. *Is a mere dream worth a discussion? Won't it only strain our peace of mind?*

As the day progressed, I tried to ease my nerves. But each time I glanced at the doorway of my bedroom, the doubt returned. I remembered each dream so vividly. Why had my baby cried in fright? Why had Samir moaned? I had distinctly heard them.

Instead of calming me, my logic was making me more nervous. I decided to quickly finish my work and visit my best friend, Shobha.

This vast bustling city of Delhi often made me feel lonely. I missed the cosy comfort of my hometown, Chamba. I loved those towering snow-clad ranges of the Himalayas—Dhauladhar, Zanskar, and Pir Panjal—that nestled my scenic valley like a mother nestling a baby in her lap. Life was so different there—peaceful and simple. The big cities failed to offer that kind of peace or security.

We had a few friends here. Shobha and her husband Sunil were the closest ones we had. As the regional supply manager in a telecom company, Samir was Sunil's immediate boss. That's where they had become friends, and soon I became best friends with Shobha.

Today, I desperately needed to spend time with a friend and share my worries with her. Riya was being fussy and cranky, too. An outing would do us both good. I would be back before Rohan and Ila returned from school. I hurriedly dressed Riya in warm woollens, wrapped a thick shawl over my flannel salwar kameez, and stepped out to a heavily overcast sky and biting icy winds of a cold January morning of the year 1964.

When I reached Shobha's house after fifteen minutes of a rickshaw ride, she was still in her nightclothes. I merrily announced, "Surprise!"

She returned my grin with a blank expression on her face. "Oh Hema, it's a little early for visits, isn't it? I haven't even finished my household chores." Then, perhaps realizing that she was being rude, she added with a balmy smile, "You look pale and haggard. Are you well? Any problem?"

"I'm okay," I conveyed softly. "I am cold. Need a cup of hot tea." I shouldn't have barged into her house without informing her. How did I forget to make a simple phone call?

With our steaming cups of tea, Shobha and I sat chatting on general topics for ten minutes. I was on the verge of discussing my bizarre dreams with her when she stood up. "Hema, I have a lot of work to finish, expecting some guests tonight. So, if you don't mind . . ."

I felt awkward. I had come all the way to see her. We had barely spent ten minutes talking and she already wanted me to leave.

I left her house but didn't want to go back home yet. I was afraid to be alone in it. I walked to a nearby park and sat on a bench. Riya ran around chasing geese near the water pond.

I sat thinking. Perhaps I was overreacting. Maybe they were just dreams. I watched Riya playing, giggling at the honking and waddling birds. Tossing worries out of my mind, I laughed as Riya came running into my arms. I bought a packet of peanuts from a vendor, and we sat side-by-side munching them. The sun peeped from behind the clouds. We sat basking in it. Refreshed, Riya and I returned home.

That evening when Samir returned from the office, he was unwell. He was running a fever. After a cup of tea, he declared that he needed rest. I got busy helping the children with their homework and preparing dinner.

I woke Samir up at dinnertime. He had slept close to an hour and still appeared tired. After a very small meal, he once again slipped into his bed. Samir had never been that listless. What was the matter with him?

After tucking the children in bed as I slipped under my quilt, my mind wandered to the past ten years of my happily married life. Samir had always been a loving and considerate husband. I loved him from the core of my heart. I wanted him safe.

What was happening was not normal. Perhaps I should speak with my elder brother, Prakash. He had always been a father figure for me. But would it be right to bother him over some dreams?

I tossed and turned for a while and then fetched my booklet of hymns. I softly chanted for half an hour. That calmed me down significantly and soon I fell asleep.

The woman I had seen in my nightmares returned that night. She arrived at the same time as always. I got goosebumps as I looked at the dark, grim image stationed at the door. Her sinister stare pierced me like an arrow. My breathing became laboured as I observed how angry she was. Why? What had I done to make her angry? I heard Samir's agitated whimpers. I heard my baby's pitiful cries. I was again helpless like a tethered hostage. From the corner of my eye, I saw her furiously stamp her foot before vanishing.

Fully alert, I surveyed the room. My heart was quivering with fright. There was an eerie void inside the door's framework that had recently been occupied by the scary apparition. *So, it's settled. She is not in my dreams. She is as real as I am.*

I couldn't leave the bed easily that morning. It was time to discuss this affair with Samir.

Samir was limp like a dead bird when he left the bed. He refused to eat breakfast. "I can't eat. I feel that I may throw up if I eat."

"Why? What's wrong?"

"I don't know."

"Did you sleep well?"

"Hmm . . ."

He looked so pale that I decided to have the discussion in the evening. "Samir, please, eat some porridge. You can't go to the office on an empty stomach." He swallowed a spoon to please me and retched. I could see he was trying to retain the food in his stomach. He gulped it down with a few sips of tea. "I don't know why I feel sick and tired. Don't feel like going to office. But I must. There is an important project coming up."

"I believe we will soon hear about your promotion?" I asked eagerly.

"The orders should have come by now."

"I am so excited. You are a sincere and dedicated worker, Samir. Your colleagues and juniors love and respect you. I'm sure they'll be happy to have you as their senior boss." Samir smiled, patted my cheek, and limped out of the door.

I kept worrying about him the entire day.

That evening at dinner I opened the discussion. "Samir, something weird is happening in our house."

"Weird? What do you mean?"

"I see a ghostly woman standing at our bedroom door just before the morning hours. She terrifies me. After a few minutes, she disappears."

Samir stared at me. I failed to see any surprise on his face. He didn't counter my claim. He lowered his eyes and went pale.

"And you get restless in your sleep. Do you see her too? You mentioned her the other night."

Samir remained quiet and glanced at our bedroom door visible from our dining space. I waited nervously. When he spoke, his voice was quivering. "I have been having nightmares these days."

I covered his hand with mine. "Do you remember them?"

He swallowed a spoonful of curd and broke a piece of bread. Instead of eating, he dropped it back on the plate and raised his head. He gazed at me with pain oozing from his eyes. "A woman in a red sari is after me . . . dragging me away from you and our children. It has happened many times. I resist—I refuse, but . . ." He stopped and stared at the main door. His expression changed, as if something had frightened him. I turned to check what he had seen. There was nothing visible to me. Samir abruptly got up and left the room.

Samir's revelation left me stunned. I sat numb for a while and then followed Samir to coax him to eat his dinner. He was changing into his nightclothes when I noticed marks on his back. He had been injured. "Samir, there are bruises on your back. Did you fall and hit your back on something?"

"I have bruises?" He tried to look at his back. "It has been hurting since morning."

"How did you get them?"

"Hema, I have no idea. I—" Samir abruptly stopped. I saw his eyes dilating.

"What?"

"In my dream, she hit me when I refused."

"Refused what?"

"Stop asking me questions, Hema. I am tired." He switched off the light and slipped into his blanket.

Samir's bruises left me horror-struck. She was physically hurting him. How? He was not sharing anything with me. He had never kept secrets before.

Life plunged into despair. The ghost's visits became a nightly routine. It had now been more than three months of living in fear. Every night I would wake up with a jolt and see her standing at the doorstep. I would begin to shiver with dread and pray to God for help. Samir would get agitated and wail like an injured animal. My baby would cry in her sleep. In the morning Samir would share nothing. My baby was too small to expound her fears. Rohan and Ila blissfully remained busy in school, studies, and friends. I made special efforts to keep them completely oblivious of the harrowing affairs going on . . . about the supernatural invasion of our house. They must be shielded from the evil.

Eventually, Samir stopped going to the office. He lost his appetite completely. He was getting weak and irritable.

I began to spot welts on his arms and legs. He tried to hide them from me. The ghost never entered our bedroom. How was she causing those injuries? The baffling mystery was making me distraught and anxious.

Samir was changing. His distorted, angry features made him look like a raging, sickly bull. He lay in his bed the whole day like a zombie. At times, he would shout at me. Our charming house had been turned into a living hell.

One day, I got a call from Samir's boss, Mr. Patel, wanting to know why Samir had taken a long leave from the office. "All his absence will be counted," he said curtly, "and it will be without pay. You must know."

This couldn't continue. I needed to do something about it. Finding him a bit calm one day, I sat with him. Lovingly stroking his head, I asked tactfully, "Samir, do you really need four months of unpaid leave?"

"I am not well."

"You need to see a doctor."

"I don't need to see any *doctor-voctor*."

"Then how will you be cured?"

"I am not that unwell." He gritted his teeth and turned his back towards me.

I maintained my cool. "If you aren't ill, why go on leave? We will soon run out of money. How will we pay the children's school fees, or even feed them?"

"I will do whatever I want."

"Samir, please, it may impede your promotion."

"I don't give a damn!" he growled.

I insisted, "How can you say that? You have worked so hard, for so many years just to realize this dream. Why—"

"You stupid woman, keep out of my life." Samir suddenly turned and pounced at me like a wild animal. "Get out of my way," he shouted and shoved me hard. I fell from the bed. My elbow hit the hard floor. I moaned in pain. Anger was oozing from his inflamed eyes like red-hot lava. He was not himself.

Tears streamed down my cheeks. "Samir, what has happened to you? You were never like this. This can't be you speaking," I sobbed.

Samir turned his back on me. "Get out of my room, bitch, and leave us alone," he hissed through his clenched teeth.

I rushed out and sat in the kitchen, shell-shocked. My whole body shuddered in fear. I rested my head on the slab and cried. My little Riya stood beside me, holding and tugging the corner of my sari. I wrapped my arm around my frightened child to console her.

Leave us alone? She was here, with Samir, trying to crush our blissful life? Samir had never been short-tempered, never foul-mouthed.

Finally gathering myself up I got back to my chores. I decided to seek Shobha's and Sunil's help. I couldn't think of anyone else at the moment. I would discuss the matter with Sunil.

That evening I picked up the shopping bag and stated, "Samir, I am going to buy groceries." He didn't respond.

Rohan and Ila stayed back to study. They locked their room from the inside. They had begun to fear their father. Though they couldn't understand what had gone wrong with their polite and loving Daddy.

Taking Riya with me, I headed straight for our friends' house. Worry kept nagging me all the way. If this scenario continued, Samir was sure to lose his job. I didn't have the qualifications to get a decent job. My children would undergo unwarranted hardships. We would be ruined, turned into paupers. Battling with my dismal thoughts, I reached Sunil's house.

Shobha opened the door in response to the bell. Music and laughter trickled out. She looked ostentatious in an orange brocade sari and make-up. An exquisite gold necklace adorned her neck. A pair of large gold danglers hung from her ears, glittering and dazzling in the evening sun's dying light. I became aware of my ordinary shabby clothes and my frayed looks. The moment Shobha saw me she lost her smile. "Oh, Hema! I didn't expect you at this time. Have you come alone?"

"Yes. Samir is unwell. I have come to speak with Sunil regarding his condition."

"Oh. You wait here. I will send Sunil to speak with you." She didn't invite me to come in. She was embarrassed by my ragged looks. I stood outside the door, fidgeting my toes, holding Riya's little hand in mine. Five minutes passed. Then ten. Riya grew restless.

Why was Sunil taking so long to come to the door? Maybe, he was busy. I was vacillating between leaving and waiting a few minutes more when I saw Mr. Patel and his wife near the door. He looked at me from top to bottom, apparently wondering why I was so bedraggled. "Hello, Hema, nice of you to have come to Sunil's promotion party. Is Samir here, too?"

I smiled. "Promotion party? No, I didn't know about the promotion. That's great news. And, no, Samir is not here. He's at home."

"Are things well with Samir? He has been a good worker, but lately—"

"Mr. Patel, Samir is very ill. He wouldn't even see a doctor. I came here to request Sunil to help."

"What's wrong with him?"

"I . . . don't know."

"Hmm. He must see a doctor."

"I have tried hard. He will have to be forced, and I can't do it alone."

"It's a good idea to take Sunil's help."

I nodded, swallowed hard, and asked hesitatingly, "Mr. Patel, Samir too is due for his promotion. Have you taken any decision in this regard?"

Mr. Patel averted my eyes. My heart sank. After a moment's silence, he shook his head. "Samir has lost his chance. Frankly, I am disappointed. Samir has always been my favourite. But some officers felt that Samir's performance has been declining over the past few months. So, instead, Sunil was chosen for that post."

"Oh, I see." I couldn't hide my disappointment, or my teary eyes. "I didn't know about the party, Mr. Patel. I was not invited." I didn't wait for Mr. Patel's reaction. Picking up Riya in my lap, I hurried away.

Why was everything going wrong in my life?

Sunil didn't tell us about his promotion. He hadn't even come once to check on Samir's condition. He and Shobha used to visit us at least once a week. Samir had been his senior. And now . . . Sunil would become Samir's boss. How was Samir going to take it?

I decided not to tell Samir about this. At least, not till he was cured.

Samir's condition continued to deteriorate. He had become almost skin and bones. His wild retaliations terrified me. I had removed all sharp objects from our bedroom. Last evening, he threw a bowl of hot soup at me when I had gone to feed him. He was becoming unhinged.

Something was wrong with me, too. Dark thoughts had started to invade me. I began to contemplate committing suicide. It was a cowardly thought, I knew. Nevertheless, this thought persisted in my mind. "End all your miseries," the sound kept buzzing in my ears, "Samir doesn't love you anymore. He doesn't need you." I knew it wasn't me. Was it the ghost who was infusing these thoughts into me? What was preventing me from taking this drastic step? My life was sinking into an abysmal gutter anyway. I was carrying on like a machine—lifeless and mechanical. How long would I last?

The children's performance in school dropped. I didn't have the drive to do anything about it. Though I fervently prayed every day. Perhaps, my prayers would rein in the evil invading us. Perhaps, this was preventing her from destroying us.

One morning, feeling lonely and down in the dumps after Samir had hurled terrible insults at me, and Riya had gone for a nap, I sat in my puja space, a corner in my bedroom where I had kept a few idols and some holy books. This was the only place in the whole world where I would get some comfort now—to go on in life.

Samir was lying in the bed. Comatose. He was making me frantic with worry. Lighting an oil lamp, I sat chanting from my booklet of mantras. All of a sudden, the brightly burning lamp got snuffed. I felt uneasy. The room had gone cold.

Simultaneously, Samir's anguished cries pierced my heart. It was as if he was being tortured. As I jumped up to help him, I saw her—a deathly pale, gaunt, scary figure standing at the door. She was draped in a red sari. It looked as if . . . she didn't have a body. Why was she here now, at this time of the day? I shivered and my hands trembled. The ghostly apparition glared at me, chilling me to the bone.

"You think you can scare me away with your chants? It is not easy to get rid of me. I have come to live here. Samir is mine now. Get out of my way," the ghost said. There was no sound. The words were forming in my mind. I was traumatized. "Stop this show. It annoys me," she commanded. "If you don't, I will harm your children."

I began to tremble like a flickering, dying flame.

Pure malice contorted her features. Numb with shock, scared for my children, I helplessly watched Samir writhe in agony. Should I obey her and give her what she wanted? Leave my home, my love, and take my children away to a safe place? Could I leave Samir alone to cope with this horror? He was so weak and defenceless now. If I went away, she would immediately wrench out his spirit and torment it forever.

I closed my eyes and loudly pleaded . . . *What has happened to your powers, God? I have been seeking your help for a long time and you have done nothing to help me. This unearthly horror can't be above you.*

At the sound of a sharp thud, I opened my eyes. She was gone. Samir lay on the floor, unconscious. I rushed to help him. A few drops of water on his face and a vigorous shaking later, he opened his eyes. "She was forcing me to go with her. I couldn't walk," he whispered.

This was it. We were doomed. She had clearly done this as a warning. She would also seize my innocent children in her snare. I broke down and cried. I felt helpless like a death-row convict kept in shackles in a dungeon.

I was desperate for help. Samir was slowly creeping towards death. That wasn't all. His spirit was in danger of being enslaved by this ghostly fiend. Who could I turn to except my brother Prakash? I had been avoiding involving him, fearing the evil woman might harm him, too. But now I had little choice. After much pondering, I picked up the phone and booked a trunk call to my brother in Shimla. After fifteen minutes of waiting, I was connected to him.

Prakash was shocked and highly concerned. I had been undergoing a terrible ordeal and he didn't even know about it. "Hema, you should have called me earlier. I would have come to help you."

"Help? How?" A sob escaped my lips despite my efforts to restrain it. "No, Bhai Ji, don't come here. I only want advice."

"What's the point if we can't stand by each other? I will see what can be done."

"I am afraid nothing can be done. No amount of prayers has been able to keep the ghostly woman away."

"Hema, don't lose hope. There's always a way. We just need to find it." Prakash's words were like a balm on a wound. "I will try and work something out. Meanwhile, stay strong." And the call ended.

I immediately regretted having involved him, knowing he didn't stand a chance against a potent supernatural being.

It had been exactly fourteen months now, since the ghost-woman had invaded our lives and gradually turned my Samir into a breathing skeleton. If we didn't find a solution now, it would be too late. I had to turn to Prakash for help, my mind argued.

Prakash turned out to be our saviour. He found a vacancy at the telephone exchange at Shimla and got Samir the job. I was jubilant when he told me this over a call. My brother has always been so clever and reliable. It didn't even cross my mind that we should change houses. I waited for the right opportunity to break the news to Samir.

The next morning, Samir received the news calmly. He listened to me and nodded. "Start packing." After a long time, he looked his normal self. I realized that deep within him, he sought an escape.

We were to leave at the end of the month, which was ten days away. Prakash sent me some money and I used that to book a cab and a truck to transport us and our belongings. I informed Samir's office of the transfer, about which they had already received an intimation. Mr. Patel sent home some papers to be signed including our agreement to vacate the house. Samir eagerly signed the papers.

Two nights later the apparition resurfaced. Since the day she had confronted me during my prayers, her visits had become sporadic. Maybe the prayers were depleting her energy. Now, she glared at me. I could sense her agitation. Her scream sent shock waves through my mind. "I know you are trying to escape. Go wherever you want. Take your children and save them. Leave Samir here for me."

I was terrified. I was also amazed that this ghastly entity had come to know of our plan. My mind struggled to focus on prayers, away from the thoughts of our coming relocation. I must avoid revealing anything to this evil spirit. I could hear Samir crying bitterly in his sleep. "Samir, be strong. Please repel the ghost who is trying to destroy you . . . destroy our lives." I whispered, "God, please help."

A painful wail drew my attention. Samir was sitting stiff

in his bed, his neck rolled back. He let out a howl like that of a tortured animal, wheezy and strained. I realized he was suffocating, desperately trying to draw in his breath. Panic clutched my heart. What was the ghost-woman doing to him? "Leave him alone, you wretched spirit, leave my husband alone," I squirmed desperately and shouted. God knows from where I got the strength to break the invisible constraint that bound me. I jumped out of the bed. The ghost-woman looked surprised. She recoiled and disappeared before my eyes. Samir flopped back on the bed. His breathing was ragged. I rushed to massage his chest. After a few sips of water, he was able to articulate a few words, "She choked me, tried to pull my soul out of my body . . ." She was so determined to have Samir. God help us. I sat with Samir, praying, helping him relax till the daybreak.

The moment I saw light appear on the horizon, I declared, "Samir, we are leaving today. Another day here and she'll kill you. I will not let that happen." Samir nodded feebly.

I called up for the transportation and hurriedly packed up. The children helped me, understanding my urgency. In the middle of all this, I managed to phone Mr. Patel and told him of our plan of leaving for Shimla that day.

In Shimla, we stayed with Prakash and his family for a week. Samir was dramatically transformed within days. He was relaxed and happy. Colour had returned to his face. It was such a relief to have sunshine back in my life.

We moved into the house Prakash had rented for us in the suburbs of Shimla. It was a small cottage in Summer Hill, located on Potter's Hill. The locality had a few houses and a small bazaar. It was only a half an hour's walk from Prakash's house.

I instantly fell in love with the charming cottage situated on a sunny slope. A glazed veranda facing the northwest side ran the entire length of the house. It provided a magnificent view of the mountain ranges and a spectacular sunset. A dense forest of pine, cedar, oak, and rhododendron trees surrounded the cottage on three sides, offering us a serene and beautiful view.

Initially, the flaming red colour of the rhododendron flowers unnerved me, reminding me of the ghost-woman. The secluded house was making me feel uneasy, too. But, I reminded myself that I had left the darkness in the past.

Distancing ourselves from the house invaded by the ghost had worked like magic. Samir regained his calm disposition.

Our children started attending a new school. Samir joined the new office. He was still very weak, a skeleton, his clothes hanging on him like on a hanger. But we were moving on, cherishing each new moment with gratitude. We were together. We were alive.

The heavenly summers of Shimla were at the tail-end. It was a warm afternoon of June. After lunch, Riya had gone for her nap. It was still about two hours before Rohan and Ila returned from school. I picked up a magazine to read and went to sit on the glazed veranda. The heat made me drowsy. My eyes became heavy with sleep and within minutes I dozed off. A knock on the windowpane woke me up. I sat up in a daze and caught a fleeting glimpse of a red haze whizzing past the window.

The veranda was supported on seven-feet-high pillars and the windows were thus about eleven feet above the ground. Only an animal as tall as a dinosaur or a winged creature could access the window. Maybe a large mountain eagle had flown past, I reasoned.

But the Himalayan eagles aren't bright red.

With my heart racing with fear, I got up to peep out. In the blatant desolation of the warm noon, the branches of the trees joyfully shook in a gentle breeze.

"Please, God, don't allow the wandering evil to cast its shadow on us again. Please, spare us a repeat of the past horrors," I pleaded.

Was I overreacting?

That night before sleeping I prayed for a long time, begging God for protection. I kept Lord Shiva's idol next to my bed, facing the door. Soon after I turned off the light, Samir began to snore. I remained awake till late in the night. It was sometime past midnight when I fell into a fitful sleep, packed with nightmares.

Samir was floating in a dark space. Blood was flowing from his eyes and mouth. With both my arms extended, I was trying hard to reach him. Somebody hit me hard on my arm.

I woke up with a start. I felt intense pain in my right arm. My vision traversed to the clock on the table and then to Lord Shiva's idol. Slivers of the moonlight navigated through the window and fell on it, making it shimmer. I avoided looking beyond. I knew she was there, at the doorstep. "I will find him wherever he is. He is a part of me now," I heard her say. With my heart beating frantically I slowly moved my gaze towards the door. The frightening shadow against the moonlight was glaringly sharp.

Did she say a part of me? What does she mean? I heard Samir squirming and moaning. I tried to divert my mind away from her. In the silence of the night, the sound of the leaking tap became all too prominent. *Drip, drop. Drip, drop.*

I came out of my trance to the sound of the dripping tap and my racing heart. I sat up and shed silent tears. The ghostly entity had followed us here, hundreds of miles away from our original home. She would be satiated only when she had wrenched out Samir's soul and taken it away with her. Had Samir known the woman before she had died? Did he have a relationship with her that he's been hiding from me? I needed to go to the core of this mystery. How would I do that?

Samir woke up late that morning and appeared disturbed and pale. Though my mind was in turmoil, I tried my utmost to be normal. I served breakfast and sent children to the school. The moment Samir left for the office I called Prakash. "Bhai Ji, she's back." I sobbed on the phone. "Please help us."

"Oh, my goodness! I'll be with you in half an hour, Hema. Don't worry. We'll find a solution."

Prakash took the day off and remained with me till the evening, but he couldn't do much except console me. He didn't know how to help me. Never in life had he heard of something so uncanny. He would have to consult someone who could deal with wandering spirits.

Where would he find someone with that ability?

Once again visits by the mysterious apparition became a daily ritual. I began to create a wall of god's idols next to the door every night, to prevent her from entering our bedroom. I knew, the day she did—it would be catastrophic.

Samir's health deteriorated and he became temperamental again. He stopped going to work and languished in bed the whole day. Sometimes he gazed at me intently, hate oozing out of his fuming eyes. Life once again began sinking into the depths of a dark abyss.

Torrential rains of the monsoon drenched Shimla for months and then retreated. Autumn brought cool sunny days. But sunshine had bid my life farewell. I continued to be encased by the clouds of misery. The parasitic ghost continued to cling like a leech, sucking Samir's life away.

Prakash continued his efforts to help us. He discussed the problem with people in his network, but nobody could provide any solution. Many were downright cynical. "A ghost visits her every day? Your sister needs the help of a psychologist." "Take your brother-in-law to see a psychiatrist."

The only rational solution suggested was to find an expert exorcist. Where would we find one? After months of search, Prakash heard about a miracle man through one of his juniors, who recommended a sage living in a forest in Theog, about seventeen miles beyond Shimla. He claimed that the holy man could communicate with the spirits of the dead.

Prakash saw a window of hope. He immediately left for Theog to meet the holy man.

On a Saturday morning in October, I prepared to receive the holy man in my house. Children happily went to their Prakash Uncle's house for the day. I tried coaxing Samir to leave his bed, but he yelled at me.

Swami Niketanand, along with two of his disciples, reached my house in the afternoon. One glance at him and I was disappointed. This man was the last hope I had! Could this puny young man dressed in a simple white kurta pyjama perform a miracle? He didn't look like a sadhu.

Swami Ji looked at me with a benevolent smile. "Hema, unless you believe, the effect of the prayers will weaken. You have been the strength of your husband. You must commit, persevere, and remain steadfast." Had he read my thoughts?

"I will try my best, Swami Ji," I said, a little hopeful.

"Take us to Samir." Once in the room, Swami Ji stood observing Samir for a few minutes and then sadly shook his head.

"You can help him, can't you?" I asked nervously.

Swami Ji smiled. "That's what I am here for."

The priests lit diyas and incense sticks in all corners of the room and then began the prayer session. As the chanting and prayers proceeded, Samir began to groan loudly like a battered man. "Hema, stop this nonsense," he yelled time and again.

"Ignore him," Swami Ji instructed.

Samir was soon shivering uncontrollably. I got worried and wanted to wrap a blanket over his quilt. The priest stopped me. "Leave him alone. It's not the cold that is bothering him."

The powerful chanting rose in a crescendo. Samir's agitations and tremors subsided. Occasionally, he moved his head from side to side like a possessed man. Gradually, he became still. He lay in his bed so immobile that I was worried he wasn't breathing.

Hours passed. I politely offered the priests to take time off. The two priests came out to drink tea and rest. Swami Ji refused. "The spirit is powerful and needs an indomitable adversary," he informed. "I'll rest only after purging the victim of this pestilence."

The white light of the day slowly turned to amber. The sun began to dip behind the mountain range. Darkness crept in slowly like a marauder, triggering a quivering in my heart. I took deep breaths to keep my spirits from faltering. Why was it taking so long?

Then, Swami Ji got up from his seat, carried a goblet of water, and sat cross-legged next to Samir's bed. "Hema, you may stay in the room if you want. But let me warn you, what you may now witness could be disturbing."

"Swami Ji, I've confronted the ghost countless times. Though she petrifies me, with you here with us today, I feel secure."

Swami Ji bowed his head graciously. There was so much humility in his gesture. He asked the other priests to create a wall of diyas and draw holy symbols of swastika and Om around us. Then the two priests left to wait outside.

With his hand lightly kept on the goblet, Swami Ji went into a trance. I noted the changing emotions on his face. At times there was pity on it, at times intense pain or anger. Was he pretending? Was he a fraud?

I began to get fidgety. Samir still lay inert. After remaining in a stupor for about fifteen minutes, Swami Ji suddenly opened his eyes. "Samir, get up from your bed. Come here and sit with me." His voice was commanding. I couldn't believe my own eyes. Samir meekly got out of the bed and came to sit next to the priest.

"Drink this holy water. It is going to cure you." Samir obediently drank a few sips.

"Samir, do you remember if a person ever offered you a sweet to eat?" the priest asked.

After a silence of a few seconds, during which his confusion was evident, Samir shrugged and shook his head.

"Think again. Didn't an acquaintance or a friend offer you a sweet dish just before you became ill?"

Samir sat silently with his head drooping like a dead leaf. Had he even heard the question? I waited with bated breath. The priest sat patiently, his eyes closed, his face shining in serenity. After full two minutes, Samir whispered, "Yes." I wondered where the discussion was heading.

"It was in a two-storeyed pale green house?" Swami Ji asked. "Two brothers live in it. One of them has a family—a wife and three children. The front door opens into the living room, the walls of this room are painted lilac. There's a maroon sofa-set in the room." Whose house was the priest describing here? I regarded him blankly. Samir was gaping at the priest. The priest continued, "There is a large painting of two horses on the wall, one white and the other brown. The white horse is injured and is lying on the ground in a pool of its blood. Blood is also oozing from its mouth."

My jaw dropped as I listened to the priest's words. He was describing Sunil's house . . . his sitting room . . . and the painting that I hated. Shobha had once joined painting classes and had made the painting that I had found revolting. Why had she painted an injured animal—a bleeding horse—in pain? Couldn't she think of something a little less macabre? I had thought then.

What had Sunil to do with Samir's condition? Where was Swami Ji leading us? He didn't know Sunil and had undeniably never been to his house! Was he visiting it now, in his mind? I had goosebumps on my arms. Samir was staring at Swami Ji with his eyes wide open in disbelief.

"I see you eating *halwa* from a silver plate. The wife prepared this halwa. Right?"

Samir was thunderstruck. "You were there, in Sunil's house?" he asked naïvely.

Swami Ji smiled. "No. But I am going through those past events now."

"What events?" My voice sounded hoarse. I was getting numb with shock and fear.

Swami Ji probed further, "Do you know of some unfortunate incident that had transpired in Sunil's house?"

"No," I replied after thinking carefully.

To my complete surprise, Samir nodded. "Sunil had prohibited me from revealing it to anyone, not even to you, Hema. He was embarrassed." Goodness gracious! Samir was conversing normally now. The evil shroud he had been bound in, seemed to have been lifted. I closed my eyes to thank God for sending us this miraculous man.

"Embarrassed? My foot! He is a devious man," Swami Ji stressed. "Speak of the incident freely, Samir. This will pave the way towards your recovery."

Samir straightened his shoulders and sat erect. Although his voice was still feeble, he spoke unwaveringly. "Sunil's younger brother got married a few months before the incident. He and his new bride lived on the first floor. Sunil lives on the ground floor with his family. Within two months of the marriage, the bride died. Sunil said it was a case of suicide. Many of my colleagues were convinced that it was murder. That the family had been troubling the young bride from day one for not bringing enough dowry. They had killed her."

"Is this true?" I asked, stunned.

"I don't know." Samir looked at Swami Ji, seeking the answer from him.

"Yes," Swami Ji said. Samir and I gasped. "He, his wife, and his brother—they murdered the poor young woman." Swami Ji thumped the floor with his fisted hand. He was angry.

"Oh my God!" I cried in disbelief, wiping my brow with the corner of my sari. Sweat had begun to collect on my forehead. "How could Shobha do it? She can't."

"The wicked hide their meanness behind innocent façades." Swami Ji took a deep breath. "Unfortunately, there's no dearth of evil people on earth . . . those who negate all the wealth of goodness that exists too."

"But Shobha was never wicked!" I debated.

Swami Ji scoffed. "That woman is vicious and greedy, a disgrace to womanhood. She's a dark conniver. She was the root cause for this murder," Swami Ji raised his voice. "She's a demon."

"A murderer?" She had already committed the murder when I had gone seeking her help. I cringed with disgust.

Swami Ji continued, "They starved the helpless young woman. When she was so weak that she couldn't even move, the three of them assaulted her mercilessly, with sticks and iron rods, trying to break her. They wanted her to compel her father to will all his assets to them—his house, money, and properties. The brave woman resisted despite the torture. It would turn her old parents into homeless paupers, she had begged. But the ruthless people were deaf to her pleadings."

"She died because of the beatings?" I asked despite my heart wanting to avoid knowing the gory details.

Swami Ji sighed. "They didn't stop there. They burnt her alive."

I couldn't believe it. Then, I remembered that I had seen it. I had had that vision in my dream . . . the dream that was still so vivid . . . of a woman set on fire. Her screams now echoed in my ears. I recalled with horror that the burning woman in my dream wore a red sari. Swami Ji's voice seemed distant, "It was a planned murder."

"The children? Did they see it happening?" I cried.

"The children had been sent away . . . to their grandparents. They are ignorant of what was going on in their house. The only good facet of this gruesome incident." After a few minutes, whilst a stunned silence filled the room, Swami Ji sighed and closed his eyes. His vision continued. "They are drunk, the two men. The greedy woman is hurriedly taking out the bride's jewellery from her closet and stuffing it in her bag." Was it this stolen jewellery that Shobha was flaunting that day . . . to celebrate the job that Sunil had stolen—the job that rightfully belonged to Samir? The thought was so offensive that it made my head spin. Swami Ji went on, "They have locked the bathroom from the outside, preventing her escape. She's burning alive, writhing in agony, her bones are broken, and she can't even stand. They are waiting for her death. All three of them." Swami Ji shook his head dejectedly and went quiet. When he spoke next, his voice was shaky. "I see them all in the bathroom, standing next to a badly burnt corpse. The evil woman is smiling. She remains inside and locks the door. The two men then break the door from outside." Swami Ji had gone pale—the scene was too horrendous for him to envision. There were beads of perspiration on his forehead.

"Oh my God!" I lowered my face into my hands and sobbed. Our so-called friends were butchers.

"They misled the police," Samir murmured.

"It's midnight, maybe early morning." Swami Ji opened his eyes. "That's the time she's been visiting you, Lalita's ghost? Isn't it?"

"Is it the ghost of this murdered woman that's been troubling us?" Swami Ji nodded. "Why us? She should have gone after her murderers," I roared.

"There was a reason." Swami Ji raised his hand to calm me down.

I remembered now that Sunil's brother had got married somewhere in Orissa, and we couldn't attend the wedding. "Was Lalita her name?" I asked.

Swami Ji nodded. He narrowed his eyes and regarded Samir. "The evening of the cremation, Sunil asked you to come to his house?"

Samir nodded. "He had said that I was his friend and must come alone."

"Friend?" Swami Ji scoffed. "Do you realize now? He is the worst enemy you could ever have."

"Samir, you don't know. He snatched the post that should have rightfully gone to you," I revealed it to him now.

Swami Ji nodded. "So, that was the reason? All the pieces fall in place now. He invited you after the funeral of the murdered young woman and fed you halwa?"

Samir regarded the priest in utter surprise. "Yes, he called me for the prayers and then took me separately to another room and offered me halwa. He said this was the traditional prasaad. But, how do you know all this?"

"Through my meditation. I saw it all," Swami Ji reiterated. "I didn't see anyone else in the room eating halwa."

"No. Only I was offered it. What was happening that day?"

"There was another man there, in black. Do you remember?"

"Yes. I didn't like him. He kept staring at me for some reason, mumbling all the time."

"He was a *tantrik*, an expert in black magic. Sunil had hired him."

"Black magic? Oh my God! Your friend did black magic on you, Samir!" I was fuming. Samir looked blank.

Swami Ji exposed more dark secrets. "Sunil had paid a huge sum to the tantrik. At his behest, he had collected fresh ashes, still warm, from the funeral pyre of the dead young woman, who had had an unnatural, agonizing death. The torture on the young woman was deliberate . . . part of the ritual . . . to make her a disoriented spirit. The tantrik performed his magic spell. The ashes were mixed in the halwa and fed to you. This was part of the ritual, a very strong kind of black magic . . . *Kalia Masaan*."

"Kalia Masaan? Never heard of it. What is it, Swami Ji?"

"It is the power attained to control the spirits of the dead through a very intense sadhana. The aspirant must spend innumerable nights in deep meditation in a *shamshan*, in the company of the burning funeral pyres and roving spirits still in their low astral plane. The angry spirits can be menacing, even perilous. It is a traumatic experience. Frightening. Most learners are unable to complete the sadhana. Only a few who persevere acquire the powers. That's why there are only a few tantriks who can perform the Kalia Masaan."

"They do this sadhana to destroy other people's lives?" I asked, incredulous.

"No. They are supposed to use their powers only for the good of humanity, to aid people in trouble. But then, there are also villains."

"How do these villains use Kalia Masaan?"

"If a person has died young or violently, the spirit remains unsettled, in the low astral plane for a long time. It has no guiding spirits to take it towards the divine light. A lost spirit, the *masaan,* is awakened by the tantrik and directed towards the target. The spirit attaches itself to the victim and begins to weaken the body. This usually kills the person within forty days."

"Oh my God! In forty days? But this spirit has been troubling Samir for a year and a half now!" I looked at Swami Ji seeking his rationale.

"It is a surprise even for me that Samir has survived for so long." Swami Ji smiled at me. "Hema, your love, faith, and prayers have been stronger than the tantrik's spell. They are stronger than the ghost's capacity to harm. They prevented the spirit from possessing Samir completely. Though it has tried to destroy him bit by bit. That's why the ghost resents you."

"How devious Sunil has turned out to be! He wanted to kill two birds with a single stone—grab the young woman's assets and Samir's job," I said, my hands clenched into fists.

"He wouldn't have rested till he had killed Samir. The devilish man knew when you left Delhi. He knew where you had gone. He had all the information from his office. The tantrik kept sending the enslaved spirit after you. He was enraged that his black magic wasn't having the desired effect on Samir."

"But why? Why did the tantrik agree to do something so hurtful? He didn't even know Samir. He had no grudge against him." The whole episode was so awful, so rotten and ugly.

"Greed makes people go to any depravity. I have witnessed it before. This tantrik uses the powers he has attained through very rigid spiritual practices for immoral purposes."

"Will you testify against them in a court? We must get the culprits punished," I said, barely able to contain my anger.

Swami Ji shook his head. "It'll be useless. Which court will take my words as proof?"

"But the murderers can't go unpunished," I exclaimed.

"No one escapes the highest court of God. Their time to pay for their foul deeds too will come. The wicked do not realize that. They are so absorbed in their arrogance that they think they're beyond retribution."

Anger was discernible on Samir's face. I was glad that he was getting his sanity and strength back. "Swami Ji, are we now safe from the evil backstabbers?" As I turned towards Swami Ji, I saw him suddenly stiffen. He was staring at the door with a frown. My eyes followed his gaze. Lalita's ghost stood there.

"I had untangled you from the fiend's clutches and sent you away to find peace. Why are you here?" Swami Ji asked her calmly. Samir and I sat dazed. Swami Ji's endeavour had been futile.

"I'm not done yet." We heard a distant, rasping voice.

"Stop troubling these simple innocent people. It's time for you to go to your realm and wait to be reborn."

"I was mistaken. Misled. Want revenge."

"On these harmless people?"

"No."

"On those who brutally murdered you?"

"Help me. I need strength. I am very hungry, weak. They starved me. Feed me meat."

"Feed you meat? How? Where? When?"

"Tomorrow night, at three, in the deep forest. I want her to come—alone. I warn you . . ." she pointed at me with her misshapen finger and disappeared.

I broke the silence that had descended in the room. "What . . . What did she say? Feed her meat in a forest? She wants me to do that?"

Swami Ji sat peacefully. Pondering.

"Does she have a stomach to put meat in?" I cried. "Isn't she just a wandering spirit that has managed to get a form?" I went on, "What should we do now? Do you think we need to follow her instructions to feed her meat? It's such a weird demand. Makes no sense. She can't eat."

"We'll have to follow her instructions." Swami Ji raised his hand to pacify me. "She has to stop hounding Samir."

"You have powers, Swami Ji. Can't you just send her away?"

"I have tried my best. Yet, she lingers. This sorcery can be best undone by the one who got this vicious ball rolling. In this case, the tantrik Sunil has hired. But we know, that's not possible. We'll have to appease her, so she stops troubling you."

"Can't we avoid that part—of going into a forest, at night?" I asked, the idea filling me with dread.

Swami Ji shook his head. "No, Hema. I know it sounds difficult, but it will have to be done. Sometimes these wandering spirits become difficult to handle. I don't want to give this one an excuse to stay on." He gave me a warm smile. "I won't let any harm come to you."

"Tomorrow night? At three? The devil's hour? The time when she materializes from the dark? She is most powerful around that time." I quivered with fright.

Samir intervened, "I can't allow Hema to risk her life. No way."

Swami Ji insisted, "Please understand. This is the spirit's last demand. If we don't fulfil it, she might become vengeful." Noticing Samir's fallen face, he added, "Don't you worry. I will keep Hema safe."

"How?"

"I have my means."

The evil ghost wants to meet me alone in a deep forest. It couldn't mean anything good. How will Swami Ji keep me safe from her? Who is this man, Swami Niketanand? How has he acquired these powers? My head was bursting with worry and fear.

That night after dinner everyone slept peacefully except me. I continued to be jittery.

The next morning when Prakash joined us, he was jubilant to see the change in Samir. When told about the ghost's demand, he became anxious. We all wondered whether it was sensible to give in to the ghost-woman's bizarre demand.

Swami Ji remained resolute.

The day went in preparations for the night. Swami Ji went to survey the area and decided upon a place where I would make the offer. "Somebody not related to the family can escort Hema till the main road. But the rest she will have to cover alone," he declared.

Who would be ready to accompany me through such an arduous task? After much deliberation, Prakash decided to approach his office peon, Basant Ram. He was the only option we had.

In the evening Basant Ram Negi came with Prakash. He was a Mongoloid featured, short but sturdy man from Kinnaur region of Himachal. He was unfazed by the fact that a ghost was involved in tonight's venture. "I am used to walking through the deserted hilly trails in the dead of the night. I have met quite a few ghosts, too. I'm not scared. Dealing with the wayward spirits is a common occurrence in the hills." He grinned with confidence. I was impressed and relieved.

I cooked my children's favourite food for dinner. They were happy and chatty, ignorant of what was going on around them.

I couldn't swallow a bite of my food. I felt sick. Abdominal cramps ravaged my body. I kissed and hugged my children before putting them to bed. I wasn't sure if I would see them again. I was risking my life to keep them safe. Would I be successful? If something happened to me, would Samir prove to be a good parent?

Silently bidding them farewell with my tears threatening to erupt, I swallowed my pain and switched off the light in their room.

Swami Ji had asked us to join him on the veranda a little before two. I was supposed to rest till then. How could I? I spent those few hours in absolute restlessness.

Samir and I joined Swami Ji on the veranda, where he sat in deep meditation. We were nervous and fidgety. Just as the clock struck two, Swami Ji put a talisman around my neck and gestured at me to leave. He would pray till I returned safely. I calmly stood up to undertake the most perilous venture of my life. I noted tears in Samir's eyes. Successfully hiding mine, I marched out valiantly like a warrior towards the battlefront.

The packet holding two kilo of raw meat was kept ready outside the door. I picked it up and proceeded to climb up the steps. Negi followed, keeping about twenty paces between us, as Swami Ji had instructed. He carried a torch but the light from it seemed insufficient.

I wondered if my children would ever believe this episode of our lives, once they grew up. Would they believe that their mother had staked her life against a supernatural being to save them and their father?

The road was deserted, not a single human walked on it at this unearthly hour. While people slept snugly inside their homes, I walked through the frightening loneliness. Ghostly whispers surfaced from the breeze blowing through the trees. The shifting shadows of the branches rushed to clasp me in their frightful grip. Nocturnal creatures suddenly howled, breaking the silence, and my heart began to race. Frightening thoughts crept into my mind. I dragged my steps. Even at that normal pace, I was panting.

I became more and more convinced that it was a trick the ghost woman had played on me, to kill me and then go after Samir unhindered. What if Swami Ji was wrong? What if his earlier success had filled him with undue confidence?

The questions bothered me, terrified me, slowed me down. I stopped to rest my pounding heart. Negi halted too, maintaining the distance, and then coughed lightly to remind me that I wasn't alone . . . a braveheart was with me.

A flying fox suddenly spread its wings, glided down a tree, and flew straight towards my head. It was an unexpected ambush. I screamed in panic and instinctively ducked, shielding my head with my free arm. The huge furry bat ominously screeched above my head before disappearing into the darkness of the cavernous valley below. I stood stunned.

I heard Negi's hurried footsteps approaching me. I gestured at him to stop. Whatever was to transpire today, it was my destiny alone. In his concern, he was overlooking the instructions given by the priest not to interfere in anything—not till the offering was made.

As I took my next step, the sound of a snigger hit me like a whip. She was here. Close to me. I sensed her presence. Was she mocking me after coercing that colossal bat into that bizarre action?

I heard Negi softly humming a song. Was he aware of her presence? Was he singing to overcome his fear?

After about twenty minutes we reached the rain shelter, the spot from where a narrow dirt track navigated down towards the deeper woods. Swami Ji had instructed me to walk alone from here on. More intrusion might annoy the ghost.

Nobody used this path at night except the nocturnal creatures. Apart from small animals like foxes and jackals, this forest was a known abode of leopards, hyenas, and Himalayan bears. What's more, I was carrying a packet that was likely to attract their attention.

Negi sat down in the rain shelter to wait. He switched off the torch. The sudden darkness was unsettling. I took a few deep breaths, hesitated, and then gathering my nerve stepped onto the two-feet-wide forest path and into an intimidating territory.

The crescent moon was at the far southwest horizon of the sky. I could barely see the path in the faint light it offered. The land would soon be shrouded in complete darkness once the moon slipped behind the mountains. I needed to be back on the road before that.

As my eyes began to get used to the dark, I quickened my pace. The dried leaves of the oak and pine had spread a thick, slippery carpet on the path. I slid on them several times and each time I grabbed the tufts of grass on the hillside to prevent from tumbling down into the abysmal dark valley. I knew if that happened, there would be no one to rescue me till the daybreak. This was perhaps the ghost-woman's plan. I doubted if Negi would be able to hear my screams. I had a feeling I had left him and the habitation far behind . . . beyond my reach. Despite all my misgivings, I trudged on.

Why would the ghost-woman want to harm me now, after having been broken out of the tantrik's spell? Was it because she still carried the remnants of loathing—loathing for those who had wronged her intensely? It should be those depraved humans—Sunil, Shobha, and their beastly brother that she should go after. Why was she making me undergo this harrowing ordeal?

In the profound silence, I began to hear footsteps behind me. They were different steps . . . unlike my shuffling ones. Someone had doggedly started following me. And, she wanted me to know. My legs began to tremble. My breathing became loud and rapid. I became convinced she would push me from behind and throw me into the ravine. That's why she had forced me to come into this wilderness where there would be no help for me. She wanted to kill me. What would become of my children? A sob escaped my lips. I resisted the urge to turn to look behind. Swami Ji had warned me to expect sounds trailing me. He had instructed me not to look back. I should have asked him the reason.

Be brave, Hema, I repeated in my mind and dragged my feet on. I walked downhill for five or seven minutes, which seemed like hours. The trailing footsteps persisted. Finally, I reached a flat area where the path widened to double its size. This was it. I was in the deep part of the forest, I concluded, and knelt to place the packet of the raw meat next to the mountain wall. I silently appealed to the ghost to accept it and leave my family alone. I wanted nothing but my peaceful life returned to me.

The breeze increased in intensity. Rustling noisily around me, the dry leaves rose like a wave to encircle me. Sudden iciness enclosed me in its tight noose. I was unable to breathe . . . I was suffocating. I tried to stand. And then, my blood ran cold. My body trembled in fright. A familiar hazy figure stood at the curve, a few feet away, eyeing me, like a predator eyeing its kill.

My heart stopped beating. Meeting her in the dark, lonely forest was nothing like the previous encounters. My legs lost all their strength and my head swooned. I needed to control my mind and my body. The ghost would take advantage of my weakness. *I don't want to die here and now, dear God. I don't want to leave my children motherless. I want to see them grow. I'll be ready to face death in my ripe old age, but not yet. Please God, help me.* I prayed earnestly.

A ghostly voice hit my ears. I felt I had put my head into a drone of bees. Her voice struck terror in my racing heart. "I want revenge. I want your body." How was I going to save myself? I was alone and defenceless in this dark forest. Despite my fright making me shaky and dizzy, I mustered the courage to ask, "Why hurt me now, and why here?"

"You are strong in your house." The words began to form in my head.

"I pity you . . . I am horrified at what happened to you. I am not your enemy. I also hate those who killed you." I was throwing every dice I had, to prevent her from destroying me.

"I need you."

"You have done me enough harm. You tried destroying my Samir."

"You protected him."

"Please leave me and my family alone," I pleaded. We are not the ones who harmed you."

A rasping whisper surging through the expanse pierced my ears . . . "They kiiiiilllll mee . . . killlll themmm . . ." A few birds perching on the trees screeched in fear. Disoriented, they flapped around me, adding to my panic.

The macabre apparition began to slither towards me like a giant python approaching its victim to swallow it alive. I gasped and stepped back. Before I could turn to rush back uphill, I felt a push. I fell with a loud thud. A sharp stone pierced my knee and scraped against my bone. I groaned in excruciating pain. She was now standing next to me. Her dark shadow hovered and drew closer. My body desperately fluttered like in nasty death throes. She was trying to enter my body . . . trying to possess me. I stiffened and resisted by shielding my face with my arms. *I am strong,* I kept repeating in my mind. And then, another shadow emerged from behind her. Another female ghost.

She had brought another vengeful spirit with her to aid her. I stood no chance against the two of them. I was doomed. I was never going to see Samir and my children again. I shivered and sobbed.

And then something strange happened. Lalita's ghost was grabbed from behind by the other shadow and dragged away. I was too stunned to understand what was happening. Within seconds, the shadows disappeared.

I was now alone. An intense stillness once again encased me. The birds settled back on the trees. The chill began to subside. I felt a calm warmth swathing me. Relief washed me from head to toe.

Who was that other apparition?

I forced myself up on my feet. I felt wetness around my

knee. It was bleeding. The pain was making it difficult for me to walk. I wanted to leave the fearsome spot as fast as possible. I pushed myself on—step by step, slowly climbing up the perilous path to return to safety. My legs felt as if weights were tied to them. I must persevere to survive the ordeal—for my Samir, for my children. Their love beckoned me. I hauled myself uphill wondering whether the ghosts were still around, assessing my strength. Were they testing my devotion and love for Samir and my children? There was no way that I could fail this test.

It took me a long time, much longer than I took in reaching the spot, to return to the main road where Negi was waiting. But where was he? The rain shelter was empty, and so was the road as far as I could see. The brave man had run away leaving me alone. Why?

My heart sank as I gazed around in despair at the intense isolation. The moon was at the top of the black silhouette of the mountain, ready to bid farewell for the night. In that last light of the receding moon, I saw it—the white packet of meat that I had left down in the forest. It now lay in the shelter, open, its contents scattered. I stared at the mess, horror-struck.

The darkness deepened. I turned and limped back homewards on that lonely, desolate road, through the pitch-black night.

A month later Samir returned from his office much earlier than his usual time. As soon as I opened the door for him, my heart sank. He looked pale and disturbed. Sweat dripped down his forehead. "What's the matter, Samir? Are you not well?" I asked with concern.

"Hema, you wouldn't believe it. Neither could I. The ghost has taken her revenge," Samir blurted as he wiped his face with his handkerchief and went to sit on a chair.

I gasped. "Revenge? How? From whom?"

"From her slaughterers."

"How do you know?"

"I got a call from a former colleague today. Sunil's house caught fire last night. Nobody knows how. Possibly short circuit in their electricity meter."

"And?"

"The fire spread fast. They are all dead . . . burnt alive."

"Oh my God, Oh my God!" I stood stunned.

"I am numb with shock. Sunil was a friend once."

"He was an evil man. They all were evil. This had to happen. The tortured woman's ghost wasn't going to spare them. I knew it. She was too powerful, too eager for revenge." My legs trembled, augmenting the pain in my injured knee. I sat down next to Samir and held his hand. "You don't mourn the death of the evil lot. They would have destroyed us if not for Swami Ji."

Samir put his arm around me. "I am thankful to Swami Ji. He saved us from them, from the ghost. You are right. Without his help, we were heading towards a sure ruin." He looked at me with love soaking his eyes wet. "Hema, it feels good to be alive again."

I nodded. "You know what, we are like the phoenix bird . . . retrieving our lives from ashes." A pale smile appeared on Samir's face. I lovingly patted his cheek. "Lalita's spirit wasn't yet ready to go on its final journey to find peace. She was angry. The butchers hadn't allowed peace to that tormented soul even after mercilessly killing her."

"Hopefully, the misled spirit will find its peace, now that it has had its revenge."

"One mystery remains. Who was the other ghost who had come to save me?"

"Swami Ji knows. Didn't you see how he smiled when you posed him this question? It is his secret."

"Samir, I don't like the fact that the children too perished in the fire." The thought saddened me. I had seen those children grow up. They were innocent.

"No, no, the children are fine. They were spared. They were with their grandparents for the night."

I closed my eyes in relief. "The ghost chose the timing well!"

"You know, Hema, they found four adult bodies inside the house. Someone else was staying in their house that night. The police personnel are trying to verify the identity of the fourth victim."

"The tantrik—that must be the tantrik." I cried with conviction. "He should have known this well—no one can escape the consequences of their Karma."

The
Resurgence

When I was born in the spring of the year 1931, in a small village hidden in a nook of the majestic Himalayas, the village *Dai* who helped my mother with the childbirth held me in her hands and exclaimed, "Good lord, he's even smaller than a kitten. He doesn't weigh more than a *savaser*." I was blue and gasping for breath. That filled my mother with anxiety and she burst into tears. Already six of her pregnancies had ended in either miscarriages or stillbirths. She desperately wanted me to survive.

Survive I did, on that tiny relentless spark of life I had within me. Had my survival been governed by destiny?

For a long part of my life, I was stuck with the name Nikku, synonymous with my appearance. It meant small in our *pahari* language. It sounded more like a nickname but nobody in my family ever thought of amending it. Everyone in school called me by this name and then it stuck to me like a cocklebur seed for a long time. Had there not been certain developments in my life that allowed me to fix the injustice to my name, I would still have been called Nikku, an impish name for a grown-up man.

We were simple mountain folks, living in a small village in Theog *tehsil*, not far from Shimla.

Shimla was the summer capital of the British rulers till I was sixteen. My memory of the struggle for India's independence was confined to the bitterness the natives had developed for the bossy white rulers due to the undue taxes they collected from us poor villagers. And then there came a day when my country's independence was declared. My whole village went down to Theog town to celebrate. A handful of surviving freedom fighters from the town unfurled our national flag and gave stirring speeches. There was an air of jubilation and I thought there would be a drastic change in life for us now. Thinking about it, not much changed in our remote village, not for a long time.

For me, the highlight of that day was the flute that my father's cousin, who ran a teashop in the bazaar, had bought me. He was a good flute player and promised to teach me to play it. I began to visit him once a week to learn.

By the time India's independence was declared, I had finished school. My village school was only till class eight. Soon, I began to help my father in his terraced fields and took our livestock to graze in the forest.

My father was a small-time farmer who earned just enough to keep us going. In the winters when we couldn't grow anything on our land, on which mounds of snow would lay claim, we didn't have enough to eat. We survived on the measly food that my mother would store for the harsh winters—potatoes, rice, and maize. Unsurprisingly, I was smaller than most boys my age. One natural asset that I was born with was my agility. None in my village, and my neighbouring villages, could match my speed. My small frame and light body became my strength. Had my father known about the advantage of being an athlete, he would have trained me for the Olympics. But I remained the sprinting legend of my area alone, a boy who could run uphill nonstop for miles in half the time as others.

I also grew up to be a fearless, spirited lad. Was I trying to hide my physical shortcoming behind a heroic façade? I became known in my region after a daring adventure. One evening just after the sun had set behind the mountains and soft twilight had begun to engulf the hills and dells, my friends and I came across a huge male leopard in the forest where we had mindlessly ventured during our games. Whilst the rest of the boys of my gang scooted away at the sight of the fearsome animal, and one of them scurried up a tree to become the witness to my heroism, I stood my ground and watched with great fascination this fierce, elegant creature sauntering just ten metres away from me. The majestic animal stopped, gazed straight into my eyes and gnarled at me, exposing its daunting canines. Imitating him, I gnarled back. The forest creature appeared confused. My sound didn't match my physique. The leopard turned and taking a long leap disappeared into the dense undergrowth, generously sparing the skinny, foolish specimen that wasn't even appetizing.

When the tale of my exploits reached my father's ears, he gave me a good dressing-down for being foolhardy. Like most teenagers, I turned a deaf ear to him.

Fearlessness became my mantra thereafter. Instead of taking my animals for foraging in the few patchy grassy plots bordering our village where most villagers went, I valiantly began venturing into the deeper part of the forest, taking our two cows and four mountain goats there. I would sit in the dense clumps of the trees growing on the forlorn hills, and play my flute. I had learnt to play it well. The forest gave me the chance and seclusion to practise unrestrained. I began contriving new tunes. As the rustic notes from my instrument drifted across the knolls and dales, I felt peace within me. I didn't have to run after my animals—they never ventured far. I understood that they wanted to stay close to the strains of my music. The small wild creatures visited me often, peeping from behind the bushes, attracted by my musical notes. The large denizens of the forest stayed away, for they didn't want to harm or scare the musician who entertained them for free.

The fresh grass for the cows was in abundance here, and so were tender leaves and juicy twigs for our goats. My father was happy with me, as our animals became healthier. Our earnings increased—we had more milk to sell.

The villagers did not dare go alone into the deeper woods. The lonely arcane forest frightened them. They were not only afraid of the wild animals—leopards and Himalayan bears that attacked unprovoked—but also of the unknown. There were stories of the presence of *chhall* and *chudails* in the desolate woods. I often narrated tales of being followed by a chudail with her feet twisted backwards, or having seen a supernatural being that kept appearing and disappearing in front of my eyes. Most of these were the work of my imagination, which became overactive when I took breaks from my flute. The simple-minded villagers believed in my fanciful yarns.

Life was smooth till I turned twenty-one. Then the events that followed couldn't have been coincidental. The mysterious force of destiny played a crucial role in forging a turning point in my life.

During one of my routine ventures into the forest, I came across a group of five strange men. Fascinated by their appearance, I stood gaping at them. Their long, matted hair, *rudraksha* necklaces around necks, red tikka dazzling against whitish powder smeared on their foreheads, gaunt bodies inside long and loose black robes—it all made them look like eerie alien creatures. Noting me staring at them with my eyes almost bulging out, one of them guffawed, "Haven't you ever seen a human being before? Or do you think we are ghosts?" A burst of laughter boomed through the silence of the forest. Flustered, I turned to go.

"Tell the people in your village not to go beyond the village boundary for the next two days. Stay at home. There is danger lurking."

I turned to behold the most penetrating eyes I had ever seen, reminding me of the piercing eyes of the leopard I had once locked eyes with. This man's eyes were hypnotic and I felt drawn to them, like a moth towards a flame, unable to look away. The sudden change in their colour unnerved me. They had turned blood red in an instant—almost the colour of a trident drawn on his forehead in vermillion. His other features were obscured under a copious growth of his frosty, grey-and-brown beard. He was distinct from the rest due to his imposing personality. He sat cross-legged on a mat, in a trance-like state, while the other men sat around him on the ground. They were all smoking chillums.

"What danger?" I asked timidly. The man had begun to scare me.

"You shall see." He dismissed me with a wave of his hand.

"Now shoo off," one of them snapped at me and I jumped in fright. The man laughed raucously.

"Don't ignore Baba Ji's prediction. He's never wrong," another advised.

It occurred to me that perhaps they were indeed ghosts. I ran away from them and to the safety of my village as fast as my legs could carry.

Those few moments of eye contact with the elderly man had a strong impact on my mind. I just couldn't remove his image from my brain. It was as if he had hypnotized me, put me under a spell, and made his way into my brain. That whole night either I thought of him or saw him in my dreams where he was leading me through dark, strange alleys and snow-clad high mountains without any visible path. And I followed him like a puppy . . . slipping, tumbling.

The next morning I realized that the warning, that I had aired the moment I had reached my village last evening, had been taken seriously. No person had ventured out to work. The villagers sat at their doorsteps, nervously waiting for the calamity to ensue. The cattle remained tied in their barns and fed on crop residue reserved for emergencies. The day passed off peacefully without any mishap and in subdued chit-chats. By the evening the villagers grew suspicious of my claim. The talk went around that I was fooling them all—"Nikku needs to be reprimanded for fooling us." "We should not fall victim to his tall claims in the future." "Perhaps, he has lost his mind." "His ventures into the forest need to be forbidden." "Nikku has come under the influence of some evil spirit."

I feared that their annoyance might turn violent. I dreaded my father's scolding. I desperately needed a hideout. I knew of one, an old oak tree with dense foliage at the fringe of the village. For hours I sat hiding on a branch, fighting a battle with mosquitoes and other blood-sucking parasites and cursed the ghostly sadhu for misleading me. My hunger pangs began to get unbearable. But I dare not present myself to the villagers for lynching. Only when darkness descended on the mountains, and I guessed the villagers had taken refuge inside their houses for the night, did I dare to climb down to reach the solid ground. By then my legs were stiff from hours of immobility. I slinked homewards through the deserted tracks.

As I sneaked into my house, the first thing I accosted was the angry face of my father. The village headman had sent him a message that he was to present me before him the next morning to explain my absurd proclamation. My father was naturally furious at me for it, and for returning home so late. He pulled my ears and gave me a hard whack on my head. His verbal anger went on for a while, after which my mother, who had been stiff with worry all this while and was much relieved to see me intact, served me hot *makki ki roti* and *cholai* saag with homemade butter. I ate with gusto.

The following morning the sun did not rise. The villagers woke up to a sky heavily overcast with thick clouds. Their previous day's annoyance at me began to waver. Should they pay heed to my warning? When I grudgingly went to the headman to face his rebuke, I saw the worry on his face. That gave me the courage to speak up. "Another day of staying home won't harm us," I suggested like a wise man. The headman nodded solicitously and passed on my advice to all.

Just before noon, the time when most villagers would have been out working in the fields or ambling in the pastures with their cattle, low, menacing thunderclouds came rumbling in hoards accompanied by intense lightning. The sky became pitch black, and the land obscured in an ominous shadow of darkness. The villagers secured their cattle in the sheds and took refuge inside their houses.

Then down it came, a pounding rain following a massive thunder and lightning so bright as if millions of high-powered bulbs had been switched on. And it poured. The like of which none had ever seen. It was as if Indra *devta*, the god of rain, had released a furious, vicious river from the sky.

When it stopped raining after about two hours, the disaster was apparent everywhere. The cloudburst had washed away several neighbouring villages and the area around our village, including the cultivated fields. Massive landslides had altered the topography of the region. A small area around our habitation had miraculously remained intact. Only a few houses in our village had crumbled under the pounding rain, whose inmates had instantly found shelter with their neighbours. There was no casualty. No person or animal had even received a scratch. The news began to trickle in, about an immense loss of life and property in the region.

We discovered that a huge rock that had slipped from its original place and had lodged itself just above the village had diverted the devastating gushes of water away from us, protecting us like the Govardhan *parvat* that Lord Krishna had lifted on his little finger to save his people from a torrential rain.

Once the residents realized the miracle that had spared us, their previous day's stance took a complete reversal. They brought offerings and treated me like an incarnation of a devta—a sacred spirit.

I felt important but knew it well that the holy man's prediction had saved my village and me, otherwise many of us could have been washed away in the flash flood. Indisputably, the man had strange powers that helped him see the future. It occurred to me that if I joined the group, I too could learn to do the same. If I could make accurate predictions and help save lives, how rich and famous I could become!

The next day I rushed through the devastated landscape to the location where I had accosted the group. I was apprehensive all the way that perhaps they had all perished in the cloudburst without a roof over their heads. I found them all unharmed and unperturbed. They had taken shelter in a cave roofed by an extended rock ledge.

I instantly dived prostrate in front of the elderly sadhu. "You are great, a godly figure. Please, please, Guru Ji, make me your *shishya*, your student."

"Go away, lad. You are too delicate to join us." The Baba smiled benignly.

"Yes, Baba Ji is right. You are best suited to be a herder," one of them stated with a grin.

"You need strict and tough practice, my boy. *Tapasya*. Sadhana. It's not child's play," Baba Ji added as others nodded. "Our way of life is tough, gruelling. You don't look the kind who'll be able to endure it." He peered into my eyes, as if weighing my loyalty.

"Why do you say so? I am the toughest and the most fearless boy in my village. Ask my fellow villagers, if you don't believe me."

"It is not easy even for the most fearless to learn Tantrik *vidya*."

"I'll learn it. I know I can. In my school, I was the best at learning," I persisted.

"Hmmm . . ." The sadhu observed me through his narrowed eyes for a minute. There was a shine in them.

One sadhu remarked, "He is a child. He doesn't know our ways."

Baba Ji glanced at him annoyingly and chided him, "You keep out of it, Om."

I should have grasped the implication of their exchange then. But I foolishly persisted, "I am not a child. I am twenty-one years old."

"You are lying. You hardly look fifteen. You don't even have a beard," Om asserted.

"I am not lying." I fisted my hands. The man was making me angry. Who was he to dissuade me, when his leader was not averse?

"Fine." Baba Ji chuckled and raised his hand, gesturing for us to stop. "We are leaving this place tomorrow. Think about it wisely, and if you still wish to join us then meet us at the foot of this hill at daybreak." I nodded zealously. "I caution you that once you join us, you cannot leave. You will have to break ties with your parents and relatives completely. Forever. Never see them again. Are you ready to do that?"

The man had cast a spell on me like a conjurer, and had my brain under his control. My mind was obsessed with a single thought. This was the life I wanted. This wasn't an accidental meeting. It had been arranged by the heavens. I mustn't let the opportunity go. Perhaps I would return to my village one day, years hence, equipped with magical powers and help alleviate the troubles and miseries of my people. "Thank you, thank you." My boyish enthusiasm brought smiles to all faces, except Om's. He was dejectedly frowning.

"Run back to your village. You don't have much time left to be with your family."

Youthful and impulsive, I had made my decision. I slyly slipped out of my house under the cover of darkness on that fateful September night of the year 1952. Wrapping my worn-out woollen jacket tightly around my body, holding on to a small bag with my bare essentials, shivering with excitement and cold, I walked down the hill to join the people I hardly knew. In my eagerness of attaining superhuman powers, I didn't even once think of my ageing parents who needed me—their only child.

The hills were still wet and slippery after the torrential rain. Most of the narrow footpaths connecting the village to the rest of the world had been washed away. The waning moon splashed the hills with its faint silver light. Had it been cloudy, it would have been impossible to reach the destination in one piece. Sliding down the hill, I contrived my path. It wasn't easy even for someone like me who had spent all his life running up and down these hills. When I reached the bottom of the hill, I was disappointed to see no one around. Had the sadhus fooled me?

The darkness was penetrating. I sat resting my back on the rocky mountainside and waited. The drying autumn leaves rustled in the mild breeze breaking the intense pre-dawn silence. The cicadas went on nonstop with their shrill chorus. The birds hadn't yet begun to stir. In the absence of a watch, for we couldn't afford one, nature was our only time source. In my enthusiasm, perhaps I had walked down a bit too soon. After hours of wait, a pale light began to spread in the sky from beyond the last mountain range and birds woke up. Soon the majestic sun rose from behind the tall mountain peak. My anxiety began to mount. There was still no sign of the sadhus. Highly disappointed, I was planning to return home when I heard some distant voices. I ran around the curve to check. Sure enough, the sadhus were cautiously descending the hill. My heart fluttered with excitement. On reaching me, Baba Ji patted me on my head . . . and just like in the dream, I followed him like a puppy.

We walked for days through the mountains, through the tough terrains, avoiding the roads and crowded towns. At nightfall, we slept under the nimbus sky laden with dazzling stars. The cold had begun to make its presence felt on the mountains, especially at night, and I shivered under a sole torn woollen wrap I had taken along with my paltry belongings. The sadhus wore bare minimum, slept without a cover, and yet they were never cold. They smoked chillums at night, filling them with ingredients I had no clue about. Till now I had only seen men in my village smoke beedis. My father didn't. He had advised me to stay away from addictions. I had till now.

On the fourth night noticing me shivering under the blanket, Om, the sadhu who had been most kind and considerate towards me contrary to my first impression of him, offered me a puff from his chillum. "Don't refuse, Nikku. Consider this as your first lesson. Without this, you won't be able to perform the steps of our sadhana." That was a good incentive for me to instantly accept the chillum and take a deep puff. Om sniggered watching me suffer a violent bout of cough. But I was resolute to prove my nerve. I managed a few more puffs before Om snatched his chillum from me. "That's enough for a start. We need to walk the whole day tomorrow and nobody's carrying the extra burden of your limp body."

That night I wasn't cold. I felt happy and liberated, fluttering in the skies like a caged bird freed after a long captivity. I had never felt so carefree and so joyful in my life.

I lost count of days and nights, ever since I had become hooked on smoking the chillum. I walked like a zombie during the day looking forward to our nightly bash. When we came across any village, we stopped to beg for rice and fresh vegetables from the farmers. They obliged us. They respected the sadhus who had renounced the world to seek God. They even offered us tea and snacks.

At night we would camp wherever we found a flat area, make a bonfire with the wood we collected from the surroundings and cook rice gruel with vegetables. During the day, we had only a handful of roasted gram to eat that we carried in our bags. This wasn't sufficient food. "Things will be better once we reach our destination," Om comforted me.

We collected leaves, flowers, seeds, or resin of certain plants growing in abundance on the hillsides. We spread them for drying when we halted for the night, repeating the procedure many times. Once dried, they were filled in the chillums for smoking. Each one of us had collected a bagful of the intoxicating supplies, to last us for months. Om familiarized me with their names—bhang, ganja, *charas*, *hafeem*, hashish, etc. I realized that this was the main reason why the group had visited the mountains.

The smoking sessions were a great respite—they suppressed my hunger and emotions. The handful of chillums went around to everyone, till there was laughter, talks of spirituality, gods and goddesses, to which I was a silent participant. Finally, I would drop dead for the night, oblivious to the miseries of the poverty-stricken nomadic life. When I was not intoxicated, I would miss the love and warmth of my home. I was worried that my parents must have been traumatized by my sudden disappearance. They had perhaps taken me for dead—killed and eaten by a panther. But when I smoked, the guilt of having betrayed my ageing parents eroded like the soil in the receding flood. By and by I became numb, hardly thought of the life left behind, became detached from all that I had once held dear.

I sometimes noticed Baba Ji regarding me strangely and wondered, was he weighing my loyalty or casting a spell on me? Could he read my thoughts?

After about a fortnight, which could have been less for I had no track of time, we reached the foothills of the Himalayas. We went to live in the outskirts of Kalka town, and laid claim on an undulating area hidden by rocks, bushes, and trees. The trees growing here were so different from the conifers that grew in my region.

We spent the day wandering around the railway station or the bus stand, bullying people into offering us alms, and blessing them with good luck. I was given a makeover by Om to somewhat look like them. He plastered my hair with mud, coated my forehead with red vermillion and used black kohl to make shapes on my face. This was necessary, otherwise nobody would offer me alms, he explained. We needed money for food and travel.

I began to notice that people were somewhat afraid of us. I overheard comments—"These are Aghori sadhus, give them alms or they will curse you." I began to wonder what was so special about this sect of Aghoris? I didn't know anything about them. Perhaps, I had made the right choice in joining them. Once I attained powers, people would be in awe of me, too.

One thing I realized was that my group avoided living in inhabited areas. The seclusion gave us the privacy to meditate. Baba Ji led our meditation sessions, though initially Rattan had been instructed to teach me the basics. We also needed privacy to smoke and drink. But I had restrained from drinking till now. After my first refusal, nobody offered me alcohol. It was expensive, Om told me. Baba Ji always drank from a fancy bottle.

After we had enough funds to buy train tickets, we travelled to Ujjain—the farthest I had ever travelled in life. I had only undertaken occasional trips to the small town of Theog. I hadn't even been to Shimla, which was barely seventeen miles away from home. Now I felt like a free bird for whom there were no impeding boundaries. New vistas were opening for me. I would roam free and travel the world far and wide.

Once in Ujjain, the incessant hustle-bustle and swarm of pilgrims invading the city from all corners of the country had me enthralled. Coming from a village with barely seven families and a population of about thirty people, the busy city not only amazed but also frightened me.

We went to live in an old, crumbling, single storey house that had been abandoned by the original owners. Om told me that the house was haunted, the reason for the owners running away. Now Baba Ji had taken possession of the house.

"You mean, he bought this haunted house?"

Om shook his head. "He didn't buy it. We started living here, along with the ghosts. Knowing Baba Ji's powers, nobody will dare challenge him."

It was illegal. But more than that, the idea of living with ghosts was troubling me. "Why do you think there are ghosts in this house? Have you seen them?" I asked, gazing around with mounting anxiety. I was afraid of ghosts. Who's not?

"Yes. We have seen them."

"Aren't you scared of them?" I asked hesitatingly.

"Nope. We control ghosts," Om spoke with confidence.

"You can do that?"

"Baba Ji can."

"Whose ghosts are they?" I hoped that he was lying, only trying to frighten me.

"There were murders here. It was a joint family. One young son murdered his wife and children, for he suspected the woman was cheating on him. The souls of the dead never got peace and continued to haunt the house. Finally, the family had to abandon the house and run away."

"Why didn't the souls get peace?"

"For those who die violently, the afterlife journey gets tough. They wander off from their path because they don't have the guiding angels."

"Then why are we living here, among the ghosts?"

"Because Baba Ji found it most suitable. Handling spirits is a piece of cake for him."

"But these ghosts can harm us."

"You don't have to worry. Baba Ji has these spirits under his control. They are his slaves now."

I was getting worried. Controlling the spirits . . . enslaving them? What was Baba Ji up to? Seeing my expression, Om continued, "That's why Baba Ji is powerful, he can make correct predictions. He has done years of sadhana in tantrik vidya, attained tantrik *siddhis*, and learnt to control the spirits of the dead people. That's what gives him supernatural powers. We are all waiting for him to teach us. Rattan is Baba Ji's oldest disciple, been with him for eight years, has learnt a few siddhis. But Baba Ji has not taught him everything yet."

"Why?" I was now worried that I would have to wait for a long time to attain superpowers. I knew Om had joined about two years ago.

"Baba Ji wants to be the most powerful. He wants to turn this house into an ashram someday, with a large number of disciples. His position among all Aghori sects will be uplifted once he runs his own ashram. That's why he is accepting misfits like you into the sect."

"Why do you keep saying that?" I yelled at him.

He smiled kindly. "You'll see."

That night I saw them . . . the ghosts. My sleep broke in the middle of the night, and I saw three white bodies hanging from a hook in the ceiling—the bodies of a woman and two children. My scream got stuck in my throat. Was I dreaming?

Was I imagining? I shook with fear and shut my eyes tightly. When I opened them again there were no bodies.

I shared my experience with Om in the morning and he smiled. "They do that to the newcomers . . . get thrill from frightening them. But they won't do anything beyond that. They are well under control."

I began sleeping with a cloth tied around my eyes. I didn't want to see the frightening vision again.

A few days later Dharamvir joined us. Though he had been with the group for about six months, he hadn't accompanied them on the trip to the Himalayas as he had caught malaria during the rains, and subsequently was too weak to undertake the tough trek. Strangely, Baba Ji hadn't used his powers to help him recover fast. When I posed this question to Om, he replied, "Baba Ji helps only his old disciples. You must first win his trust. Dharamvir and you are too new. So, don't expect any attention from Baba Ji."

Now seven of us—Baba Ramdeen, Rattan, Chetan, Dev, Om, Dharamvir, and I—lived in that three-roomed primordial haunted house situated on the fringes of the city. Mould was growing on the walls that hadn't been painted on for so long. Many windowpanes were missing and had been replaced by newspaper sheets stuck with the wheat flour paste. That partially managed to protect us from the cold draught of the winter. There was no furniture, so we slept on mats spread on the cold, hard floor. We lived a life of austerity.

Baba Ji had the largest room to himself with a proper bed. The rest of us occupied the other two smaller rooms. I opted to share the room with Om and Dharamvir. Rattan, Chetan, and Dev kept to themselves, always acting superior to us.

The courtyard in the centre with its walls blackened with the soot of cooking fires was our kitchen. The original kitchen remained unused, perhaps because it was small and dark. We took turns to cook simple but sufficient meals here and I felt somewhat restored. The smoking sessions thrived with the usual revelry.

If we were not out collecting alms, for which usually Om, Dharamvir, and I were sent, we meditated in the most secluded spots at the banks of the river Shipra. The Aghori way of worship was quite different. The mantras they chanted too were strange.

We often went to Mahakaleshwar temple, the temple dedicated to God Shiva in Mahakala form, the God that we Aghoris venerated. We hung around the temple complex, collecting alms from the generous pilgrims. Many devotees occasionally fed us sumptuous meals. I looked forward to them.

I soon struck up a friendship with Dharamvir. We both were still different from the rest. Dharamvir had short hair as well as a short beard. My sparsely growing beard hardly covered my face. I now had matted hair that had grown to be a little below my shoulders. I never washed and combed them. To give them the special sadhu look, Dev would give me a hairstyle. He was an expert in weaving hair with needle and thread into *jattas,* he had told me.

Both Dharamvir and I had begun to dress in black robes over our pyjamas. The others now wore vermillion loincloths. They also smeared ashes on their bodies and I wondered why. There were a few things I found baffling about the group. They disappeared on certain nights. No one offered to take Dharamvir or me with them, or reveal where they went. When they returned late in the morning, they would be smeared in fresh ashes from top to bottom, resembling ghosts. Were they burning wood to make mounds of ashes and then bathe in them?

I asked Om about it, for he was the most easy-going and approachable. "We are worshippers of Mahakala, Bhairav, the dark and fierce manifestation of Lord Shiva. We believe it makes us fearless. Therefore, we follow Mahakala traditions. Lord Shiva too covered his body in ashes."

"You burn mounds of wood to make ashes?" I asked innocently.

Om frowned at me. "Nikku, you ask too many questions. Have patience. You'll be told things at the right time."

"When will be the right time?"

"That Baba Ji will decide."

I was becoming unsure if I wanted to be like them, soiled in ashes. That would hide my fair and rosy complexion that I was proud of. Though my complexion was progressively turning sallow.

Another thing I found strange, rather revolting, was that my group members kept human skulls with them, and used them as tumblers for drinking liquids—water, tea, alcohol. Many times they also mixed drugs with their alcohol and drank the potent mixture from their *kapalas*. That's what they called the skull they carried—kapala. One day I hesitatingly asked Om about it. "Why can't you use a cup or a glass?"

He laughed. Then picking up the skull he owned, he smugly declared, "You better get used to our ways. You will have one soon, once you are initiated."

"No, no. A glass is fine for me."

"Nikku, you have to adapt to our ways if you want to be an Aghori."

"Drinking from a skull disgusts me," I said.

"We Aghoris get powers by doing things that are repulsive to others. That's how we get superhuman powers. I'm still trying, need to learn a lot. Baba Ji has attained a lot. You will learn by and by." Om patted my back and said, "I am not supposed to reveal much to you. Only Baba Ji will do when the time is right."

"But how can drinking from a skull help?" I persisted foolishly.

"The spirit of the person to whom it once belonged continues to be attached to it, and we try to keep that spirit under our control. That gives us powers."

"You mean you swallow the spirit each time you drink from the skull?"

Om burst out laughing. "You have no idea about the Aghori way of life, do you? You are a rookie who joined us without knowing what you were getting into. Now you have no choice but to learn. And don't ever blabber your silly ideas in front of Baba Ji, or for that matter in front of any other member. You can get into serious trouble. Baba Ji won't tolerate it."

I began to get worried. My idea of becoming a sadhu was to meditate and pray to God. It was He and He alone who gave powers to the chosen few. That's what I believed. I made up my mind that I was never going to use a kapala and disrespect the person who once lived an honest life, worked hard, laughed, and loved. It was a strange and revolting practice. All Aghori practices had begun to repulse me. Om was right. I had joined the group without knowing much about them.

Half a year had passed, and no one had spoken about teaching me anything. There wasn't much interaction between them and me either. Beyond collecting alms, I did nothing else. What was Baba Ji waiting for?

During the nights when Dharamvir and I were alone in the house, we would sit together sharing our views and the lives we had left behind. Dharamvir had similar views to mine. He too was getting unsure if he wanted to adopt the Aghori way of life.

Dharamvir belonged to a village in Rajasthan. After a family conflict, he had left his home. He confessed that his anger was as intense as a volcanic eruption, but he was learning to control it. It was in a bout of fury that he had left his family and vowed to spend the rest of his life as an ascetic.

Like me, he had had a chance meeting with the Aghori group and was spellbound by Baba Ji performing miracles. He too had become obsessed with learning the tantrik vidya to attain power over others. Foremost, he confessed, he wanted to take revenge on his cousin and his wife, who had cheated on him and his father and taken possession of the properties they had equal rights to. This was a God-sent opportunity, he believed—his meeting the Aghori group.

Now, he was remorseful that he had left his parents at the mercy of his scheming cousin. "I plan to leave this place and join the ascetics living in the Himalayas. But before I travel north to the lofty mountains, I will visit my parents and set things right for them."

Dharamvir had also downright refused to get hooked on drugs. He was the only one among us who would go early to bed to avoid our smoking sessions. That was quite annoying to Baba Ji. "You can't become an Aghori till you smoke this stuff. They take you to an elevated level of consciousness and only then can you perform the Aghori rituals," Baba Ji said. But all those efforts to force Dharamvir to smoke failed.

I too had tried to coax him. "How will you become Aghori if you shun their basic practices?"

"I don't think I want to become one. I'm not cut out for it. I'm planning to leave soon," he replied curtly. "I find some of their practices disgusting."

I nodded. "I am never going to keep a kapala," I stressed childishly.

Dharamvir smiled and gazed into my eyes with a look that was akin to pity. "Nikku, go back home. You'll not survive for long among these brutes."

I didn't understand Dharamvir's remark till I began to grasp a dark side of Baba Ji. I realized people often came to seek his help for harming others. I overheard snippets of conversations about taking revenge, hurting businesses, or ending someone's life. Having been brought up in simplicity, where an upright moral character was mandatory, these shady deals began to shake my faith in Baba Ji.

One day I was in the courtyard cooking rice for everyone when a young man came to meet Baba Ji. I didn't intend to, but it so happened that I overheard them.

"Baba Ji, finish off my neighbour Bhaskar. I'll give you five hundred for the job." The man was offering him money for murder? My heart sank.

"Why do you want him killed?"

"His wife Chando and I are madly in love. Bhaskar is a pest, an obstacle. Unless he's removed from our path, we can't be together."

"Then go and kill him yourself."

"And spend the rest of my life in a prison than with my Chando?"

Baba Ji laughed gaily. "You want me to go to the prison instead?"

"Baba Ji, you are joking. I know about your powers. Why, many people know about your powerful black magic. And the law cannot point fingers at you. Even the policemen are afraid of you."

Baba Ji smirked pompously. "Hmm . . . five hundred is too less. I need to build my own *matth* here. Alcohol and drugs too are expensive now. Fifteen hundred rupees and I'll do it."

I began to shake. From unease to anger, from fear to shock, my emotions were changing rapidly like the colours of a chameleon. Baba Ji was using his powers for hurting people. This was downright wicked and sinful.

"Baba Ji drinks the most expensive foreign-made alcohol. Wonder where he gets the money for it." I remembered Dharamvir had pondered aloud just the previous day. This was where the money was coming from, by performing black magic to kill innocent people.

Then an incident transpired that left a fatal blow to my faith in Baba Ji and triggered my desperation to escape. It also became obvious to me that I had gotten entangled in a barbed wire, and freeing myself from it would be a herculean task.

Dharamvir should have waited for the opportunity to quietly leave and go his way. That's what I had begun to plan—to hide part of the money from collecting alms. My scheme was to buy a train ticket to escape at the first opportunity. But Dharamvir was naively daring. One evening, as we sat down with our chillums for a smoking session, he approached Baba Ji and sat next to him. "I have chosen the wrong path," he said. "I was mistaken. The Aghori way of life isn't for me."

"So?" Baba Ji granted him full attention, stroking his beard, something he did when he was annoyed.

"I want to leave."

I watched with alarm as Baba Ji's face instantly contorted in anger. His fisted hands were ready to strike Dharamvir. "Now you want to leave and reveal our secrets to the public? No way. You can't leave. The choice was given at the beginning. You were clearly told then that once you join us, you can't leave."

"I had no idea that you would try to turn me into an addict and a cannibal."

"How dare you?" Baba Ramdeen's voice boomed. He was now shaking in anger and I in fear. "You have crossed the borders of my tolerance. Now taste the punishment of your own making." Baba Ramdeen gestured at Rattan. He nodded and made eye contact with Chetan and Dev. I watched them with trepidation.

Dharamvir got up to go. "I am leaving tomorrow. Dare not stop me!"

He had barely turned to go when the three men pounced on him. After the initial struggle that was futile, for Dharamvir stood no chance against three sturdy men, he was beaten black and blue and dragged into the dingy and filthy kitchen that was never used. Rattan returned after a few minutes and took a thick rope from Baba Ramdeen's room. They were going to tie him up. I watched the proceedings in muted shock. He wasn't a criminal, couldn't be treated like one. Joining or quitting the group should be an individual choice. But could I dare to reveal my thoughts? I trembled and took deep puffs from my chillum.

Once Dharamvir was locked inside the kitchen, Baba Ramdeen sent Dev and Chetan on an errand. Dharamvir kept hammering the door and shouting. "Don't pay him any heed," Baba Ramdeen warned, eyeing me. I sat like a zombie— frightened and immobile. An hour later the men returned with a few packets. Om and I kept sitting in a corner, watching the proceedings. We dared not aggravate Baba Ramdeen's ire.

Baba Ramdeen went to sit outside the kitchen with his kapala and some other stuff. He began to chant mantras. I grasped that he was performing his black magic. I became worried for Dharamvir. Could I help him? There seemed no way. Dharamvir, who was intermittently shouting to be released, soon fell silent. After half an hour Baba Ramdeen opened a packet, picked up a ladoo, mixed it with the ash from the other packet, and sent Rattan to feed it to Dharamvir.

For the next few days, I had no idea what was happening with my friend. There was strict vigilance outside his prison and I was specifically prohibited from going anywhere near the room. I didn't have the guts to defy the command.

Not long after, Dharamvir's tortured wails began reaching my ears at odd hours. What was wrong with him? Was he in pain? Did Baba Ramdeen have no pity in his heart? He was torturing a harmless, good man and didn't even feel guilty about it?

Then one night when his pitiful cries had gone beyond my endurance, I got up to go to Baba Ramdeen, to request him to stop torturing my innocent friend. He had crossed the limits, I wanted to tell him. As I reached the door of my room, I stood aghast for a moment and then instantly hid behind the door. I peeped through the narrow slit at the hinge and witnessed the most harrowing scene.

Dharamvir was lying on the floor outside the kitchen, almost lifeless. Baba Ramdeen and Rattan were sitting next to him. A grisly female ghost was floating in the air, hovering over Dharamvir with her face close to his. My eyes bulged out in terror, and panic seized my brain. In that instant, I knew I stood no chance against Baba Ramdeen. If I lodged a protest, I would be facing Dharamvir's fate.

I watched with alarm the victimized man's body going into throes as he struggled to breathe. She was ostensibly sucking out his breath. My whole body shivered at the creepy sight. Then the ghostly figure evaporated. "She's well under my control." I gritted my teeth at Baba Ramdeen's boastful laughter. He was evil. There was no point in begging for Dharamvir's life. He was a dead man now . . . a specimen for Baba Ramdeen to test his powers on. I was frantic for my safety. How would I ever be able to escape from such a monster?

Dharamvir was dumped in a corner of the courtyard—on display. I couldn't bear to look at him. He had turned into a skeleton and lay comatose, in his own muck.

That night, as my spirits sunk to their lowest ebb, I lay down on my mat and cried. I was in shock. Om held my hand and I found it shivering. The noble man too feared Baba Ramdeen, I realized, but he never dared to express it openly. "Om, why is Baba Ji being so cruel to Dharamvir? Why can't he spare his life?"

"Shhh . . ." Om lightly put his finger on my mouth. "Speak softly. Otherwise, we too will be targeted." He whispered after a brief silence, "Baba Ji has cast a deadly magic spell on Dharamvir. It's called Kalia Masaan. He has fed Dharamvir ash collected from a funeral pyre and attached a spirit of the dead under his control to slowly suck the life out of Dharamvir. He has no escape. He'll die soon. I have seen this happen before, to another man, who had similarly defied Baba Ji. It gives Baba Ji the chance to practise his skills. I believe it also amplifies his powers."

"What is Kalia Masaan?" I asked nervously.

"It is a very strong kind of black magic. Only those who play with the spirits and have bound them as their slaves can do this spell."

"Can't it be undone?"

"Only by the one who executes it. Or, by an equally strong opponent, the one who too has help from the world of spirits."

"Om, can't you do it? Can't you somehow save Dharamvir?" I asked anxiously.

Om shook his head. "No. In our group, only Baba Ji has the powers. He says one day he'll choose some among us to pass on his knowledge. But when that'll happen, only he knows. I too am waiting."

"Please don't kill innocent people when you have the knowledge," I whispered, my hands folded in appeal.

Om gazed at me kindly. "Rest assured I won't. I wish I had chosen a better guru. But I will have to stick with Ramdeen for many years now. Once I learn the siddhis, I'll help people, alleviate their suffering. The genuine Aghori Gurus never harm others. They use their tantrik vidya for the welfare of people." I grasped that Om was the only upright Aghori in the group. No wonder he was the only one who had tried dissuading me from joining them. Perhaps he feared that one day I too would land up in a similar hopeless situation as Dharamvir . . . a sample for the experiment. Perhaps that was what I was. Ramdeen, the man I now hated, was waiting for an opportunity. My thoughts sent jitters down my spine.

I slept badly that night and the nights that followed. Dharamvir lay in the courtyard, neither dead nor alive. His feet and hands, which had strangely turned charcoal black, twitched continuously. He didn't ask for food or water, neither was he given any. Finally, a few days later he died. His body was taken out in the middle of the night and disposed off. How and where? I had no idea. "This is what happens to the traitors," was Ramdeen's farewell comment to him. For a moment, he glanced at me and then walked away. I secretly shed tears that night and wished Dharamvir's soul would escape from this man's malicious hold and attain peace.

The incident magnified my despair. This was pure slavery. Was I now stuck here, with this group, for the rest of my life? How long would I survive in the company of this vindictive bunch? It was true that the Aghoris had warned me in the beginning. But I was, like most people of my age, highly impulsive and rash. That was probably Ramdeen's trump card, to have a large group of gullible youngsters like me under his control. He had caught me in his web the day he made those predictions that became true. It suddenly occurred to me that my decisions were not mine. Ramdeen had subjugated my mind that day in the forest.

I learnt to hide my anxiety behind a serious façade, though my mind continuously worked towards finding a way to escape. I now began to miss the mountains even more. They beckoned me, infusing me with nostalgia for the beautiful, carefree life I once had. It was as if my spirit had been left behind and I must return to retrieve it. Only when I was under the influence of drugs, I forgot my longing. The moment my mind cleared, my memories awakened and I missed the warmth of my simple home and my parents. How callous I had been to abandon them. Repentance, like a potent acid, was eating me away.

Fortunately, the following days, Ramdeen kept busy to pay me any attention. I too kept my distance as much as I possibly could.

One evening, Ramdeen announced, "Next month we are moving to the main Aghora Matth, before the beginning of the twelfth year of the Kumbh Mela. I will be among the privileged few who will take the first *Shahi Snan* in the holy river." He smiled smugly. I hated him. Ever since he had killed Dharamvir, I had begun to detest him as much as I feared him.

Then Ramdeen focused his attention on me. He had not shown me such courtesy in a long time and I became flustered.

My legs almost collapsed under me. I was losing bladder control, so petrified I was of this wretched man. "I think we should begin the boy's initiation as Aghora, before he too begins to change his mind." He guffawed boisterously, patted his potbelly, and smiled pompously while my shivers intensified.

Three days passed in utter dread. I kept waiting for the ceremony I had no interest in. I had tried reducing my smoking to almost half in the past few days, for I wanted to quit the addiction. I had a feeling that as long as I remained intoxicated, I would remain under Ramdeen's control.

Then late one night, Om and I sat in our room chatting, as Chetan sat outside our room guarding it. Ever since Dharamvir's episode, I was never left alone. There was always someone guarding me. They didn't trust Om, I judged, so it was either Dev or Chetan.

Ramdeen, Rattan, and Dev had gone out on an errand. I had realized through their urgency that they had gone on an important mission.

It was around midnight that I was disturbed out of my sleep as the three men returned from somewhere in a hurry. I peeped through my door out of curiosity. I found them hurriedly washing their blood-smeared bodies under the courtyard tap. Had they got involved in a fight and were injured?

Then I saw Rattan approaching my room. I rushed back to bed and pretended to be sound asleep. Rattan shook me. "Wake up, Nikku, hurry." Both Om and I sat up reluctantly and Rattan offered me a chillum. "It's exclusively for you, with a special concoction. Baba Ji has specially prepared it for you," he declared with a grin. "Smoke to your heart's content, for tonight you are going to become a man from a boy." I nodded without comprehending what he meant. *A man from a boy? But I am already a man.* "Om, you too are to come with us."

Om looked visibly worried, and I wondered why. I became vigilant. Something was up. I wanted to remain fully alert, so I faked smoking the chillum as I lay on my mat. "Om, Is Baba Ji going to make me an Aghora today?" Om looked down, refusing to open his mouth.

Ten minutes later Rattan again barged into our room. "Time to initiate your learning. Tonight is auspicious. Baba Ji is waiting for you. Hurry. Get up!" Rattan commanded, peering at me. Instantly alert, I jumped out of my bed.

"Take a quick bath under the tap and wear this." He handed me a saffron loincloth.

When I stepped out, with my teeth chattering and body shivering after the cold-water bath, I found the group waiting for me at the gate of our lodgings. Om approached me with the excuse of making me wear the loincloth properly, which I had wrapped around like a lungi. His hands were shaky. I saw fear in his eyes as he whispered, "Be careful tonight, Nikku. Don't do anything foolish. It can be dangerous. If you get an opportunity, save yourself." My spirits dwindled. I wished I had smoked the chillum. My head had begun to throb.

Ramdeen looked distinctive with a copious bunch of rudraksha necklaces covering his hairy chest. The prominent trident-shaped vermillion tikka covered his nose and forehead. He wore an exceptionally tiny loincloth, of the same colour as his tikka, which barely covered his genitals. He looked even more fearsome than usual. The procession, with him in the lead and I in the middle surrounded by the others, all in their tiny loincloths and bags with unknown stuff, marched through the cold black night.

We walked on till the habitation vanished. A pack of stray dogs rushed towards us menacingly, barking and yapping. I felt so helpless without the protection of even a single layer of clothing on my body. Ramdeen calmly raised his hand and released a series of sounds. The dogs instantly became submissive and retreated.

We walked on by the banks of the river Shipra. The dark night grew darker still, till it engulfed the whole landscape in its macabre cloak. I gazed up at the starlit black sky. "It is *amavasya*, the new moon night, the most important for our sect," Rattan, who had appointed himself as my special escort, perhaps on Ramdeen's directives, spoke and then began to chant. Others joined him. I walked on silently. After about half an hour, we turned left and took a narrow path lined with *kikar* trees and thorny bushes, where we could walk only in a single file. Then lights appeared all of a sudden . . . like magic, glowing and glowering. I noted a few fires burning, distant from each other. Their fiery glow had set the river's quivering water blazing. My heartbeat doubled. To what kind of place had they brought me?

The procession halted at the entrance. There was a board on display, but I couldn't read it in the dark. A strong stench of burning flesh hit my nostrils. I realized with dismay that it was a *shamshan ghat* and those fires were the burning bodies of the recently dead. Why had the Aghoris decided to bring me to this place in the dead of the night, where the last rites of the dead were performed? Had they been lying about my initiation? Was my life in danger?

A man came to meet us at the gate. He and Ramdeen had some discussion in whispers. After he was handed a bundle of money, he pointed towards the far end of the cremation ground and disappeared.

Carefully evading the fires burning the dead bodies of once loving and loved people, or hated and feared goons . . . all equal in death, abandoned by their families at this dark hour to slowly smoulder into ashes, we moved on.

My heart was trying to jump out of my dry and bitter mouth. What kind of initiation into the holy life was this? I counted six smouldering funeral pyres before the group halted near the last one, distanced from the rest. Beyond it, the landscape was once again shrouded in darkness.

I was shocked to perceive a naked female body lying prostrate on the ground. Her face and neck were black and distorted with burns. I had never seen a naked woman before. Had they removed the dead body of the young woman from the pyre before it could burn completely? Wasn't that against the religious codes? And why were only the upper parts of her body burnt? My legs became unsteady. What were we going to do with the dead body?

"Sit down," Ramdeen barked and the group instantly responded except for me. Rattan, who still stood as my guard, obviously to prevent me from escaping, now held my hand tightly and pulled me down. I lost my balance and rolled on the ground. Ramdeen stared at me through his flaming eyes. I quickly sat up and then subtly inched to sit behind him, where he couldn't see me. I sat with my chin rested on my knees, hugging my legs tightly with my arms, trying to prevent their shaking. Contrastingly, the other sadhus sat crossed-legged around the funeral pyre burning without a body, their backs straight and stiff. Rattan continued to be my sentry.

Dev took out a cage from the bag and kept it next to me. A beautiful white owl sat in it rotating its neck all around and viewing us all with its beautiful limpid eyes. I extended my hand to touch the handsome creature and instantly received Dev's blow on it. He stared at me indicating that I was to leave the bird alone. What was this gorgeous feathered friend doing here, I wondered. How was it needed in my initiation as an Aghori?

Dev opened the cage and caught the owl, pressing its wings down with his hands. He brought it to Ramdeen, who chanted something in the owl's ears. To my utter surprise, the bird began to nod. Ramdeen took out a knife from one of the bags and cut the owl's wings and threw them in the fire. I almost threw up. The owl remained passive. After a bit more chanting he began cutting the owl's talons . . . one by one while Dev held on to the tortured bird. The bird shrieked in pain. Dev held the owl above the fire, making drops of blood drip into it. As if it wasn't enough, Ramdeen next made a cut in the poor bird's neck. The bird was still alive, its body fluttered to escape the torture. Its blood now poured into the fire in an unbroken stream. I shut my eyes and moaned. I could feel the bird's pain. It made me nauseous. What they were doing to the poor helpless bird was atrocious . . . horrific cruelty. Ramdeen continued to chant. The bird's tortured screeches began to subside. I opened my eyes to find the bird's body lying on the corpse's face and Ramdeen sitting next to it. Soon, his chanting rose to a crescendo. Chetan passed him a huge plate filled with bright red powder mixed with things I was unfamiliar with. The fire rose and hissed as Ramdeen began throwing the substance in it.

The rituals continued. The fire slowly began to wane. Thick white smoke replaced it and began to rise in whirls. My eyes were getting heavy. And then all of a sudden, I jolted awake. What was that? The smoke formed a figure of a shapely woman, with long tresses of hair blowing as if in a strong breeze. The smoke figure was distinct, solid. Ramdeen stood up and then went to squat on his haunches atop the woman's corpse, one foot on her breasts and one on her belly. His voice was commanding. With each mantra that he uttered, I watched with bewilderment as the smoke took the shape of a rope and twirled around the female form. It was as if a body was being tightly bound with a rope. Whatever magic it was, it was incredible. I stared in disbelief.

"You are being bound to this earthly realm. You'll either submit to me . . . be my slave till I am alive, or you'll rove aimlessly on this earthly plane eternally. I will not allow you to reach the realm of the spirits." The booming sound of the Aghori terrified me. Who was the man addressing? This figure of smoke?

A woman's shriek pierced through my heart. It was coming from the dead body. The face of the dead woman moved to one side with a jerk. I couldn't believe my eyes. How could a dead body move and scream? All the Aghori sadhus sat immobile, mumbling, as if this was nothing out of the ordinary. Ramdeen returned to his original position. "Time to initiate the boy," he barked.

Rattan got up, held my arm, and tried to pull me up. I mildly resisted and looked around like a frightened mouse caught in the jaws of a hungry snake, about to be gulped down. No one paid me any attention. I realized I would have to submit; there was no other option. Om had warned me.

I stood up on my shivering legs. Rattan walked me to a smouldering pyre a little distance away and picked a handful of ash from the pyre. He smeared the ash on my chest. I tried shoving his hands away. "Wh-What are you doing? This is dead man's—"

"Shhh! This is the first step towards you becoming an Aghori. We play with the dead, control them, make them work for us. Haven't you seen Baba Ji trying to bind the spirit of the dead woman?"

"Do they ob-obey you?"

"The docile ones are easy to control. But it takes time to break the stubborn ones. That's what Baba Ji is doing, trying to subdue the spirit of the dead woman. She's becoming difficult. You'll help him in the task now."

"How? I don't know anything."

"Shut up, boy, and stand still. Don't ask too many questions or Baba Ji will be angry with you. If that happens, you are doomed." I nodded reluctantly. Soon my entire body was covered with the ash of a dead person, from head to toe. A dead person's burnt flesh all over my body. I was disgusted. I felt nausea rising in waves leaving a bitter taste of bile in my mouth. I swallowed hard to keep my food from jetting out. I was led back to the group. Ramdeen gestured, and I was taken to the partially burnt dead body of the woman. "Remove your loincloth," Rattan ordered. I froze. Now I had to get naked in front of everyone? What were they going to do? "Possess her body, as a man should." I stood stunned. Was he asking me to have sex with a dead woman? Have sex for the first time in life, in front of spectators, and with a dead body? I sought Om in desperation. He sat with his eyes closed, ignoring me. The rest were keenly watching me.

Ramdeen said, "Mating with her will initiate your process towards becoming an Aghori of our sect. Go ahead. Before we all feast on her remains. You will have the privilege of the first bite of this flesh that we now own." So this was what they did when they disappeared at night. They violated the dead in every sense. They didn't stop at smearing ashes on themselves. They cannibalized the dead.

I didn't dare to move. What could I do? If I didn't obey Ramdeen, I'd be dead. If I obeyed, I would live. But for how long? And could I live after committing such sins?

Rattan ripped off my loincloth and shoved me towards the dead woman whose burnt face was featureless and repulsive. "Quick. Go ahead, lie on top of her, or Baba Ji will be annoyed," he whispered. I gagged. I couldn't possibly do what they were asking me to do. This was sickening. "He's getting stubborn. Wasting time. Cut off his *ling* and shove it into the woman's body." I began to shake like a dead leaf falling off a tree. And then I saw her . . . a floating female form with clear features emerging from the darkness. She had the same shape as the young woman lying in front of me—thin and curvy, but her face wasn't burnt. And she wasn't naked. She wore a flowing sari. She was dusky and beautiful. With blood flowing down her neck she drifted toward me, slowly, menacingly, with an ominous rage as if daring me to even touch her. I realized that it was the ghost of the dead woman, which was being bound by Ramdeen. The ghost would now kill me. Terrified, I shrieked and jumped five feet up into the air. In the process, I slipped out of Rattan's hands. I didn't miss the opportunity and dashed away from the scene as fast as my legs could carry. A woman's mocking laughter followed me. I also heard shouts and footsteps chasing me. It was now a race to save my life and I sprinted away like a gazelle being chased by cheetahs. My pursuers had no idea about my speed, which I knew they wouldn't be able to match in any way. Within a few minutes, I had left them all far behind. Their shouts and yells began to fade. The ghostly laughter followed me for a while and then died down.

I didn't pause. I ran like I had never run before, tearing through the darkness, through the brambles, unmindful of my body being shredded by the thorns. I stopped running only when I knew I had managed to create a safe distance between my chasers and me. I was breathless, but if need be, I could sprint another four miles nonstop. I thanked my stars that I had not bragged about my gift of speed. Otherwise, they would have been more vigilant.

I had now reached the outskirts of the city. I stopped to swallow mouthfuls of air, and realized I was naked. Fortunately, at that hour of the night there wasn't any human around in this sporadically inhabited area. A few stray dogs barked and rushed towards the intruder in their nightly territory. Seeing my ghost-like form coated in thick ash, they stopped. I shouted at them. They scurried away to safety.

I chose the shadowy parts of the lanes to proceed towards the city. I was afraid of being caught. Ramdeen would not spare me. He'd torture me before killing me. He would then possess my spirit and enslave it forever. I began to foresee my dark future. It made me once again pick up my speed. This was the only way to keep myself warm and alive . . . for the time being.

My mind was working as relentlessly as my legs now. Where could I go? At all costs, I had to avoid meeting this Aghori group again. They were dealing with the dark side of the supernatural, entrapping spirits of the people who had had violent deaths. Copulating with the corpses. And eating them? My God! There had to be a limit to degradation. All this stupidity to attain superhuman power? Was the power worth losing one's sanity? What was I thinking when I joined them? A sheer madness on my part! I must leave this city immediately and go back home. But how? I needed money. I needed clothes to cover my naked body. There was some money lying in my bag. But I couldn't go back to the Aghori dwelling. I'd be caught in a minute. An excruciating death awaited me there.

Before I realized it, I was standing in front of a large temple complex. A young temple priest sitting at the gate stared at my naked ash and blood smeared body with a dropped jaw and then dashed in through the gate like a wild cyclone. I stood shivering, my hands unsuccessfully trying to conceal my nakedness, wondering where to go. I hadn't yet made up my mind when the man was back with another elderly priest. Before they could open their mouths, I blurted, "Please help me . . . save me. I was with an Aghori group. I have run away from them. If they find me, they'll kill me."

"This is God's abode. No one is denied shelter here. Please come in."

I was given warm water to bathe and then a herbal mixture to apply on my cuts. To my immense relief, the young priest produced a set of clothes. After hearing my story, the senior priest was furious. "Ramdeen is a scoundrel, unlike genuine Aghori babas, who never harm anyone. I have heard numerous tales of his dreadful exploits." Well realizing the peril I was in, he immediately sent the young priest to buy a ticket for the earliest northbound train. Meanwhile, he offered me hot tea and sat with me.

"You are right," I said. "Ramdeen uses spirits under his control to kill. He killed my friend in front of me and I couldn't do anything. I am petrified of him."

"That's why you must leave immediately. Otherwise, no matter where you hide in this city, Ramdeen will find you. He's notorious for entrapping unsuspecting youngsters and using them for his black magic. He's getting powerful ever since he attained siddhi a few years ago, following which he has become arrogant and greedy . . . influenced by unholy forces."

"Can't he be stopped?"

"Very tough. Everyone in this city knows that it's risky to stand up against him. He can destroy lives."

Fortunately, the railway station wasn't far, and the young priest returned with a ticket to Ambala within half an hour. Giving me some money from the temple funds, the nobleman sent me to board the homeward-bound train. I sat on a rickshaw's floor, hidden under a blanket, looking like a bundle of luggage. I fell short of words to express my gratitude to the priests. To me, they were like angels, who had saved my life.

Initially, my parents couldn't recognize me. I had been away for barely nine months, but my emaciated body and transformed avatar sent them into shock. Then, their joy knew no bounds to have me back. They had lost all hope of ever seeing me again. The word spread fast. Soon the whole village was at our doorstep to celebrate my return.

I felt ashamed of the pain my thoughtless action had caused my parents. They had aged so much in a short time. I never shared my misadventure with my parents. After the initial enquiry, during which I told them that I had tried becoming a sadhu, they never pestered me for more information. I went back to helping my father on his farm and looking after our livestock. Thrice a week I walked down to the town to sell our vegetables, milk, and homemade butter. I was trying my best to return to a normal life. But could I?

Months passed. I lived in perpetual fear of Ramdeen. Winters came. My village hid under a thick blanket of snow. Life became slow, easy-going. I relaxed thinking I had been spared. At the end of March, the bright sun helped to melt the snows and the cold began to ebb. Concurrently, I began to feel a presence around me. The ghost of the woman I had seen at the Ujjain crematorium began to appear at night just as I was about to fall asleep. I was sure Ramdeen had sent his enslaved spirit to kill me. I began to expect that he would visit in the summers, and with the help of the ghost, kill me. I began to dread my fate, thinking I would end up like Dharamvir.

I needed help to get rid of the ghost. Could I find someone here who was powerful enough to thwart Ramdeen's powers?

Perhaps, I should try to contact Om, though that could prove dangerous. But only he could find me help. I didn't want my parents harmed. I realized that in the present circumstances, it would be best if I stayed away from my village.

While all of this was taking place, there existed a thought that kept showing up in my mind of its own accord. A thought that was increasingly becoming an obsession. It was, as if, being decreed into my conscious and subconscious by a higher force. I wanted to immerse myself in the service of God and His creatures for as long as I lived.

I told my parents that life of a recluse was my calling. My parents didn't raise an objection, as long as I didn't stay too far from them.

I chose a hidden spot in a dense grove of trees. It was about half an hour's walk from my village. With the help of my father, I built a small wooden hut.

I began my life in isolation in the serene and dense forest of pines, oaks, junipers, and cedar with a sprightly stream flowing nearby, supplying me with unlimited fresh water. This was a heavenly place to spend the last days of my life. The ghost was going to find me here, too. I presumed my days were numbered.

My parents and other villagers visited me here occasionally, bringing me supplies, making sure I wouldn't die of cold and hunger. They also accepted me as their holy man and sought advice on matters they couldn't handle on their own. But I was just a novice.

Meditation was one good aspect I had picked up during my stay with the Aghoris. Om had taught me some techniques to reach a higher level of consciousness. I often thought of him and missed him. He had been the only good man in that group. The rest were just a bunch of opportunistic villains who stalked the gullible and the weak to exploit them.

The forest, like a true friend, instilled immense peace within me. I had brought along my old flute and played it sometimes. The fauna and flora of the forest were now my companions and together we extended our adoration to our Creator. When I wasn't praying, I was thinking . . . thinking about the meaning of life, about the spiritual world, about the coexistence of good and the evil that perpetually surround us or live within us. I thought about the choices we make in life, and the role destiny plays to make those choices for us.

As my mind calmed down, things began to become more lucid. I grasped that by my needless anger, unkind words, the chase for power, egoism, I had been destroying the very essence of peace and happiness I sought in life. The only time I could be happy was when I helped others without a craving for a reward—*Nishkam Karma* as Om had explained from a few readings of our Holy Gita.

It was the end of the fourth month of my solitude. So far, I had been left in peace by Ramdeen's ghostly slave. I had begun to relax. Then one evening, as the day and the night had begun to blend into each other, creating a soft mellow spread of haze on the landscape and I sat battling with my inner dilemmas, I was jolted out of my reverie. The woman's ghost had come to sit calmly on a rock right across me. I was startled. "What do you want?" I asked her crossly, shivering with fright. "Why can't you let me live in peace?" A wave of panic was surging through me. I assumed that this was my most vulnerable moment—perhaps the final moment of my life. I could outrun a human. But, could I outrun a ghost? I had no choice but to confront her boldly.

She smiled and then communicated with me. She was speaking but there was no audible voice. Her unspoken words were like an impression playing in my mind. This was quite an extraordinary experience.

"Don't be afraid. I mean you no harm," she conveyed calmly.

I scoffed at her. "Haven't you been sent by Ramdeen to kill me?"

"I would never kill you. You are a good human. You are destined to do bigger things with your life. You are to help people in need."

"That's exactly what I wanted to do. I wanted to learn, but got involved with the wrong people."

"I know. I saw it all." She laughed. "What a fiasco you created that day! I am grateful to you for it."

"Grateful to me? Why?"

"The distraction you caused for that vile man broke the spell he was casting. That facilitated my escape, too."

"You are powerful. Why hadn't you escaped earlier, before Ramdeen tried his tricks?"

"I was in shock . . . still drifting around my body. Didn't realize he would try to bind my soul to become his slave."

"How did you reach here?"

"I have been following you . . . from the train journey to your village, and now here in the forest. All the while I've been trying to get your attention."

"If you were following me, why didn't you speak with me earlier, like you're doing now?"

"I didn't have the powers. I had to learn."

"Learn how?"

"Through my guides, my angel guardians. They help me. Teach me."

"Why don't you contact someone else and leave me alone?" It suddenly occurred to me that I wanted to stay away from things I didn't understand.

"I have chosen you for you are a facilitator, a good medium. There are only a few humans who have the ability."

"Oh!" I shrugged. I wasn't sure if I wanted to associate with her—the spirit of a dead woman. Ramdeen controlled some spirits, misused them. I wanted none of it. I tried diverting from the topic. "Your neck has healed today. The first time I saw your spirit at the Ujjain cremation ground, you were bleeding from the neck. As if someone had slit it."

"Someone had. I didn't die a natural death. I was murdered. I wanted you to know."

"Oh! Really? Why? Who murdered you?"

"Who do you think?"

Why was she asking me? Then the answer struck me like a blow on my head. I recalled that there had been blood on the bodies of the three tantriks that night. Now I knew that they had returned after killing the woman and then tried to enslave her spirit. No wonder only the face and neck of her body had been burnt. They were hiding their crime. And that man we had met at the entrance of the crematorium had been their accomplice. He had been paid to keep quiet about the gruesome murder. Or he had no choice. Like others, he was afraid of Ramdeen. "Was it Ramdeen?"

"You are smart."

"But why? Why did he kill you?"

"I was an easy victim—a young widow unwanted by the family, living alone outside the temple complexes, without protection."

"That was no reason to kill you. There are so many destitute women in Ujjain."

"There was a reason. I was smarter than the most, and wanted to learn. I secretly began following the tantriks, watching them at their sadhana. I learnt the mantras they chanted. I also acquired a few siddhis. I then learnt that Ramdeen was attempting to attain some powerful siddhis and I began following him secretly. Eventually, he caught me. By then I had learnt a lot. Ramdeen challenged me and realized I had become his rival. He wanted me to become his paramour, wanted to exploit me sexually. I refused that downright. Soon after, as I slept outside a temple, he and his two accomplices killed me."

"Oh my God! The rogue slit your throat."

"His co-conspirators did that, while he held me in his tight grip and watched me dying. Then he wanted to seize my spirit, which would be more powerful than any he had under his control. That night at the cremation grounds, he used his most potent spell. He was going to use you as part of that spell, like the white owl. You too would have been sacrificed in that ritual. He would have wrenched out your spirit to yoke with mine to give me, his to-be slave, potent powers. Fortunately, you managed to escape. I was right behind you then, running away from the vicious net of that tantrik." She giggled. "You run real fast!"

"What a scoundrel Ramdeen is!" I was aghast at what the man was capable of. I was outraged to know that he was going to kill me that night. Would he have tortured me before killing me, like he had tortured the owl? It was a providential escape. "He killed my friend, too, through his black magic. Do you have any idea what has happened to Dharamvir's spirit? Is it trapped in Ramdeen's unholy snare?"

"The angels took Dharamvir's spirit with them before Ramdeen could possess it. It's you now, who needs to remain vigilant. Ramdeen is in league with the devil."

"I am afraid Ramdeen will kill me soon."

"He's trying to. His group is planning to visit your village soon."

"Oh! Please help. He may try to harm my parents and the people of my village."

"Do not worry. Many noble spirits want to aid you. Together we'll save you. Ramdeen will not be able to reach here. Be assured."

"Thank you. Thank you!"

I realized I needed her and the protection she was offering. Without it, I would soon be dead. More than my life, I was worried for my parents. Ramdeen might go after them before killing me to teach me a lesson.

The spirit looked at me for a few seconds with a smile on her face. "You'll help mitigate sufferings of the good people," she said. "But you'll not seek fame and riches. The moment you do that, you'll fall from our grace."

I nodded. "I don't want any of it. I did once—when I was a foolish, immature boy. Now I have no desires for worldly possessions. This is where I'll spend the rest of my life." I pointed at my modest hut and the forest.

She smiled. "That's why you are the chosen one. I'll come whenever you need me. You just have to summon me with a pure heart. Only you'll be able to see me, not the people who will seek your help, unless I want them to."

I came out of the trance. The night had dispensed its darkness over the expanse. The jungle's nocturnal sounds were coming alive. I sat in peace and pondered. How would I fight the evil sitting here in this forlorn forest disconnected from the world? Perhaps, I just needed to drift along with the winds of destiny.

The spirit of Chhaya, which was her name when she lived in a body, became my spirit guide, my guru, and my shadow—down the road of life. Thus began my tryst with spirits and spirituality. Whenever I needed her, I would go into deep meditation, allowing a free flow of our interactions. She helped me in my yogic advancement, taught me the *ashta* siddhis and guided me towards the path of illumination. From Nikku, I became Swami Niketanand. People began to pour in from far and wide seeking my help. Chhaya was the pillar I leaned on, to help people in distress. She let me take full credit for all the help we rendered. Her spirit was beyond any desires. So was I. But I had to be known as a miracle man. Otherwise, how could I reach out to the afflicted?

Ramdeen's clout didn't last long. A few months later, before he could execute his plan of destroying me, he died. In his arrogance, he carried the notion that he was invincible. False pride had tarnished his mind and turned him into a monster. Each time he tried destroying others, he received a portion of what he had directed at them. The role of Karma to shape destiny is more powerful than he could envision. He died a most agonizing death.

It was a freak accident. The bus was parked for the night at a bus depot. The depot was on the way to the cremation grounds, the route that Ramdeen and his cronies often took. They walked oblivious to the dark clutches of death waiting to grip them in its lethal claws. The moment they arrived in front of the depot, the bus went straight for them, with meticulous precision—without any driver—rolling and gathering speed to run over Ramdeen and Rattan. Rattan died instantly. Horror-struck and helpless in front of a powerful supernatural adversary, Chetan and Dev watched their allies being crushed under the unforgiving contraption of metal and rubber. They were spared to tell the tale.

Ramdeen didn't get an easy end. He had to endure excruciating pain for hours, stuck under the wheels of the bus. The souls that he had tried to enslave in his lifetime, had become the cause of his doom.

I know that it was a premeditated murder by the angry vengeful spirits. Worst still, Ramdeen's spirit is now doomed to remain unsettled and troubled.

Ramdeen's death resulted in setting Om free. He wasn't with the group that fateful night. Even if he were, the good soul wouldn't have been targeted.

He came to visit me a few months after Ramdeen's death. I could see an enormous change in him. He was relaxed, carefree, and forthright with his views. He confessed to me what I had suspected—he had always wanted to escape from Ramdeen but was petrified of him. "God paved a way for my freedom. Who am I to question the ways or the events crafted by Him? Ramdeen had to pay for his Karma. We all do."

Om went to the higher reaches of the Himalayas in search of his spiritual self, to find the meaning of our existence. I never heard from him again. But I know, he is free . . . a liberated spirit . . . tranquil and blissful. So am I.

There are messages from the realm of spirits.

There are whispers, signs, dreams, and visions.

Concede your mind and heart to listen and receive.

Acknowledgments

Even though it is my fifth publication, the experience has been as gratifying as it was with my first book, and with all the others. This wouldn't have been possible without so many generous, supportive, loving, and kind people around me, especially my family. You all are so dear to my heart . . . Inaara, Aaran, Nisha, Amber, Peter, and Aman. This book is for you all.

I am highly indebted to Vandana Sharda, Pranav Shukla, and Shweta Sirur, for sharing their paranormal experiences with me, which laid the base for a few stories in this volume. Thank you all!

I am grateful to you, my dear nieces Nidhi and Manisha, for your help and continuous support.

I would like to express gratitude to my publishers at Prakash Books—my long association with you has been the most rewarding. I highly appreciate your unremitting support, Shikha Sabharwal and Gaurav Sabharwal. You are two highly enterprising people and have taken your establishment to another level. Thank you for growing, and helping others grow.

I am grateful to my editor, Garima Shukla, for her patience, helpful suggestions, and analytical work on my script. I appreciate Gavin Morris for the great cover design. To the Fingerprint! team, a big thank you! You all are the backbone of the organisation.

I owe an enormous debt of gratitude to all the readers of my literary works, whose support has played a great role in keeping me motivated.

Above all, I bow in reverence to God, for He alone is the one who illuminates my path, and leads me through the ups and downs of life.